Praise

A N   O u

of t h

R E P U B L I C

"Siddhartha Deb has written a novel that reads the way life on
the frontier border between eastern India and Myanmar —
the former Burma — feels. In a jungled, mountained world
where each action is veiled in several meanings, and where a
tangle of unseen boundaries leaves equal amounts of menace
and friendliness everywhere, Deb's story moves inexorably
toward a goal both alluring and terrifying."
—Donovan Webster, author of *The Burma Road*

"Deb writes with engagingly simple prose, providing insight
into a corner of the world little known about. . . . The book
gives a compelling account of an unstable region's hopes and
frailties by way of an individual's tortuous soul search, grab-
bing you with its well-honed suspense, as both Amrit and
India's northeast teeter between peaceful resolution and
abject disrepair."   —*Time Out* (New York)

"Deb is a fluid, thoughtful novelist intent on retracing his steps
around the periphery of his country — around the very idea of
the nation itself. . . . As young writers increasingly lay claim
to different regions of India, Deb rediscovers this faraway
corner of the northeast."   —*The Village Voice*

"Deb writes with a thoroughness of detail and a precision of
style that recalls Joseph Conrad and Graham Greene. . . .
[Deb's] talent is undeniable."   —*The Nation*

© Jerry Bauer

About the Author

SIDDHARTHA DEB was born in northeastern India in 1970. He worked as a journalist in Calcutta and Delhi and has written for the *Boston Globe*, the *Guardian*, the *New Statesman*, and the *Times Literary Supplement*. He lives in New York and Calcutta.

AN OUTLINE

of the

REPUBLIC

AN **ecco** BOOK

HARPER PERENNIAL

NEW YORK • LONDON • TORONTO • SYDNEY

An Outline

of the

Republic

A NOVEL

Siddhartha Deb

HARPER ● PERENNIAL

A hardcover edition of this book was published in 2005 by Ecco,
an imprint of HarperCollins Publishers.

First Harper Perennial edition published 2006.

Designed by Claire Vaccaro

The Library of Congress has catalogued the hardcover edition as follows:

Deb, Siddhartha.
An outline of the republic : a novel / Siddhartha Deb. — 1st ed.
p. cm.
ISBN 0-06-050155-3
1. Journalists — Fiction. 2. Erotic films — Fiction. 3. Calcutta (India) — Fiction.
4. India — Fiction. I. Title.

PR9499.3.D433O98 2005
813'.6 — dc22

2004058348

ISBN-10: 0-06-050157-X (pbk.)
ISBN-13: 978-0-06-050157-0 (pbk.)

06 07 08 09 10 ❖/RRD 10 9 8 7 6 5 4 3 2 1

I came back from that frugal republic
with my two arms the one length, the customs woman
having insisted my allowance was myself.

The old man rose and gazed into my face
and said that was official recognition
that I was now a dual citizen.

He therefore desired me when I got home
to consider myself a representative
and to speak on their behalf in my own tongue.

Their embassies, he said, were everywhere
but operated independently
and no ambassador would ever be relieved.

SEAMUS HEANEY

Do you see the story? Do you see anything?

JOSEPH CONRAD

contents

shadows

* 1 *

They gave me the vaguest of assignments before packing me off to the region, introducing the subject late one night in the company urinals. It was a dimly lit room, the low-powered bulb dangling from the ceiling creating more shadows than light in that space where all things spoke of age and ill maintenance. The brass fittings were tarnished, the toilet seat broken, the marble tiles cracked and stained, but Sarkar made the job seem urgent as he sidled into the stall next to me. "Get ready to leave soon, Amrit, maybe the day after tomorrow," he said, shaking slightly and drawing short, urgent breaths as he pissed into the toilet bowl.

I ignored him, but he had already veered away from my assignment to the business of seizing untapped opportunities in the region by launching a new edition, so that I heard disjointed words and phrases—"markets . . . subscribers . . . captive audience"—spiraling upward against the tinkling sound of urine falling on porcelain. The water from leaking bowls and the partially clogged gutter lapped at our feet, and we had to walk out of the bathroom on tiptoe. We made our way down the stairs, past the administrative floor sunk in darkness and the peon in charge of the office keys, nodding in his chair, to the night cars hulking in the open quadrangle at the back. The drivers on duty were playing cards, sitting cross-legged on a sagging string bed, out in the open instead of in the dispatch room that smelt of diesel, engine oil and the greasy after-trace of fried food. A small square of sky was visible above us, framed by the crumbling edge of the *Sentinel*'s century-old building, the smooth slate surface of the night dimly reflecting the halogen lamps on Central Avenue.

"The region's untapped, Sarkar?"

We had been sending a *ðak* edition to the region for thirty or forty years. In the morning, well before the first shift came in, one solitary subeditor sat with the paper and prepared the *ðak* edition, transforming outdated news into fresh, relevant information by the simple expedience of advancing the datelines by a day and adjusting all references to "today," "tomorrow," and "yesterday" in the reports.

"What?" Sarkar was already in the car. "Oh, I see," he said, sprawling on the backseat of the Ambassador. He raised his voice as the driver started the car and the printing machinery behind us jerked into life with a series of heavy thumps. "Be positive, Singh. Do something different for a change."

Like everybody else in the office, Sarkar called me Amrit except when annoyed. Then it became "Singh" to my face and "the mad Sikh" behind my back, and I saw myself briefly through their eyes: black shell glasses, wild untrimmed beard, no turban, six foot tall in a land of short men. Some of the younger subs and reporters thought I didn't understand Bengali, and I had heard them say on occasion that a Sikh without a turban—someone like me—was equivalent to a Bengali without a brain.

I didn't care too much about what they thought. My enemy was within, alert to the slow decay of my ambitions with each day I came into work, sometimes telling me that the very age and repose of the *Sentinel* building had seeped into me. I was a discontented man, but without the will or belief to act on the impulses that seethed inside, and the gibes of the young journalists floated by like the days and years spent at this job.

Sarkar asked the driver to wait so that he could have the closing words in our brief exchange. "Look, Amrit. This is a special opportunity, this series on the region. Testing the waters, that kind of thing. We begin with your stories, perhaps we can send you again, and, who knows, maybe the old man will want you to head the satellite edition we will set up there eventually."

The old man was dying, though. The paper, part of a fortune acquired by him after a beginning selling life insurance door-to-door, was far from his thoughts as they cut and patched his body at the most expensive hospital in the city. And eventually was as good as eternity at the *Sentinel*—just as the immediate departure Sarkar had spoken about turned out to be a month from the day he first mentioned the assignment.

IT TOOK THEM THAT LONG to make up their minds to send me to the region, which was a good thing because it gave me time to set my own little scheme into motion, for the photograph to make its way into my hands. And provincial though I was in many ways, I had foreign contacts—one foreign contact, who had come into my life abruptly a year or so ago. I got in touch with Herman the German when I found the photograph; a magazine he wrote for was interested enough in the image—and the story behind it—to send me an advance for initial expenses, along with a note as to the kind of article they would like. "Something exemplary we are looking for," their instructions said. "A portrait of the mystery and sorrow of India through the story of the woman in the photograph."

The note made me nervous. The burden of its expectations was heavy, especially because in the assignment and promised fee, I sensed a possibility of breaking free from the pattern of my life so far. It was a start, a small first step toward cutting loose from the office that increasingly resembled a wreck, leaving behind the debris of Central Avenue once and for all. For a while I had been thinking of quitting and working on my own, but it was Herman the German who showed me that there was a clear, discernible way toward such a goal, even as he pointed out to me that the *Sentinel* was a dead end. Now, with that note in my hand, clipped to the photograph, I could imagine leaving the *Sentinel* and becoming an independent journalist, doing what appealed to me rather than participating in a tired game that had lost all meaning. I will be free, I said to myself when the magazine sent me the note and the advance, even though I wasn't sure what that freedom would be like, what its shape would be, and what new prisons it would lead me to ultimately.

So it was that when I finally found myself on an Indian Airlines flight to the main city in the region, I thought not so much of Sarkar and the *Sentinel* and its office intrigues as of the possible future and my uncertain route toward it. As the small Boeing began its descent toward the shifting, banking plains of the giant river valley stretched out below us, the fall of the aircraft similar to the plummeting sensation in my stomach, my fingers left damp patches on the thick white envelope I clutched tightly to my side. Inside were instructions and the photograph that had aroused the foreign magazine's interest. The clouds disappeared, giving way to dense green hills, the runway a little tentative in its role as a landing strip as it emerged from the profusion of shrubs and bushes. A bag fell out of an overhead compartment somewhere as the aircraft bumped its way to a stop, and I wondered how I would find the small, expressionless woman in the photograph, how I would make her story my story, perhaps my best story yet.

❖ 2 ❖

The city I flew into was a mere starting point for my journey—a place to begin asking questions about the photograph and the situation it depicted, a spot for marking time so the *Sentinel* editors would think for a while that I was doing stories for them—but in its own way it clarified what I could expect as I struck deeper into the region. That initial, aerial view of a green and fecund valley gave way to the camouflage of army uniforms and the dour faces of soldiers once I set foot in the city. The monsoons had turned the ground soft and squishy, and the brown silt of the valley lapped at the black boots of the soldiers. Along the main road, which turned into a narrow, twisting highway once one left the offices and shops behind, there were new buildings being put up. Together with the soldiers and their sandbags, the half-finished structural frames rising from piles of sand, cement, and gravel gave the city an air of impending siege, as if they were erecting not shopping centers and government offices but fortifications for one last, decisive battle.

Too many shootouts and bombings had taken place in recent times for the government in Delhi to trust the local administrators and police, and the army had been put in charge of the checkpoints in and around the city. These barriers kept people off the streets at night, but the sprawling shape of the settlement, its proximity to the river and the heavily forested hills, and the presence of many back alleys meant that there were always enough entry and exit points for the insurgents. They occasionally appeared in the city in Maruti vans with smoked windows or on small, 100-cc Japanese motorcycles, taking the corners at great speed as the streets emptied rapidly of pedestrians in a ripple effect created by their squealing tires.

It was an old city, recorded in the memoirs of a Chinese traveler nearly two thousand years ago. Not surprisingly, little of the place he wrote about had survived; just the wide, severe river that rested like a somnolent leviathan next to the shapeless modern settlement, and the temple up in the hills where they performed animal sacrifices throughout the year, the waters of its lake a dull red from blood or mercury deposits. Now the grandeur of the city's ancient names seemed oddly misplaced, perhaps even borrowed from Delhi or Bombay, when I read them on the signboards outside new apartment complexes and suburban developments clustered around the oil refinery on the eastern corner.

The distant past, in any case, was of no use in understanding the present or the future here. Further to the east, in the states bordering Burma, there was some talk of a ceasefire between the government and insurgent groups operating there.

But even if that truce trickled all the way back to this city by the river, it would not erase the thick sewer smell tinged with petroleum fumes, the hastily assembled office blocks and shopping centers, or the unfinished flyovers rising out of the hollow basin of the city. In the evening, as the traffic on the main streets died away and the settlement was plunged into darkness, the partially constructed flyovers looked like derelict jetties protruding toward a sea that had retreated some centuries ago. Nothing could have been more forlorn. It seemed to me that the region had been forgotten by the world, and in the absence of connections with what lay beyond, an entire society was trying to create itself from selected memories and incomplete knowledge.

The people were like that too: provisional, uncertain, their responses taking place within single, discrete moments, their personalities determined by the whimsy of immediate acts, so that no story taking place in that region was ever quite complete, no individual a rounded figure, and the outline of the region itself was traced by blurred, fluid boundaries that shifted back and forth with each fresh incident.

SOON AFTER MY ARRIVAL, I went to the cremation ceremony of a man who had been gunned down by insurgents outside the house of a big transport operator. It seemed like a reasonable thing to do at the time. I was hanging around waiting for Robiul, the *Sentinel*'s retired stringer, to give me some leads about the photograph. I had spoken to him from Calcutta, but he had gone away for a family wedding shortly before I reached the city, leaving a brief note for me at the hotel to say he would be in touch when he returned. There was no way of knowing when that would be, and I thought the cremation ceremony might provide a story for the *Sentinel*. At the very least, I would get my feet wet, seeing at firsthand the effects of the insurgency and violence on ordinary people.

Then again, maybe the people at the cremation weren't ordinary. No one was clear about what had led to the incident, but people knew the victim was a former insurgent, a "lieutenant" who had gone into some kind of shady business after surrendering and receiving amnesty a couple of years ago.

The cremation ground was nothing more than a bare, treeless stretch of land on the outskirts of the city, unmarked except for the pyres that resembled uneven mounds of earth from a distance. It spilled over to a section of riverbank used by fishermen, and the partially charred logs near their fishing boats suggested a strange plague of fishes beached in a moment of great calamity. The atmosphere was humid and still, the mood uneasy, and the entire scene seemed a little surreal, especially when I saw the airy nets and sails of the fishing boats floating between sky and river like strange, intricate kites.

A few cars and the beat-up van that had served as a hearse were parked next to the small thatched tea stall on the road. There were other shops selling flowers and lamps further down, but the spot picked for this ceremony was at the very edge of the cremation ground. I arrived there with a local reporter, discovering that policemen and journalists outnumbered the small group of mourners. It had rained earlier in the day, and the lieutenant's relatives and friends—shabby men in their thirties and forties with a pale young woman among them—shuffled uncertainly amid the mud and the ashes. The policemen and journalists were visibly impatient, while in the background, the fishermen putting away their boats and gathering their nets paused occasionally, observing the crowd dispassionately.

The mourners looked warily at the fishermen and us, a clot of suspicious and hostile figures drawn unwillingly into this final ceremony, going about their tasks almost as if they expected to be challenged at any moment. The men appeared ragged, their untucked shirts fluttering in the heavy, water-laced wind that came in from the river. When they spoke among themselves, they huddled close together, initially communicating in whispers and murmurs that gradually became sharp, shrill cries, their little arguments over the rites flaring up and dying unresolved amid the repeated fumbling of the thin, nervous priest and the periodic bursts of static-ridden commands from the police walkie-talkies.

It was not a hero's funeral. The mourners did not appear to be well-off, and many of their arguments were about the cost of the cremation. The priest had been talking to the men insistently for a while before some of them reached reluctantly into their pockets, ignoring the woman standing nearby with her purse open. Finally, they came up with an assortment of notes and small change. One man was dispatched to the shops further down to procure the item needed for the ceremony. The priest took up his chants again, the onlookers shifted around, while the bald, corpulent lieutenant looked on silently, lending a touch of grotesqueness to the proceedings, as if some old parable about the limitations of the flesh were being enacted.

I felt an unlikely wave of sympathy for the lieutenant as they argued about the proceedings with his body, and my attention was drawn to the young woman as she separated herself from the unhappy, querulous group. She walked toward the corpse and bent over it, not crying—as far as I could tell—

but almost contemplative, her fingers twisting a strand from the stale marigold garlands, her long, loose hair falling over her face and obscuring it from the onlookers. Her shoulder blades were visible beneath the thin cotton of her shirt, and she seemed frail, her smallness accentuated by the corpse spilling over the sides of the pyre. But there was a bond between them yet, a relationship that had not quite ended, and I was aware that she still saw something in him that the rest of us could not. The unshaven Brahmin conducting the cremation did not feel the same way. He spoke sharply to a couple of the mourners assisting him, and another tired argument broke out between the priest and the men about her presence. The woman raised her head and listened to them quarreling. Then she rose and began walking toward the parked cars.

My fellow observers had exchanged knowing glances when she first approached the corpse, and I thought I had heard something that sounded like "college girl" from one of the journalists, a man with a mustache like a worn toothbrush set on a drunkard's swollen face. She was very young, probably no more than nineteen or twenty, I saw as she approached us. "Engaged to the lieutenant," my companion explained. The journalist with the swollen face heard. He smacked his lips appreciatively and said, "It was all a matter of money, you see. When he had money. This ripe young thing and that fat, bald man. Such a mismatch. He didn't look any better even when he was alive."

There were some titters, which died abruptly as the woman stopped and looked at the man who had spoken. I couldn't see the expression on her face, but the journalist dropped his gaze, opened his notebook, and began scribbling rapidly, his tongue sticking out with fraudulent concentration.

There was something dreamlike about the pause — the woman looking at us, the journalist pretending to write, the other men shifting around uneasily, and the slow, circular chants of the priest that only emphasized the déjà-vu quality of the moment.

"Go on," she said, speaking softly.

The journalist scribbled harder.

"You're writing down everything, are you? Make sure you tell your readers what a mismatch it was."

The journalist looked up, but not at her. He turned and tried to catch the eyes of his colleagues, his scraggly mustache quivering, his face twisted in an expression that was meant to indicate amusement and show us he was not nervous about this unexpected challenge.

"What makes you better?" she asked. She moved toward him, and he stepped back hurriedly, awkward on the sloping ground. "What makes you people any better, standing here and watching? Aren't you all part of it, the payoffs, the bribes, the scams, the backroom deals?"

"Don't get angry, sister," the journalist finally replied, swallowing nervously and looking around for some support from the other reporters.

"I'm not angry, brother, but I'm thinking that you won't look any better when it's your turn on the cremation pyre."

The journalist winced, while some of the other men began laughing. The woman looked at us, her face flushed with anger.

Below us, unheeding of this exchange, the fire had caught, leaping from the pile of wood below the corpse, the smoke and flames gathering in intensity and rising to merge slowly with an ochre sunset that was itself a vast radiance over the cold sweep of the river.

"None of you will look any better when your time comes," she said.

The men stopped laughing. It was the sort of comment that sounds like a curse even in this day and age, and it coincided with a fierce crackling of the logs. A couple of bones exploded at that very moment, and some of the men started, stepping back hastily. The woman ran past us into one of the Ambassadors and slammed the door.

A fresh quarrel had broken out between the priest and the mourners, who were getting ready to leave. The policemen, their duty done once the body had been consigned to the flames, began clambering back into their jeep hurriedly, and the journalists turned to follow so as not to be left without an escort on the uncertain road back to the city.

The woman sat in the car, her face visible through the open window, an incongruous and enigmatic figure in that setting of cynical middle-aged men come to see the sharp, sour end of a life lived without much promise. She did not look up when our vehicles rumbled past her, but when I turned back, I could see her, small and indistinct, making her way back toward the pyre.

I didn't file anything on the cremation or the killing, although I heard enough rumors to suggest that much remained unresolved about the story. It was like all the other events that caught my attention sporadically as I stayed on in the city, incidents flickering and dying out like fireflies in the dark night of the region. Going to the cremation ceremony had been part of maintaining the appearance of a big-city journalist looking to file some of the usual stories, and at first I dutifully spent time meeting people and exploring the city. Nothing got written though, and soon enough I only had to go back to the hotel room and feed a fresh sheet of paper into my Baby Hermes to usher in the doubts and the worries, smothering all hopes of finishing a story that would keep Sarkar satisfied for a while.

Inevitably, the clacking of the typewriter came to a halt before I had hit the stride of my first sentence, and into that sudden silence other sounds flowed: the deep-throated rasp of buses and the high-pitched clamor of passengers and coolies outside, the neutral television voices and the clash of plates and glasses in the dining room below, and, entering my consciousness at the end, the monotonous clatter of the pale yellow ceiling fan over the narrow bed, where the photograph waited for me, along with the note containing those troubling words, "Something exemplary we are looking for."

Why look for the exemplary in that picture, in that unusual situation? I thought savagely. Take my life if you want the exemplary. But they wanted a story about the woman, the insurgency, the old war, and I had agreed to this combination in my conversations with Herman. So I forgot about the report I meant to prepare for the *Sentinel* and looked at the picture and the note. Then I panicked and dialed Robiul's number, even though he had told me he would call when he returned. As I listened to the melancholy ring of the unanswered phone, Robiul, the woman in the picture, Herman's magazine, and my hopes of being free seemed like disparate elements in a particularly troubling dream, insistent through the long nights of my stay in the city even while their secret connections remained unavailable to my conscious mind.

· 3 ·

It was in such a state of disorientation, when I had put down the phone one morning after trying to reach Robiul, that I became aware of a pounding on my door. It was the man in the room next to mine. He had arrived the night before, a brisk figure wearing a beige safari suit and smelling of aftershave even from a distance, a briefcase of shiny fake leather in one hand, brown paper parcel in the other. The last buses coming in from the districts had long been garaged when he walked into the small reception area in the hotel, and at first I'd thought he had perhaps come in on a train running very late.

The aftershave, however, had seemed an unlikely touch for a tired railway traveler, and there were other things about the man that made him hard to place. The suit suggested a government official, while the flashy briefcase with the large golden clasps looked like a small businessman's sign of social advancement. Joseph, the worried-looking Malyali who was the hotel manager, hesitated as the newcomer handed him the parcel, and all of it seemed unnecessarily clandestine and mysterious for that shabby vegetarian hotel concealed behind the bus stand.

It was barely ten in the morning when the new arrival began knocking on my door, hammering on it with such intensity that when I opened it and saw him there, I thought his briefcase had been stolen. I was mistaken; he merely wanted to convey his joy at finding me in such close proximity. "Singh-saab," he began as I stood there. "I am Tripathi, your neighbor. I'm in the next room." He still smelt of aftershave, and although the finely embroidered *kurta* he wore sat a little tightly

his beer belly, he was an elegant figure as he smiled enthu-
ically at me. "Joseph told me everything," he said, taking a
glance into my room. "Usually insist on having no one
d me. But Joseph assured me that I had been put next to
journalist from Delhi, and I thought, better some lively
ny for a change than the usual dull safety. Long way
ome for us, isn't it? Yes?"

ace fell a little when I told him I had come from Cal-
but he quickly brushed aside this minor detail with a
question that made it amply clear which aspect of my Sikh her-
itage he was interested in. "Drink? Scotch whiskey? One *chota*
peg to greet the day?" He was halfway into the room already. I
only managed to get rid of the idiot by pretending I had to call
someone urgently, dialing Robiul's number because that was
the first one that came to mind. I must have promised to meet
him later though because he reappeared in the evening, smiling with the pleasure of conspiracy, a bottle in each hand, followed by two hotel attendants carrying glasses, soda, and
ice—as if the sole intent of his journey to the city had been to
get drunk with me.

Tripathi was an odd drinking partner to have surfaced in
that hotel, a place populated mostly by petty officials and gar-
rulous pharmaceutical salesmen sent up from their headquarters in Calcutta. He had seemed eager for drink and company
in the morning, but as he cleared the table and fussed over the
glasses, I discovered a pent-up aggression and unease under all
that politeness. "Say when, Singh," he said smartly as he
reached for the bottle and twisted the cap off. I found the af-
fectation interesting—I didn't know anyone said that outside
of novels or old British films—and asked him to stop when he
had poured me a generous measure. Tripathi kept pouring, not

looking at me. "Say when, Singh. When. Say when." It was a contest of wills, as if he was establishing his superiority before we could drink as temporary equals. I reached for my glass without a word and he stopped, reluctantly.

This was an awkward note on which to begin our session, and we drank mostly in silence at first, the only sounds in the room the crunching of stale peanuts, the clinking of glass and bottle, and the hiss of Tripathi drawing on his long filter-tipped cigarettes. He asked me a few questions about my work, looking out through the window as I answered, unconcerned about maintaining a façade of interest. For all his air of sophistication, he seemed uncertain of what to make of me. I felt that he was hiding his confusion behind a condescension tinged with a slight disbelief, as if he didn't really accept I was a journalist.

"Cheers," he said, refilling our glasses. "Don't suppose you have a visiting card on you, do you?" I dug out the little plastic box with my cards and gave him one. Tripathi looked at it carefully and put it away in the breast pocket of his *kurta*. "Must tell Joseph to give you a packet of tea," he said, as if finally satisfied with my credentials. "Usually bring him a couple of packets. Top-grade stuff, first flush." These last words were the equivalent of his visiting card, and he stood expectantly after speaking them, his head slightly cocked. When I didn't oblige with questions, he lit another cigarette and went to the window, blowing smoke out into the alleyway behind the hotel. His long, white *kurta* billowed in the breeze from the fan, making him look quite tall and graceful, and as if satisfied at last with the pose he had struck and the camera angles that captured him, he began talking about himself.

"Yours humbly is an assistant manager in a tea garden," he

said with a quick tilt of his head. "Perhaps you know everything there is to know about the industry?"

"Status-conscious job, isn't it?" I asked him. That explained some of his affectations, and I found it easy to imagine him in white shorts, tennis racket to one side, getting an evening drink at a planters' club. I was surprised when he looked back at me morosely.

"Assistant manager, Mr. Singh, not manager," he replied. "There is a difference between the two, although this may not be immediately obvious to outsiders. One is king, the other a mere slave. No prizes for guessing which role I would rather play."

He drank and puffed on his cigarette for a minute or so and then turned to face me. "I will never be made manager, Singh. It is not fated for me." There was a change in his voice. I had been distracted by a hotel boy ambling down the corridor with a soda bottle in his hand, and I looked at Tripathi with surprise. He seemed to be on the verge of tears. "Never. My destiny. Nothing left. Doesn't matter now," he said, slumped on the bed. "Garden's been sucked dry. Tea industry dead."

He glared at his glass, picked it up, and drank noisily. He had taken small, almost delicate sips at his whiskey so far, but once he began ranting he drank as if he were gulping down air after a sprint, stumbling over his words occasionally and making it difficult for me to follow what he was saying.

"Every single motherfucker's busy squeezing, Singh. The manager, the owner in Calcutta, the insurgents with their demands for protection money, and you know what, Tripathi may have been taking it up the ass for fifteen years, but he's getting out now while he still can."

His face had become flushed, his hands shook, and the room

was full of cigarette smoke. A motorbike spluttered into life in the alleyway, and Tripathi started, spilling ash on the floor.

In the beginning he had seemed like a sophisticated man temporarily trapped in squalid surroundings, but now the small room with unpainted wooden furniture, rickety fan, and wavering termite trails on the wall seemed like the most natural setting in the world for him, giving me the impression that he had been here many times before, telling his story over and over again to a series of unfortunate listeners incarcerated with him in this shabby hotel.

He leaned toward me and whispered, "Fucking place is corrupt from top to bottom, Singh, I tell you. I don't mean just the garden, I mean this whole place. You can smell the corruption, even touch it."

He stuck his hand through the open window and waved at the air. All I could see outside was the alleyway, littered with white plastic bags and pint bottles of cheap whiskey, the wall of the cinema hall daubed with posters announcing showtimes for *My Wife's Secret Lover* and *Double Fighter*.

"All of them—the local people, the settlers, the insurgents, the government shits. Money needs to be taken to the insurgents and the sucker of a manager won't go. Why? He's got family and kids, he's too scared, and the owner sits in Calcutta and cooks the books; so who has to visit the insurgents and listen to their crazy talk about exploitation while handing them the money?—it's your friend Tripathi. Not anymore. It's over, Singh. I have a plan, and I am putting it into effect any day now."

We had worked our way through the first bottle and I was hungry. Thinking it likely that the rest of Tripathi's account would be extended, I suggested we go down for dinner, hoping to bring the drinking to an end and make his story a little shorter. Tripathi sat up straight on the bed, as if he suddenly remembered the persona he had assumed in the beginning. "Yes, early to bed and early to rise. Same thing in the gardens." He stood up stiffly and bowed. I repeated my invitation to dinner. "This is good enough, Singh," he said. "Joseph will give you tea packet, don't forget now. Top-grade stuff. First flush. Cheers. Say when. Early to bed." Then he emptied his glass and left, stumbling at the threshold.

IT WAS WITH A CERTAIN amount of surprise, then, that I moved to make room for Tripathi at my table twenty minutes later. His eyes were red, he hadn't changed his clothes even though he had spilt whiskey on his *kurta*, but he had brought his briefcase to dinner with him. He placed it carefully on the table as if planning to show me commercial samples, and collapsed onto the plastic chair, drawing it toward me, so that our knees were almost touching as I turned to face him. Apart from three pharmaceutical salesmen playing a game of cards in one corner, the dining hall was empty.

"You've heard of the corruption here?" Tripathi asked, bringing his face close so that I could smell the drink on his breath. There were bags under his eyes and his face was heavy with the alcohol. "Don't know if I mentioned the corruption everywhere, eating all of us up from inside. I'll tell you, Singh, I'll give you a good story to write. Joseph, come here, get the bloody table cleaned. A good story. First-grade story. Top-flush."

One of the hotel boys came and waited for Tripathi's dinner order, but Tripathi waved him away. Joseph arrived, shuffling across the dining hall in his rubber slippers, still wearing his shirt and tie, looking as though he had been preparing to get into bed.

"Mr. Tripathi, sir, some problem with your room?"

"Sit down, Joseph. Sit and listen carefully, and speak only when I ask you for your opinion." Joseph looked at me hesitantly, uncertain if he was dealing with two drunks or one. He too was a long way from home.

Tripathi watched Joseph closely as he sat down, then turned and stared at me coldly.

"You have your notebook, Mr. Reporter? I don't know how much homework you've done before coming here, Mr. Journalist, Mr. Singh-without-a-turban—are you a Punjabi Hindu or one of those freaky modern Sikhs who cuts his hair?—but you should know that I find your appearance suspicious. I have reason to be suspicious, Mr. Singh, because there is much cause for suspicion around here."

He raised his head and looked piercingly at Joseph and me. Then he surveyed the dining hall, staring belligerently at the pharmaceutical salesmen, who immediately became engrossed in their game of cards. "I have to tell you a story? Who said so? Why should I? Well, all right. Since you insist, Mr. Reporter, I will tell you the story of my life."

He put his hands firmly on the briefcase and began.

"I'm a troubled man, Joseph. It's lonely in the gardens if you have the assistant manager's job. It's different if you're the manager. Then there are things to do; you can spend time in the club, take your wife and kids shopping in the district headquarters, dispense favors to the small bureaucrats, stay chummy with the big ones. If you are a fucking labor, even then there are things to do, if it's only blowing the entire week's pay on cheap liquor. It's me, the man in the middle, who's stranded with all the worries. Can't associate with the labor types or the clerks, because that would give the company a bad rep, and of course I can't be with all the managers when they get together at the club, because I am not of their social status. They do have a separate room in the club for the assistant managers, a cheap imitation of the main bar, and you can see the other fellows like me in that room, all the assistant managers trying hard to imitate the managers. They try to talk like the managers, but of course their English isn't as good. They copy the kind of clothes their bosses wear, but their clothes are made of polyester, the styles out of date. The quality of the alcohol is inferior—they drink the Indian-made whiskey and not the foreign stuff—and the men are all balding or with white hair. All you have to do is look into their eyes to see that they're just barely a step ahead of the clerks.

"I can't do any of that pretense. I'm too good for that—dammit, I should have been the manager if I had the right connections—and I stay on my own, lonely, the man in the middle, with my quarters exactly halfway between the manager's bungalow and the labor lines. It's on a slope, so that the labor lines are below me and the manager's bungalow above. No one has a house higher than the manager except God.

"Fifteen years like that, Singh, with the garden yields getting poorer. The new owner stopped investing long ago, we have begun making payoffs to the insurgents after some kidnappings and murders in neighboring tea estates, labor has been in unrest, and we are selling off shade trees for timber in order to make the account books look right. I'm marking time, Singh, without any idea what I will do when the garden closes down.

"Bad, yes, but it's even worse because of the stress about taking money to the insurgents. See, I have no say in the matter. They make their demands directly to the manager, the manager talks to the owner, and then I go on a certain date with a briefcase full of cash to the middle of a jungle to meet the boys. Everyone calls them the boys, you see, and they're about just as unpredictable as children. The boys are frightening, Joseph, because there's no telling what they will do one day if they become upset for some reason. They could shoot me, string me up from the trees, and no one would even find my body. I could be eaten by animals, without so much as a cremation, and I have started to feel with each trip I make that such a day will come sooner rather than later. The garden can't keep making payoffs on nonexistent profits, and I have begun thinking that the owner and the manager will leave me holding the bag. An empty bag.

"I am a man pushing forty, barely keeping things running and waiting day after day for even this limited life to end, either because the boys blow off my head or because the garden closes down, or one leads to another. It's no surprise, then, that my sleep starts getting messed up and I start having this dream, every other week or so at first, then with greater frequency, until I know the dream so well that I feel I've lived it and not merely dreamed it, and that it's more real than the things I do when I am awake, that this is all my life is reduced to now, the living of a single episode over and over again. Listen carefully, all of you.

"Things are slightly unclear when the dream begins, with different aspects, but mostly it involves me getting into a car with some people, maybe with my hands tied, and there are some oddly shaped, flat-looking buildings around me. There is this worry in my head as I get into the car about the briefcase I am supposed to take to someone—surely the boys?—and how I must be certain that the case is with me, how I have to be sure about that even though it is difficult to do much when your hands are tied. The dream shifts, and I see a constant stream of images: I'm looking at the briefcase, checking the money in it, counting the cash, putting it somewhere safe, misplacing it, opening the briefcase to check that the money's still there and being interrupted at that point by something else, on and on until I am exhausted and about to wake up from sheer panic.

"Then comes the point where the dream settles down, and I am on a motorcycle, riding behind someone. I can't see the rider's face, not even when I look into his mirrors, and the wind rushes by ruffling my hair, and it's quite chilly. We're riding along one of those typical hill roads, with a drop to our left and thick forests on the right, the road climbing slightly. I am sure that it is day but there isn't all that much light, as if the sky is overcast or because the trees are hanging over the road and blocking off the sunlight. We've been riding for a while when I see a little track to my right going into the forest. The motor-bike rider goes past it, perhaps twenty or thirty paces, and then comes to a stop, keeping his engine running. No words are spoken between us, but he waits there without turning around, and I know I am supposed to get off and walk back and take the track going into the forest.

"I don't want to do this, because even if I can't see the face of the man driving the motorcycle, it's still not as fearful as going into the forest on my own. If we just kept riding, I know this deserted stretch without any sunlight will end. The hills would open up, we would come across houses and shops and other people, and everything would become better.

"But I do as is expected of me and get off the motorcycle. I feel a weight in my hand, I look down, and I know I have the briefcase with the money. I feel much better. I tell myself in the dream that nothing can go wrong now, and with that in my mind I enter the forest. I start walking along the narrow path curling through the trees, and it's so humid that I am soaked in sweat. Finally, I come to a clearing in the forest, and I wait there. It's a strange clearing. The trees all around somehow manage to close the sky off, and I wait in this tent in the forest for the boys to come and relieve me of my money.

"When the boys appear, I recognize them immediately, even though they appear a little strange. They are wearing rags, and they have leaves and twigs in their hair, but I don't feel sorry for them or anything because they still look menacing. There seems to be something important about the way they are dressed, but just as I am about to figure it out, I get distracted by an open space to the side. You know how it is that when you're in a forest, there is a kind of openness only the sky or water can have, and I peer at this open space, trying to figure out if what I am looking at is a pool. I get entranced by what I am seeing, because it seems to me that through the gap in the forest I am looking at a strange kind of horizon, something familiar and yet not entirely recognizable. What I see in the distance is a city, maybe not a city, perhaps a factory, maybe some strange collection of buildings. I keep looking, and I feel dizzy, as if the forest is turning on its axis, and then it strikes me that what I am seeing in the distance is really Delhi, but Delhi as it would appear if you were standing on a giant map of India and viewing the distant skyline of the capital from the dark forest of the region, and then I can see everything—to the west another skyline that must be Bombay, and closer still Calcutta, and Thai trawlers sneaking into the Bay of Bengal—the whole country visible in an instant to me.

"Then I am facing the boys again, watching as their leader approaches me. I smile at him in the dream, I bow low like a Japanese businessman, and I feel reasonably confident as I clutch the briefcase and feel its weight. I kneel carefully, place the briefcase on the ground, and get ready to open it. Then I don't want to open it anymore, because I know what has gone wrong."

Tripathi paused and licked his lips. He wiped away the saliva from the corners of his mouth before continuing.

"I don't mean I am unable to open it because it's locked or anything, but now I know things have gone wrong in spite of all my preparations. I must never forget the briefcase, and I haven't. It's not empty, but whatever is inside the briefcase, it's not money. No, it doesn't have the money that they want. There's some other thing in the briefcase, newspapers or rags or something, and although I have no idea how I know the money is not inside the briefcase, I do know that if I care for my life, I can't let them open the briefcase in front of me, even though one of the boys is already bending down to open it, and I start running, and the forest starts whirling around me and the trees begin to rain a thunderstorm of dried leaves and I wake up screaming."

Tripathi was crying, his head resting on the table. I looked at Joseph, and he tentatively put a hand on Tripathi's shoulder, but Tripathi jerked away violently, his hand striking the briefcase on the table and knocking it to the floor. It flew open, revealing stacks of blue currency notes, still stapled together in thick bunches with the pale pink receipts of the issuing branch on top of each bunch. The pharmaceutical salesmen gasped, and Tripathi stared at the money with a horrified expression on his face.

Joseph started and rose from his chair. The salesmen stared on, all pretense of being involved in the card game forgotten. Tripathi dropped to his knees and began to close the briefcase, but Joseph was already walking away. Tripathi snapped the catches shut, looked wildly at me, began to say something, and then ran toward the elevator after Joseph, changing his mind halfway there and heading for the stairs instead. I waited until both men had gone and, ignoring the salesmen rolling their eyes at me, made my way back to the room.

In the images that came to me that night in my sleep, I am certain I saw Tripathi's briefcase, but it was not full of money. The case was open, illuminated by a band of yellow light that came from an open window in an otherwise featureless room. I was a great distance away from it, and had to move in a slow, complicated pattern to reach it. (When I thought about it in the morning, I realized that although the floor had been blank, I had been moving like a piece in a chess match, limited to squares of the same color and restricted by the arbitrary rules of the game.) When I finally approached the briefcase, I found that its velour-lined interior was stacked with postcard-sized photographs, tied together with rubber bands. The photographs were of a number of different women. Some were familiar — the woman I had come to find, the lieutenant's fiancée, a former girlfriend, my aunt Harpreet — but most were unrecognizable, and regardless of whether I knew them or not, they all stared sullenly and expressionlessly at me as if I had imprisoned them in those pictures.

❖ 1 ❖

Too many unlikely events had come together in the brief to
find the woman in the picture; Sarkar's sudden assignment for me, the discovery of the photograph, the meeting
with Herman the German more than a year ago now. There
was no common thread between any of these disparate events,
nothing other than me, as if I had pulled them all together un-
knowingly, like some magnet that doesn't comprehend how or
why it attracts metal.

I could remember a time when I would have thought nothing of such circumstances, during that phase of my life when I
quit more than one steady job to try something new or interesting. But that had been in and around Delhi, that unreal city
where fly-by-night schemes bloom in all seasons, and the atmosphere had been different as well: in those days, I could return to Delhi with my money exhausted and still find, within a
month or two, some big paper to take me on. That changed
when the newspapers became concerned with balance sheets

and new management principles; it was a sign of how far the *Sentinel* had fallen from its position as the preeminent English daily that it was willing to hire me, no questions asked, when most offices in Delhi had closed their doors in my face.

This was why Sarkar's talk of a regional edition surprised me. The *Sentinel* hadn't done anything new in a hundred years, and even the Calcutta edition was losing ground to a stripling rival paper that had come up right across Central Avenue — but the idea of sending me to the region didn't die away. The chief reporter mentioned it sarcastically as he scanned whatever news I had rustled up from the municipal corporation, and the gossip trickling back from editorial meetings indicated that my assignment was mentioned regularly amid the perennial discussions about marketing strategies and revenue streams. Sarkar had been talking to a reclusive financier who was willing to support the launch of a new edition, someone who wanted the *Sentinel* to begin by giving more attention to the border states. The signs were far too numerous to ignore. At some point even I accepted the trip as a possibility and began thinking of it as an opportunity to propose an article to the magazines Herman had spoken of so enthusiastically.

I had been skeptical when the gangling German first suggested I could make a living writing for editors he knew, but then he had appeared in my life with an idea that sounded preposterous and turned out to be a commissioned piece. "A story on shit," he had said, sitting cross-legged on the floor because I didn't offer him a chair. "How in the world's filthiest city the stuff is got rid of. Story on Calcutta sewer system." I stared at the German, thinking about his wonderful reduction of the city I lived in to one choice epithet. I looked at his scraggly blond beard, at the battered soles of his large hiking boots and the old rucksack he had dumped on the floor, and I wondered if I should listen further or throw him out. He looked no different from the backpackers who congregated around the cheap hotels on Sudder Street, perhaps good for a little social work with slum children and pavement-dwellers but not much more than that.

He must have realized what I was thinking. He was almost level with me, even from the floor, and he reached across and handed me a card with the name of the newspaper or magazine he was doing the story for, something called the *Wochenpost*. He was looking for an assistant who would be more than an interpreter, he explained politely, preferably a local journalist who knew the terrain and had sources in the municipality.

Later, I would find out that there was a term for people like me who helped foreign correspondents. But I didn't know I was acting as Herman's fixer when I took sick leave for a week to work with him, translating and taking him around, making phone calls to sources I had. The reporting for the feature was routine, if quite strenuous. Together, we interviewed the reptilian clerks at the municipal office and laborers working in the sewers. We bought a colonial map of the sewer system of the White Town from a knot of hostile and suspicious officials at the Survey of India office, and went off on a whim to the great compost ground along the Eastern Metropolitan Bypass, where Herman was mobbed by villagers trying to sell him cauliflowers. But it was in the evenings, as we drank Patiala pegs of Old Monk rum at Olympia Bar and swapped stories, that Herman became my guide and interpreter.

His infectious energy blurred and shuffled the finite boundaries of my life, not so much through what we did as what we spoke about. We were by no means unequal in our stock of stories. His were about memories of the Berlin Wall coming down, the difference between Germany and England (where he had traveled a lot), and the work he did in theater before turning to journalism. I told him about the Wagah border point where I had watched the ceremonial headdresses of Indian and Pakistani soldiers bobbing furiously as the sun set over their parade, of the rooftops in Mathura erupting in plumes of color during the festival of Holi, and about the murder of one of the Dalai Lama's aides in Dharamshala during a chilly, dry winter amid rumors of the resurrection of an old Tibetan deity called Shugden Dorje. But it was the meaning Herman could impart to experiences, whether his own or mine, that delineated the difference between us. He saw possibilities where I did not, and I don't mean merely in the crude sense of turning these stories into articles. He saw experiences as important, as possessing a shape, whereas for me they were merely transient moments flitting by as they transformed themselves into memories.

Without Herman's entry into my life, it had not been too hard to maintain the illusion that the *Sentinel* was merely a temporary stopover, a resting place until I found something more suited to my abilities. But I envied Herman and his easy freedom, the way a German speaker could land up in a distant foreign city and go about reporting a story, and that envy led me to exaggerate my stasis to him. He asked me how long I had been with the *Sentinel*. "A lifetime. Ten years, what does it matter?" I said mockingly, but when he pinned me down, I was forced to admit that I had been working at the *Sentinel* for over seven years. The stories I had told him of places like Mathura and Dharamshala were from the distant past; I hadn't left Calcutta in a very long time.

A life without shape, almost without meaning, it seemed to me. Herman didn't quite see it that way. He liked the stories I told him, even if they were from long ago, and at some point he began insisting that I think of writing for the English-language magazines he knew in England and Germany. I wasn't sure about these publications, especially those in Germany that were published in English—were there any?—but it was good talk. The alcohol made the exchange rates sound even better than they were in reality; just one article, and enough to live on for two to three months, along with the possibility of doing something more interesting than the routine municipal squabbles and skullduggery I reported on for the *Sentinel*. Another life, another me, I thought. Only when I raised my head and noted the flushed faces and loud voices and exaggerated gestures of the rest of the clientele in Olympia did I realize that everyone there was immersed in a parallel life, existing for the time being in an alternate universe where the failures and miscalculations of the present one had been washed away cleanly.

Herman didn't let up. He was relentlessly enthusiastic whether drunk or sober, and even after he went back to Germany he sent me a letter or a scrawled postcard every now and then. I didn't know much about his personal life, but I sensed that in his own way, he too was lonely and disaffected. Sometimes he called me late at night when I was at home, and we held long, rambling conversations that indicated both of us were drunk. When I told him I might be sent to the region on an office assignment, he seized the opening. "Now is your chance, Amrit. There could be many interesting stories there." I thought so too, because foreigners were rarely given permission to cross the Inner Line into the insurgency-ridden states. "New life for you, my friend. You will come here after that, on a ticket I will send you. Will meet people, get fresh assignments. We will drink in Berlin, but no Old Monk here; I am so sorry." Then he changed tack. "It will be the fiftieth anniversary of World War II soon, and there was a campaign in the region, was it not?" I decided to do some reading and look through old reports and files in the office. Without Herman's prodding, I would not have come across the photograph.

He called a couple of weeks after our first conversation about my assignment, his distant voice competing with the rumble of the occasional taxi heading toward Rasbehari Avenue and the sound of stray dogs barking into the sweltering Calcutta night. There was loud music on his side. Berlin sounds, I thought, with vague images of a Western city culled from films and books. When I mentioned the photograph, it seemed too insignificant a find for someone in a place so far away.

"Found a photograph in the library, Herman. Looks interesting, but I don't know how it got there."

"Old photograph?"

"It's new, not archival or anything like that, dated couple of months ago in the caption. Postcard size. Color."

Our words overlapped because of the delay, and sometimes we spoke at the same time and then both stopped, letting the dogs and the taxis and the Berlin pop music take over.

"Black-and-white? No? Color? Describe photo."

"Okay, here's what is in the photograph. It's a picture taken in a room, with three people in front of a wall, a woman and two men. The wall's blue, quite faded. The woman is small, with high cheekbones, narrow eyes, young, in her twenties, looking at the camera with no expression on her face. She's wearing a traditional-looking long skirt with some kind of red pattern on it. Her face is pallid but that may be because of the flash. There's one man on each side of her, slightly in front of her, closer to the camera, so that only their heads and torsos are visible. Can you hear me?"

"Go on, Amrit."

"The men are both masked. They are wearing identical checked scarves covering their heads, and one end of the cloth is wrapped around the lower part of the face, so that only their eyes are visible. They are big men, with broad chests, wearing white T-shirts. Each man is holding an automatic rifle in one hand, AK-47s, their barrels pointing up."

I heard the humming of the song in the background, electronic music with regular beats like the heart of some giant beast.

"You ready for the last bit, Herman?"

"Yes."

"On the back, there is a caption scrawled with a ballpoint pen. It says, 'The MORLS leadership today exhibited a porn film actress as an example and warning to the people of the state. They shot her as punishment to impress upon the people the importance of desisting from all corrupt activities encouraged by Indian imperialism. It further exhorted the people to lead a sound moral life as a harbinger of liberation.' It is dated two months ago, and . . .'"

"So recent?"

"Yes."

"What is the MORLS?"

"Some kind of insurgent group in the region."

"Who sent the photograph? Did you ask?"

"I don't know, Herman. The office says that when our old

stringer, Robiul, retired, they hired another man on a trial basis, so it may have been part of the stuff he sent. There was no story accompanying the picture and they never carried it."

"And who is this stringer?"

"I have his name, a phone number, no address. They didn't use his stories and didn't retain him. I spoke to the accounts manager, who said they sent him a check by registered post to cover the few weeks he worked for us, and it came back. Address unknown."

"They didn't call him?"

"They didn't try. The accounts manager said it's not his headache if someone doesn't want to get paid."

"Where was the photograph taken? Which is the place?"

"The place is Imphal, Herman, the capital of the state of Manipur. It's in the region they're sending me to, but much further east of the city they want me to report from. Manipur is on the border with Burma, an old kingdom that was conquered by the British and then made part of the Indian republic. The people there aren't happy and there are many insurgency movements. There are secessionist struggles in almost all the states of the region."

"Burma," I heard Herman say thoughtfully. "Good stories in Burma, Amrit. Great stories in Burma. SLORC, Aung San Suu Kyi, the quest for democracy. I am such an Asia junkie, Amrit. So excited. How much to report. Not much written about."

"I can't go to Burma, Herman. I don't have a passport and I doubt they would let me in anyway. But Manipur? That's a possibility."

Herman asked me to try calling the stringer, to find out about the group and the woman and see if other newspapers had carried the story. I came up with nothing except for scattered references to MORLS, the rebel group. The missing stringer's phone and fax didn't work, so I got in touch with Robiul, the *Sentinel's* retired correspondent, even though he was not based in Imphal but in the big city by the river that was the first stopping point for anyone visiting the region. Robiul said he would try to help, and Herman seemed convinced it was a good story: sex, violence, political turmoil, the remoteness of the border, with the World War II campaign against the Japanese like a heavy, detailed backdrop in an old painting. These were Herman's terms, not mine, and he talked the story idea over with me until I sent him a proposal that he forwarded to the editors of a magazine in Tubingen. He was vague about what kind of magazine it was, but that hardly mattered. They were interested in the story. They wanted me to write about the woman in the picture.

It wasn't like anything I had ever done in my life, but the check the magazine sent me, drawn on an Indian bank and in rupees, that seemed real enough. Herman had carried his part out, and there was nothing left for me but to try and write the piece when the *Sentinel* finally sent me to the region. My only worry, apart from actually getting the story, was that I hadn't told Herman the entire truth about how I came across the photograph. The circumstances were too odd, and didn't seem relevant at the time.

* 2 *

The insurgents had been in the region in one form or another for nearly four decades, crystallizing around different ethnic and tribal identities as a distant government in

Delhi alternated between complete neglect and brute force. This city by the river and its uncertain state of siege was only the most recent symbol in a series of secessionist wars, some of them as old as modern India itself. As I traveled deeper into the interior, I would find myself traveling a route riven by conflict, with shadowy armies meeting each other in fierce but inconclusive encounters.

Much of the region had been treated as different from the rest of India by the British, divided by an Inner Line that only colonial officials and Christian missionaries could cross freely. It was an area of perpetual separation, a museum collection of tribal territories and princely states curated over by a resident commissioner, and by the time of independence the notional line had become an unbreachable wall. The politicians and administrators in Delhi who determined how the region would fare in the fledgling nation should have anticipated this barrier, but their knowledge was partial, their lack of imagination absolute.

They faced the alienation of the local populations with contempt, a potent mixture that, like hot air meeting cold in the skies over the hills, produced thunderstorms of rebellion and repression. The Nagas rose first, then the Manipuris, then the Mizos, Assamese, Bodos, and Hmars, and now intelligence reports spoke of as many as a hundred and fifty groups swirling in the vortex of the region, a discontented army of teenagers and young people sworn to similar but separate causes, moving stealthily along arms routes from jungle camps located in Bangladesh and Burma.

The group that had a role to play in my story was one of innumerable minor outfits, a significant presence only at the very end of the highway that began just behind my hotel at the interstate bus terminus smelling of vomit, diesel, and pungent betel nuts. Nobody here knew much about MORLS and the woman it had exhibited at the press conference. Nobody cared, not when there were more immediate worries at hand, with shootouts and encounters interspersed with uncertain stretches of peace.

Peace in this city didn't mean quiet. Political scandals pushed their way into the vacuum left by the pause in violence, with accusations directed at politicians and government officials about embezzled money, hidden mistresses, and secret deals with insurgents, while humming in the background of all this was a constant crisis about funds. The state employees received salaries so infrequently and randomly that people queued up early outside their offices whenever word went round they would get paid that day. I saw these mobs on a couple of occasions, with clerks and minor civil servants trying to push their way past the people ahead of them, while encircling this crowd, squatting on the potholed roads, were vendors who were owed money by the government workers. Everyone was desperately trying to get a share of the cash before it ran out, so that even a routine transaction took on the air of a siege, a feeling of things about to collapse that affected the peasants selling vegetables as well as the salaried workers.

AMID ALL THIS, still waiting for Robiul to return to the city, I was referred to a cheerful but tired-looking official who had served briefly in Manipur. The official was a Syrian Christian from the southern state of Kerala, a dark, suave man who had gone to college in Delhi and appeared eager to return there once his stint in the region was over.

I met him in his office, making my way with difficulty through the crowd of hopefuls who had gathered for an arbitrarily announced payday. He asked me to accompany him to his house. "We can talk more freely there," he said, gesturing a little hopelessly at the melee near the cash counter on the department floor. The working day was nearly over, the cash had long since run out, but there was still a jostling, shoving throng yelling wildly at the cashier, who was shouting back, empty hands raised high in the air as if he were being held up in an old western. The official shook his head regretfully; he didn't have to worry about his salary since it came from Delhi, he said, but it was hard for some of his local staff.

He lived in a government area cordoned off by barricades, the roads, gardens, and bungalows clicking into a neat grid that comprised a striking contrast to the unfinished flyovers and buildings of the main city. His bungalow was at the end of a long row, quite isolated and dark, and I waited among the shadows in the verandah while he turned the lights on room by room with a slightly detached air, as if the place didn't really belong to him.

The bungalow was musty, and there were signs of disorganization that didn't go with the neat, polite man who had invited me there. A window with a missing pane had been crudely sealed with a piece of cardboard. The drawing room we sat in was big and unused, with dustballs on uncarpeted sections of the floor, mildew on the walls, and cobwebs on the ceiling. Only one small corner of the room looked inhabited, with a pile of books and magazines sitting on a coffee table, the glass top slightly askew on the old, burnished tea plant that served as a base. The official's rubber slippers were lying under the armchair, and he put them on while his driver made us tea. "Bungalow's much too large for one man," he said, as if registering my curiosity about the untidiness. "But the civil service would lose its reputation if it started thinking small."

I had liked his controlled manner earlier, noting the dignity with which he treated his unpaid staff. I didn't get the impression, for instance, that he was raking in money through bribes and payoffs. Perhaps he didn't need to; his father was a small industrialist in the south, he said modestly, which probably meant that he didn't have to strain beyond his salary to provide for his children and his retirement. The quiet of his bungalow, however, was in its way as oppressive as the chaos in his office.

"Make yourself at home," he said politely, picking up a bunch of leaflets on wildlife sanctuaries on the coffee table, putting them down, and turning to a book on the birds of India. His face lit up momentarily when I asked him about the book. "You are interested in wildlife? No?" He became remote again. "Yes, something about Manipur, about MORLS, wasn't it?"

I waited for him to continue.

"Why bother?" he said. "The political turmoil is quite inconsequential. The birds, the animals, the flora, that is what lasts."

I began to say something about how it was difficult to ignore the upheaval, but he interrupted me.

"You must learn to differentiate between the superficially intriguing and the truly interesting. For instance . . ."

He reached for one of the leaflets and opened it to a small map.

"There you go. Manipur. The Moirang Lake, perhaps as remarkable a water body as you will ever come across." He paused, waiting to see if the name meant anything to me. "The people there live in floating huts on the lake, with this incredible environmental sense, in complete harmony with the ecology." He pushed the leaflet toward me and I saw the lake, a small splash of blue near the highway snaking into Burma. "Complete harmony," he repeated, and I wondered if the phrase came to his mind often, like some exercise in meditation, a mantra that he used to invoke impressions of the lake as he was being driven from the lonely bungalow to his dilapidated office along streets full of soldiers.

"Hog deer," the official muttered, more to himself than to me, moving the lamp closer to take another look at the leaflet. "Barking monkeys, jungle fowl," he went on, and the names were both soothing and incomprehensible. "There is only one other thing to see when you're in Manipur, although it must be said that you're best off not going at all. That is in the lake area as well, the Prosperity Project."

"What's that?" I asked. "I was told not to expect much in the way of prosperity except among the drug lords."

"You wish to know about the Prosperity Project? Imagine then, if you will, an environmental project—otherwise I would have no interest in it—but also think of a completely integrated developmental setup. An alternative community that has everything—AIDS clinic, agriculture and handicrafts training, a drug rehabilitation center—and manages to address all the problems that plague Manipur. And the director, Malik, he's almost become a local man after all those years out there."

"A social worker running an NGO?"

"No, Mr. Singh, not a social worker running your average NGO. Instead, a man who is a remarkable thinker." The official hesitated, trying to find the right words to describe Malik. "Almost a visionary, I would say, were I inclined to use such words. In my official capacity, I wouldn't, you understand. But if I were speaking off-the-record, I would say he is an inspiring figure in a place where so much is bleak. A creator of order in the wilderness. A messenger of hope for an area plunged in darkness. An emissary sent from the heart of the republic to its borders." He paused for breath and looked a little self-conscious about his sudden burst of eloquence. "Don't focus only on the despair in the state, Mr. Singh. Write about what has been achieved. Visit the project, talk to Malik, listen to him, and perhaps he'll even help you with your insurgent group."

"What does MORLS stand for?"

"Movement Organized to Resuscitate the Liberation Struggle," he replied tersely.

" 'Resuscitate the liberation struggle'? What could that possibly mean?"

"Everything, if you have an automatic rifle to back it up with. And MORLS may not have very much else, but they have the weapons."

He paused, the subject of the insurgent group apparently distasteful to him, and I wondered why he had agreed to talk to me at all. Perhaps it was no more than loneliness, a yearning evoked by memories of the social life he had in Delhi, but ultimately this desire had not been fulfilled by his conversation with me. On our drive to his bungalow, he had hinted he found his work here quite hopeless, caught between a lack of funds for regular projects and the greed of fellow officials and politicians, but my presence in his house had produced a cautious reserve that I took to be the bureaucrat in him reasserting itself—perhaps because he felt that an unknown journalist was not to be trusted with significant information.

"Look, the insurgents are a police and army matter, and my department in Manipur was food and civil supplies. Not that there was much in the way of supplies to control out there. The state lies at the very end of National Highway 39, and it's a bad route where landslides hold up trucks when the insurgents aren't carrying out massacres. A state with the highest rate of educated unemployed in the region, rampant drug use, promiscuity, AIDS, and regular violence with government forces as well as ethnic clashes. MORLS is a symptom of the upheaval in the state, no more. It's a small group, a roving armed band, and I was given to understand by local colleagues that it has no coherent goals."

I told him about the photograph, and he nodded.

"Trying to capture the high moral ground. They've done things like that before, ordering college girls to stop wearing jeans and instead dress in more modest and traditional clothes, going after prostitutes and drug users. They even shot a couple of exam runners a few years ago."

"What are exam runners?"

"Oh, just people who help students cheat during college exams, so that they can be added to the mass of unemployed youths in the state. They stand near the windows and pass answers to the examinees. You have them in other parts of the country too, but perhaps not with such fancy names. That is MORLS for you, a group going after petty criminals and weeding out what it sees as immorality."

"Are they popular?"

He shrugged, looking irritated.

"You will have to find out by going there, won't you? Ask Malik. He knows some of them. Negotiated with them about the traditional clothes business and somehow convinced them not to go after young women in Imphal. A very persuasive man, you see. As for their popularity, there was one story that went around about a young heroin addict who couldn't kick the habit in spite of going through a number of treatments. They say he got a package from MORLS one day. There was a note that said, 'Can't stop? Take this and you'll never need drugs again.' There was a bullet in the envelope. People said that the addict was so scared that he quit right away. Did the people in the state start admiring MORLS for that? I don't know. Their attitude was ambiguous, which is perhaps why you should see Malik. He is a subtle man, an individual who understands ambiguity, and that may explain how he succeeded where all others had failed."

That was all the official had to tell me, and I left him examining the lake on the map, humming the names of birds and animals to be found there; had I not found him to be a serious, intelligent man I would have suspected him of making up the names. "Do meet Malik," he said without looking up as I left. "Cats that like swimming in the water," I distinctly heard him murmur to himself as I stepped out to the front porch, but it seemed evident that he was speaking of a species of his favorite wildlife rather than about Malik or MORLS.

I LEARNED A LITTLE more about MORLS in the newspaper offices in the city. There were a few file photos of the group, pictures of insurgents training in the jungle and a surrender ceremony in Imphal about a year ago. The men in the jungle seemed smart and photogenic, posing with AK-47s and rocket launchers for the camera, the trim lines of their camouflage standing out against the tropical backdrop of the jungle. Those in the surrender pictures looked less polished. Dressed in cheap civilian clothes that had probably been issued hastily by the army, the insurgents approached the politician garbed in white as if they were sleepwalkers. The shine on their faces when filmed in the jungle was gone, and they looked bone-weary and blank. The machine of the state had broken them and was ready to process them into something else; it was better if they didn't think about what they would have to become in the service of the entity they had fought against for so long.

This was a start, but it wasn't anywhere close to the woman exhibited at the press conference. In any case, the caption itself was ambiguous. Did they kill her afterward? If so, wouldn't the caption have said that? It would have been news, the killing of a porn actress by insurgents in a frontier state, and even the *Sentinel* would have devoted a single-column item to it. Or did the word "shot" mean *injured*? I called a couple of people in Imphal to find out, speaking first to a local journalist who had written occasional pieces for the *Sentinel*'s rival in Calcutta and then to a police officer from the central services. Neither told me anything I didn't already know; such things happened all the time, they said. The police officer hadn't even heard about the woman and the press conference, while the journalist remembered none of the details. It wasn't exactly news, he suggested, since the incident had taken place a while ago, but I should come to Imphal and take a look myself if I thought it worth the effort. He asked me to pick up some Navy Cut cigarettes for him if I decided to make the trip; they were going at high black-market rates in Imphal.

I WAS WAITING for Robiul to come back before I went to Imphal. The weather changed again, and the overhang of large dark clouds above the city melted into heavy rain, producing flash floods and filling the narrow lanes branching off the main road with black, knee-deep water. The rain seeped through the roof and window into my hotel room, soaking a corner of the bed until I moved it, hoping that the wet patches near the ceiling fan wouldn't cause a short circuit.

The weather made the waiting seem even more endless, evoking a state of crisis to which there could be no possible human response. The interstate buses were delayed or canceled due to landslides in the hills, and the hotel was overrun by stranded travelers. The conversations in the dining hall were about trains, flights, taxis, about getting out and getting home before all modes of transportation broke down. There was no sign of Robiul, but I kept waiting, ignoring the friendly overtures of the three pharmaceutical salesmen who had been witness to Tripathi's outburst.

Strangely unaffected by the rain and influx of new guests, they went out to work in colorful ties, holding briefcases with the names of their companies—Pfizer, Hoechst, and Glaxo—stenciled on the sides. Around seven in the evening, they came back with their trousers rolled up above the ankles, hair wet and plastered to their scalps, briefcases held high like the swords of a victorious army. Pfizer and Hoechst were in their late twenties, handsome in a smooth sort of way, while Glaxo was an overweight, middle-aged man, who nodded vigorously at everyone and said, "Business is never bad in this line. There exists no place in the world that does not need my medicines." After they finished dinner, Glaxo usually extracted an old pack of cards, which he shuffled laboriously before dealing them out with loud slaps. Pfizer and Hoechst made jokes about their bosses in Calcutta and the officials and doctors they had met, occasionally asking me to join them in the game. It wasn't hard to refuse. The only game they seemed to know was Bray, and they never tired of it, peeking into each other's cards and delighted at the jokes being told, a happy adolescent family among the atomized guests scurrying through the hotel.

I usually sat in the dining room watching television, and when even the indefatigable salesmen began yawning, I went into my room and thought about the photograph. I knew that waiting was a bad sign, the sign of a man who wasn't much of a journalist. In Imphal, I could have looked for the stringer who had taken the photograph now in my possession and talked to people: the journalist who'd asked for the cigarettes, other reporters who had attended the press conference, policemen filing a report, men running local video-rental places who might know the woman in the picture from their dealing in porn tapes.

But I needed to hear from Robiul before moving on. I wanted him to tell me that the story was possible. What if the woman were dead? Or even if alive, what if she couldn't talk, her tongue cut out like that of some rape victims? And even if she was alive and I found her and she talked, did I have it in me to write the story the magazine wanted? How would I do that—taking the waxing and waning of daily life on a frontier state, the scattershot of violent incidents that together created no larger pattern at all, the roll call of strange, alien names that played indefinable, unclear parts in each incident, the patchy history of a distant region—and somehow fashion all this into a coherent story. And an exemplary one at that?

Once I stopped believing in the story, I stopped believing in the possibility of a different life. The story would make me free, Herman had said. It was the first step in a journey toward my independence, finding out if I could emerge from the stupor of the past seven years to start a new life. People do it,

Herman had said. They change careers midway, go to college again, begin anew, because the self is not a fixed, immutable thing but a core around which our hopes and acts fashion fresh layers of being every day. There are no laws that say that you cannot become much more than your environment asks of you, nothing that prevents you from seizing the circumstances and shaping a unique role for yourself in the flux.

Robiul was such a person to me, because he had proved that people can achieve this even in the backwaters of the world, even when they are so old that no new life will measure up in span to the former, discarded one. I hadn't known much about him before my recent interest in the region. He had been one of a number of quiet, unremarkable stringers working from the districts and far provinces. Just a distant voice on the phone, a sender of telex messages with facts and quotes, a name in an occasional byline, a man collecting a small monthly retainership and article fees to supplement his main job as an English lecturer at a local college. If he became seen as anything more than this in the office, it was only at the moment of his resignation, when he turned down an offer to make him a staffer, with all the benefits that implied.

The details of his dispute with the *Sentinel* editors were revealed only in fragments, but it seems the process began when he came to Calcutta to ask permission to write a special story. A local boy, someone whose parents he knew, had been murdered while on a new job in distant Bombay. Robiul wanted the *Sentinel* to put their man in Bombay on the murder, although he would be more than willing to go himself if they agreed. The paper did what it was best at doing: Sarkar listened to him and pretended to be excited. Then he asked Robiul to go back home while they planned the piece. Of course, he promptly forgot about it as soon as Robiul was out of the way. No malice was intended; it was just unimportant to Sarkar and the paper. If it had been a Calcutta boy, someone from a well-known family, things would have been different.

Robiul sent a stream of queries for a month, and when it became clear even to him that nothing would come of it, he resigned.

They offered him a permanent position then, but Robiul didn't change his mind. The telex he sent with his rejection had been passed around the office. He was tired of a decade of work in which the paper had ignored his best efforts in the same way that his region was ignored by India. "Much water under the bridge," Robiul said at the end of his message. "Like Thomas Hardy poem. Years like black oxen. Broken by their feet." People were uncertain if it was Robiul or the region that had been broken by the passage of time.

I sensed a defiant man in the message, a guess that was confirmed by his friendliness when I phoned him from Calcutta for help with my story. A man who felt defeated would have been bitter and resentful: Robiul's openness was possible only because he was sure of himself. It gave me some reason to feel hopeful in the middle of all my uncertainties, and I thought in a vague way that Robiul would bring me luck.

❖ 3 ❖

The call from Robiul came after nearly two weeks of waiting, on an afternoon when I had just finished a strained conversation with the *Sentinel* office. A hostile and suspicious Sarkar had finally got in touch to find out why I hadn't sent any stories and what was making me stay in a hotel with just one telephone line. I managed to deflect his suspicions with hints about the investigative piece I was working on. It was necessary to think on my feet, so I gave him something about the murder of a former insurgent in mysterious circumstances and how the powers involved were trying to cover it up as a simple revenge killing. The cheap hotel was part of waiting for a contact, someone who had insisted on meeting at a fairly anonymous location. It sounded a little thin even to me, but Sarkar gave me another week.

"What gave you the idea I wanted special investigative stories?" he said. "But I will let your behavior pass for now, and you can finish this one. Be proactive, Singh. Look, I need color pieces, things about local festivals, wildlife sanctuaries, shopping. Feature-like things. Do they have adventure tourism?" I told him that everything was an adventure out here, but Sarkar was deaf to irony. "Find out if they're planning adventure tourism. If not, suggest it to them. Then do a story on it. Look, we have to pull in advertisers. It's a potentially good market, but we need your stories to gauge how people will respond to increased coverage from a national daily. The financier wants to see us doing something."

I remembered that Sarkar had wangled a semester at some small American university on a cultural exchange program run by the U.S. consulate. He had come back with the convert's zeal, full of snappy phrases like "wave of the future" and "consumer markets" that emanated from him like an aura.

"Do me a favor, Singh. Just forget about the insurgency after this," he said before hanging up. "And be with-it. Region's opening up, remember, with new business opportunities. Just be with-it. I'm counting on you, Amrit."

When the phone rang again, I picked it up with great reluctance. "Robiul here," the voice rustled. "Amrit, I am back in city. Will be with you shortly, say half hour." I began to tell him where I was staying, but he interrupted. "Know where you are. Thirty minutes, not a second more." I put away the bottle of warm beer Joseph had sent and cleaned myself up. Then I took out the picture and sat there holding it, as if it were a talisman that would invoke Robiul.

He came into the room with a light knock, his flowing gray curls and the loose white shirt he wore over his trousers giving him a misty, spectral appearance. His touch was cold and clammy as we shook hands, his demeanor and appearance more that of a provincial poet or artist than of a newspaper stringer. When I gave him the photograph, he took it from me without a word, like a bereaved father come to collect the belongings of a dead child. After he had finished scrutinizing it, he turned it over to read the caption. Then he gave me a wry smile. I strained to catch his words as he spoke, finding his falsetto somewhat disconcerting.

"Picture was sent by Thoiba. Referred by me for *Sentinel* stringer position last year."

"Where can I find Thoiba?" I asked.

Robiul shook his head gravely.

"Thoiba dead."

He continued in rapid-fire phrases, as though he was composing a story for a telex operator hunched over his machine. "Not violent incident. Bus plunges into gorge while avoiding oncoming truck on hairpin bend along Aizawl highway. Four spot dead. Driver and three passengers." He stood up. "Come. Brief walk to bus stop. Then my house."

We left the hotel, making our way past the small travel

agencies and restaurants that encircled the interstate bus terminus, and approached the narrow footbridge spanning the railway tracks and platforms. Where the bridge began, just beyond track four, beggars had dispersed themselves along the stairs; in the middle of the footbridge, somewhere between platforms two and three, a police officer stood on guard with two constables, an obstacle around which the busy stream of passengers, coolies, and local men with their bicycles eddied and swirled cautiously. The constables, scrawny men in white uniforms, alternately watched the pedestrians and the officer, the latter usually immersed in deep thought, eyes closed. He was much larger than the constables, and the black butt of his revolver peeped out like a timid bird from the holster on his ample waist. Every once in a while, he emerged from his trance to point out an approaching figure. The constables reached out with their sticks and tapped the chosen individual, bringing him to a halt and making him open his bags in the center of the bridge, damming the flow of traffic and creating a great flurry of activity at one end, where the beggars began working the stalled crowd with enthusiasm.

The whole thing was an impressive exercise. I doubt the policemen ever found the bombs or guns they were looking for, although when I suggested this later during a chance meeting with the officer in charge of the railway police, he angrily fished out a sheet of paper and began reciting from it: "One thousand four hundred numbers of gelatin, five hundred numbers of detonators, and sixteen numbers of bundles carrying fuse wires." It sounded like a very strange shopping list, but he was really trying to impress upon me the many seizures his men had made in the past few months.

Robiul nodded pleasantly at the beggars and the constables—the officer mercifully had his eyes closed—and took me across to the main platform. A large group of coolies and relatives was awaiting the arrival of a long-delayed train from Delhi, kept company by the sharp ammonia stench of urine and the smell of human excreta lying between the tracks. Robiul apologized for having taken so long to return to the city; a family wedding had taken him to a small town upriver and then he had been held back by the heavy rains. "Most anxious to help you with your story. Unusual story." He looked up at me and smiled reassuringly. "Many unusual stories here, of course," he said. "Never an end to them."

The sky had finally cleared after the steady downpours of the past three days, and the city felt unexpectedly pleasant as we left the station behind, entering the main thoroughfare where hibiscus and jacaranda flowers were in bloom. The colonial-era offices and college buildings looked well-maintained, and the trees were quite unlike the grimy, skeletal structures visible on Calcutta roads. Even the large, slightly desolate pond off to one side looked as if it would have been an attractive space if there had been more people around. A lone young woman, pretty in spite of her bright slash of lipstick and gaudy *salwar kameez*, paced around the perimeter of the water. Occasionally, she glanced at the distant policeman perched on his little traffic island, or at the single men in Maruti cars who slowed down as they passed by. Further along we came across a sand-colored paramilitary van, and when the soldiers clicked at us with their tongues to use the opposite pavement, the atmosphere of everyday ordinariness was dispelled.

Robiul's voice seemed to become clearer and less of a falsetto as we walked, and he talked about the photograph I had shown him with a mixture of sadness and irritation.

"Young woman led astray," he said, shouting above the noise of a minibus that bore down upon us and then veered away at the last moment. "Extremists, every man jack here. The militants, the army, our young people, your old officials."

"Will I be able to find her?"

"If you're lucky," he shouted back. "Usually quite easy to find someone there. People know."

"Small-town thing?"

"Sure." He pointed at the jumble of shops lining the streets, with young men perched on scooters and motorcycles outside the tea stalls. "But when people go missing and the army or the boys have something to do with it, then nobody seems to know. Locals, outsiders, it doesn't matter." Robiul's white clothes were getting splattered with mud from passing vehicles. He didn't notice. "I will help, yes. You have decent ambitions." He stressed the word "decent." "Personally though, Amrit, I have left all this behind. The news, the head-lines, the stories. Things are not always what they seem, and you think you are doing the right thing when you are only making it worse. I am finished with all that. I have chosen." He made it sound like a terrible oath. "Chosen the sane, middle ground. Path of detachment. No more extremes."

A gap appeared in the pavement ahead of us, a missing flagstone with a flashing glimpse of the swirling, dark waters of the sewers below. Robiul deftly stepped off the pavement to the road, guiding me along with a light hand. "Gets worse where you are going. Proceed to Imphal for story, but proceed with caution. Avoid extreme reactions, avoid involvement, and concentrate on practicing the journalist's objectivity. Detach-ment." It was strange advice from a man who had quit because he wanted to pursue a particular story. "You are coming from the outside, you say? Good. Detached observer. Find your subject, interview subject, get out. No involvement. No further complications."

The torrent of speech was dammed temporarily by the discovery of a minibus that went to his neighborhood. It was a long ride past half-constructed buildings and more unfinished flyovers, but then we were in the outskirts with small houses set amid the thick foliage of the hillsides. The major landmark in the area was a cigarette factory near the road, its brown walls starkly visible amid the lush, wild vegetation everywhere. I had a sense now of what the city had been like in the past, before the insurgency and the building boom took over with their odd juxtaposition of violence and money, and I thought the place a good refuge for Robiul, far removed from the trauma of headlines and news reports.

His house was a ramshackle old bungalow with whitewashed walls and an unpainted tin roof, fenced in by a wild jumble of lantana and bamboo. The room that served as his office resembled the external surroundings, its random collection of papers and books suggesting that much had been left to nature and chance inside as well as out. The Olivetti typewriter sitting in the middle of the desk, its keys brushed smooth with use and age, resembled old lawn-mowers one sees in gardens run wild, more part of the landscape than an instrument of order and reason; the literature textbooks, news clippings, and press releases had crept up over the years like wild grass—and it seemed that Robiul's talk of the sane, middle ground came out of a sharp sense of having lost control. A colored print of Mecca on the wall indicated that he was a Muslim, although I had had no inkling of this so far, and I felt that all the clues to his character were hidden in the mass of papers and objects in that room.

"The woman in the picture, Amrit? You can perhaps find her. The local contacts will know how you should go about it. There are others who might help as well, particularly a man called Malik. But for the background to the story? Talk to local sources about MORLS, but don't probe too deep."

"Why?" I said with some surprise. "Not that they're more important than the woman, but they are interesting for some sense of context. It would be useful to interview some members from the group."

"Context?" Robiul asked. "You live in this country and you do not have the context? Did the Khalistanis in Punjab not go around telling women how to dress? You were in Punjab for some years, you told me, reporting the end of Bhindranwale's men. Did you miss everything that happened? Are there not groups in Kashmir that flung acid on women without the veil? And don't we know that there is another movement gathering force, bigger than the Khalistanis and the Kashmiris and the insurgents of my region, men in khaki shorts whose center of power is not in some border state but in the heart of the republic itself?"

He was speaking in full sentences now. The dust and scattered paper and books that had seemed so chaotic at first seemed to give him a solidity he had not possessed before, almost as if he were an image developing slowly in a chemical solution. Under those loose clothes, he was a small and old man, even though he held himself very erect. He didn't look dreamy any longer, the way he had in the hotel room, and he brushed his hair away from his face with a barely contained intensity as he spoke to me.

"We are quite lost, Amrit. All of us, and that is why I know you have had the context all your life. You may be a stranger here, but you are no stranger to your country. And things aren't that different here from anywhere else, perhaps more extreme, yes, but not a different order of things." He waited while a servant brought strong Assam tea and little sweets made from coconut paste. "I should be clearer about what I want to tell you. This group doing the press conference, this MORLS, it bothers me more than any other insurgent group I have written about in twenty years. You must be aware that sometimes the government encourages a particular set of people to pose as an insurgent organization in order to discredit other outfits, in order to control things. You follow me?"

"It worked well for them in the Punjab. Turning the battle between police and insurgents into a blood feud."

"Here, too. In Manipur, the Kuki tribe has been fighting the Nagas for all of last year. Villages burnt on both sides, passengers pulled out of buses and gunned down. Now, who were the Nagas attacking before that? The Indian government, the paramilitary, the police. How did the Kukis get arms suddenly so that the Nagas were kept busy fighting them? You see. But there is more. There is always much more.

"Sometimes the intelligence agencies arm certain people. But often it's also political parties supporting one group or the other, even individual politicians using an insurgent group as muscle. And some of the insurgent groups are not much more than armed groups looking to make quick money. There are more than a hundred insurgent organizations in the region, nearly fifteen in Manipur alone. Who knows anything about all these groups except for their names? You think they all have manifestos, a party structure, a central command? Who is to say which is an insurgent group and which is not when strangers come knocking in the dark with their faces covered?

"Concentrate on finding the woman. But do it fast. Get your information, go home, write the story. There is a lull in the violence because of the peace negotiations going on, so you may as well go now. But don't hang around. The longer you stay, the more complicated the story gets."

He began doodling on a piece of paper, producing three circles that looked like balloons or like trees drawn by small children. He added straight lines to the balloons, and they became the bulbous heads of stick figures. Then he put in more lines, so that the stick figures were holding guns with stocks and triggers and muzzles. "She would have been a local woman, quite young, probably not staying with her family because it would have been too shameful for them, what she was doing. Imphal is a small town, you see, and everybody knows everybody else. It is quite possible she has no family to speak of, at least no father, and that she had to support herself and her mother. You are interested in motive, how she would do such a thing as act in a porn film? Blackmail, probably by someone she trusted. Not difficult at all. You sleep with a woman, take some pictures, threaten to expose her. Or you dangle the possibility of film roles, saying what has to be done at present is only a necessary step on the road to fame. The MORLS seems to be made up of stupid brutes, but they must have had some evidence about the film. And there would have to be an outsider involved in the making of the film, by which I mean someone from mainland India, from Calcutta or Delhi or Bombay, someone with the money and technical resources."

"Murky," I said.

"Sad," Robiul replied. "A sad story. Like the story of my people, my region." He handed me a thick envelope. "Contacts in Imphal. Phone numbers, addresses, names. Some background information. Read at leisure."

I took a quick look at the contents of the envelope. He had collected clippings for me and painstakingly typed out two full sheets of information with phone numbers and addresses. He had also added little notes about the people. "Treat what he has to say about the Nagas or other ethnic groups with some skepticism. He is something of a chauvinist." At the very end of the list, there was the name I had heard of before—"Malik, Director, Prosperity Project, Moirang Lake region"—and next to it the cryptic comment, "Possesses good information, but what are his sources?"

Robiul walked with me to the bus stop, holding a large steel torch that lit up the overgrown path leading down to the main road—a national highway that disappeared into the hills of Meghalaya where the green of the river valley gave way to a more ethereal blue. The neighborhood had been a pleasant sight when I arrived in the afternoon, but although the sun was just beginning to set behind the hills, the place was now deserted, the cycle repair shop and tea stall I had seen on my way here shuttered down. At the bus stop, there were only two other passengers waiting for a ride into the city center, Bihari milkmen squatting on the ground with large metal cans, while from a temple further down the road came the sound of a *kirtan* being performed, a hypnotic, wailing voice appealing to God the beloved, its sorrow punctuated by the sound of little hand-cymbals. As Robiul and I waited in the twilight, he pointed out the posters of local insurgents on the walls of the bus shelter, the rising sun of their organization pasted like an indigenous brand name next to the advertisements for soap, washing powder, and cigarettes put out by the big companies.

CHAPTER THREE

◈ **1** ◈

The photograph of the woman had surfaced in the office morgue—so called because of the anticipatory obituaries of public figures kept there—at the end of a long day full of small irritations: the usual bad weather, long traffic jams, promised stories that turned out to be dead ends, and a couple of hours wasted in the office library looking through its disorganized files. As if this was not enough, I was on duty as the solitary night reporter, and by the time the reporters' room emptied out with a scrape of chairs and hiss of matches, the dry throat and stiff back bothering me all day had flared into the unmistakable signs of a Calcutta viral fever.

Around eleven, when the early edition had been closed and I had one more hour to go, Pandey came into the room. I didn't look up, but he stood insistently by my side and I gathered from his mumbling that he wanted to close up for the night. This was unusual: he was on duty outside the reporters' room, and both of us had to stay till midnight, his task being to sit by the door while I waited near the phone for a possible front-page incident. I showed him my watch, but he gave me a sly grin and suggested that I go to the morgue. He had seen me leafing through files in the library, and winked and gestured at his keys to indicate that he could let me in if the morgue happened to be locked.

Pandey was the oddest of peons in this office full of curiosities. He had a pale bald head with a big mole on his forehead, thick glasses that exaggerated a severe cross-eyed gaze, and a pair of mismatched legs, the right shorter than the left. If anyone said anything about his legs, which the younger reporters frequently did, he replied with choice obscenities that began in loud Bhojpuri and trailed off into English. But he was a canny fellow, rather good at judging people, and he had figured out that his chances of getting home early would improve if he suggested something of interest to me. He jingled his keys again, saying that there were enough files in the morgue for me to spend my remaining hour fruitfully, and it struck me that perhaps he was right. It was unlikely that anything major would happen in the city at this hour, so I took my bag and followed his limping figure down the editorial corridor with its row of unmarked doors.

The room Pandey led me to was on the third-floor landing, facing the men's bathroom. I had never been there before, but I knew that, apart from being a repository for obituary files, it was used as an office by two sports stringers. They must have left the room unlocked, because I didn't need Pandey's keys to get in. He turned on the light, pointed at the shelves on the walls, and left. I could hear him going down the staircase—the bent, shorter leg leading the way as if the other leg was at fault. Next to the door through which I had entered, there was a framed certificate on the wall, the crinkled sheet of paper barely visible through the stained and oily pane of glass covering it. Opposite this was a desk piled high with yellowed invoices and vouchers left behind by the sports stringers. Behind the desk was another door, while the walls held deep shelves which ran all the way up to the ceiling, protected from the dust by sliding glass doors. It felt like a room that had been created out of a larger one, something that was quite common in the vast spaces of the *Sentinel* building, and I wondered how long they had been using it as the morgue.

I looked at the folders in the shelves, realizing that they held much more than anticipatory obituaries: photographs, election results, maps, press releases and dispatches that had never been carried. The bottom shelf to my left was filled with a bunch of files marked "Regional," and it was here I began my search, ignoring those folders named after public figures or political parties. Each state, and occasionally a district, had a "Miscellaneous" folder to itself. These looked promising, with odd news items that would never qualify as front page stories but were likely sources for the kind of things that might interest a foreign magazine. As I worked my way along the row, however, I discovered it ended in *K*. I looked around the room, checking all the shelves—even rifling through the desk of the sports stringers—but there were no other folders for states.

The tiredness of fever, the absurdity of the incomplete and random records, and the abandoned atmosphere of the morgue seemed more than anything like an uneasy hallucination, and I wondered if I had stumbled into a story of some kind. Nothing after *K*. Did the premonitions of the death of public figures also stop at a certain place in the alphabet? Perhaps there was a secret arrangement to the order of the folders, a coded message or signal that I would have to unlock over the years. Maybe I had uncovered my real vocation in the *Sentinel*, the central meaning of my life.

I found that I was leaning over the desk, laughing out loud even though my throat hurt. My voice sounded distended in the room, and the expense vouchers of the sports stringers fluttered to the floor as I slapped one hand on the desk, still laughing; only the sound of someone going into the bathroom made me sober up. I decided to put the Kerala folder back in place, turning it over to smooth out a bent corner before slipping it into the shelf. The word "Continues" had been scribbled on the back, with an arrow next to it in red. Continues where? Inside secret recesses in the wall? Then I thought of the other door, right behind the desk.

I pushed at it, the door feeling heavy and creaking in protest as I applied my weight to it and felt around for the light switch. It was as if I had stepped through a mirror; there were similar shelves along the walls, a framed certificate hung slightly askew next to the door, and another desk. Checking the shelves on my left to see if there were folders for the other states, I found they were there all right, continuing from *K*. It was as I pulled at the folder on Manipur that the photograph fell out, lying at my feet like a note that had been hidden there exclusively for me.

I looked at the woman sitting on the chair and her expressionless face, at the eyes of the two men—almost hidden in the shadows of their scarves—and felt something that was a mixture of unease and triumph. I sat down at the bare desk, and after I had read the caption, I went through the rest of the folder methodically to see if there was any more material related to the picture. But the other stuff was commonplace: press releases from government agencies and local sporting clubs, typed reports about a visit by a central minister and mass demonstrations after incidents with the army. The photograph was an anomaly in this folder, a window to a distant place, quite unlike the mass of words and papers that offered no images of Manipur at all. The place simply did not exist in my mind, but the photograph had offered me a glimpse into that faraway corner of the country, and I sensed that at last I had found a possible story for Herman.

With twenty minutes to go before the midnight car left for the south, I decided to take the picture with me. I glanced quickly at the shelves to make sure I'd not missed any other files, and as my gaze fell on the third row from the top, I felt as if I were looking into another mirror or threshold. The shelf was filled from end to end with a series of identical books, nearly fifty of them, each with gold lettering displayed on a bright orange background. They looked new, and the words on the spines glittered even in the dull light. I slid the glass door to the side with difficulty and pulled out a book from the end. The copies were tightly packed and I struggled to extract one, but once I'd done so, the others filled the empty space as swiftly and silently as water closing over a gap created by a rock thrown into a pool.

I sniffed at the tome in my hands; it was an old, satisfying smell, hinting at bookstores and libraries from long ago. Unmarked except at the edges of the thick pages, which had a slight yellow tinge to them, the book had the logo of a typewriter on its title page. Below this were the words:

Eastern Eyes

Euan Sutherland

Printed by the Imperial House

9 & 10 Chowringhee Square

Calcutta

1946

The "Imperial House" baffled me, although I knew the rest of the address well enough: the book had been printed here, in this very building, but in the days when the *Sentinel* had been a colonial paper called the *Imperial*.

Somewhere an old grandfather clock struck twelve, its faint booms echoing through the cavernous interiors of the building. I didn't want to miss the ride home, so I stuffed a copy of Euan Sutherland's book into my bag, checked the photograph was still there, turned the lights off in both rooms, and left.

❖ 2 ❖

R obiul had told me to fly to Imphal, no more than an hour's journey by air on one of the Boeings run by a regional branch of the Indian Airlines. "Get in quick, get out quick, and make sure you have seat reserved for return flight." The airfares were subsidized, and in spite of aging planes and uncertain schedules, flying was faster and more dependable for long trips than taking one of the buses departing from the nearby terminus.

But Robiul called with bad news early in the morning, just as I was about to head for the city booking office. "Do not attempt to get ticket," he said in his usual falsetto. "All flights to Imphal canceled for remainder of month. Engine trouble with both aircrafts." He sounded agitated and somewhat uncertain, and I had the feeling—not for the first or last time during those months in the region—that something was being kept back from me. I asked Robiul if I could hire a car and driver to take me through the shortest land route. "No short routes here, only long, indefinite ones," he replied. "The road is so bad, Amrit. We will not be able to find any one driver and car to take you through the entire stretch." It was an uncertain journey by land, he said with reluctance as I pressed him for details; maybe a thousand kilometers of bad roads across three states, with floods in sections of the plains and landslides in the hills. I got the impression there was more on his mind than canceled flights and bad roads, that he had perhaps changed his opinion about my going to Imphal, although I had no idea how that could possibly affect him.

"Do recollect the amount of time it took me to get back from wedding," he said. "If you get stuck somewhere in middle?"

"But I am stuck in the middle," I said. "My story's in Imphal, and home, I suppose, is somewhere in Calcutta. What on earth am I doing here?"

"Yes, I know. You have only been waiting here to see me. Now that you have seen, you must move on." He made up his mind and began talking rapidly. "Only way is along Highway 39 through state of Nagaland. Perhaps from here to the refinery town near state border with Nagaland. Then one must take Highway 39 all the way across Nagaland to Manipur. Maybe four or five days' worth of journeying."

I liked the quaint term he used, "journeying." There was a certain weight to the word that reminded me of the way people had talked thirty or forty years ago, when going somewhere involved important and difficult decisions, and traveling was not to be taken lightly. Robiul took my pause as hesitation. He started telling me again about how it would be impossible to find a driver willing to go all the way: different tribes, separate police forces, too many insurgent groups for a single man to depend on the protection money he paid out in any one place.

"What about taking the buses, like most other people? Anyway, I'm not even sure I can afford a driver and a car both there and back." From what I had heard, it was possible that the buses would end up costing me more than a plane ticket and even then leave me stranded somewhere on the road.

Robiul remained silent. I heard the dopplering blast of a truck that was coming from or heading for the interstate highway, and then in the quiet that followed, what sounded like the clanging of a temple bell, sonorous and slow.

"Bus is possible," Robiul replied. "But sometimes buses get stopped. Accidents take place."

He didn't say who stopped the buses.

"Even a journalist with a press card can have difficulties on such occasions. Then, such a bad time of the year to be journeying. Landslides and broken bridges can hold up road traffic for days." He tried one last time to dissuade me, but when I remained adamant that I wanted to head for Imphal right away, said I should take the bus if I was determined to go.

"Fine," I said hastily. "Maybe I'll find a driver with a car somewhere along the road. Maybe I'll find something else worthwhile."

"So you will, Amrit. You should stop overnight at refinery town on border before starting out on Highway 39. I will see to government accommodation at refinery guesthouse. Once you reach Kohima, it will be possible to have car and driver arranged for the rest of the Nagaland-Manipur route. That part perhaps will not be so difficult if the cease-fire between government and insurgents holds."

I said nothing, reflecting on the uncertain road ahead, wondering how long it would actually take to reach Imphal and if I would be better off waiting for the flights to resume.

"You are sure you want to do this, Amrit? You are sure about your story?" Again, there was the sound of a truck in the background, over which the high pitch of Robiul's voice screeched sharply. "If it is only a problem with *Sentinel* job, I know an editor at other Calcutta paper, who is originally from this region. He may be able to offer you a position with his paper. I could ask. That would be simpler than this . . ." He fumbled for words before continuing. "This wild venture. Amrit, even if you do the story about the woman, it is not certain to me at all what you will do after you leave *Sentinel*. You say you will cash in your retirement fund, but how long does that last? I speak from personal experience."

I was touched by Robiul's concern, but also impatient to be done with the discussion. He was old, I thought to myself, and perhaps I had been wrong about him. Maybe he had been broken by the years of unrewarding work in a provincial city. "Amrit, I have not revealed before. The lecturer position, I am due for retirement very soon, so I work part-time for Marwari concern to earn extra money. Job involves writing tender applications and letters to government agencies and suppliers. This is no country for old men."

"I wish I had known."

"No, Amrit, it is not that important. Have been very glad to see you. But this German friend of yours, if he loses interest in you? What is this magazine you are to write for? Do German magazines take English articles, and why should they be interested in the backwaters of the backwaters? All these questions bother me."

"They bother me too," I said. "They've been bothering me ever since I left Calcutta. But I have to try this because there's nothing else to do. There hasn't been anything else to do for a very long time."

"Then call me if you need help or more information. Have spoken to people in Imphal. Keep in mind what I say. Don't dig too much into MORLS. And don't go to Burma alone. Take reliable local man with you before you cross the Burma border, even if you are sightseeing only."

"Burma? Why does Burma keep coming up in conversations about Manipur? I have no interest in Burma."

"You will please listen to me, Amrit. In Burma if they discover you are journalist, they lock you in four-by-four cube, throw away the keys, and forget about you. Don't take camera if you go, no press card, just plain tourist looking to buy foreign-made goods, maybe wanting to make some money. That they like. Remember what I say."

The bus to the refinery town left at eleven, so I had Joseph get me a ticket while I finished packing. I discarded all the news clippings that I had gathered as a possible insurance against Sarkar checking up on me. All the stories went into the wastepaper basket: encounters between insurgents and the army, political scandals, a mortar attack on the state assembly just before I got here, the killing of the lieutenant, this last item accompanied by a picture of the lieutenant's fiancée amid the wilted marigold garlands. I felt a brief sense of exhilaration as I dropped the articles one by one into the bin, aware that I was finally beginning my journey, cutting my ties to the *Sentinel*, and, in a small but satisfying act of revenge, leaving Sarkar ignorant as to my whereabouts. I paid Joseph in the lobby, asking him not to tell anyone who called where I was going.

As I stepped back, a woman approached, accompanied by a small boy. I heard their voices behind me and felt a tug at my shirt. It was the boy, who pointed at the woman. She was coming toward me, one hand brushing her hair back from her forehead—the only sign she was nervous or self-conscious.

"You're the reporter from the big paper," she said. It was not a question, but the voice was pleasant, the accent hinting at missionary-run schools and an expensive college.

I thought she looked vaguely familiar, and realized I had seen her at the cremation, drifting back alone to the funeral pyre as the rest of us departed from the scene.

The pharmaceutical salesmen, who were just starting their day's work, scrutinized her as they came out into the lobby, slowing down so as to take a good look, drawing themselves up straight and adjusting the small knots on their big ties. She ignored them, staring at me with such intensity that I began to feel awkward. "I want you to do a story about the killing of my fiancé," she said.

"Leaving the city. Bus to catch," I said in reply to this odd request. I gestured over my shoulder in emphasis. She didn't say anything immediately. Instead, she reached into her hand-bag without taking her eyes off me and pulled out some papers.

"My father was involved in the killing. Santanu, my fiancé, was set up."

"I'm sorry, but talk to some of the local reporters. I'm leaving for Manipur."

"It'll take you a year to get there by bus," she said. "Why aren't you interested in my story?"

We had moved into the reception area to let other people pass through the door. I had a better look at her now, surprised she had so much authority for a young woman. She was taller than average and light-skinned, the elongated shape of her eyes indicating that she was from the region. She was attractive, and it seemed understandable that the pharmaceutical salesmen and petty officials suddenly had things to ask of Joseph, crowding the little lobby and looking at her. The wariness she had projected at the cremation had given way to a determined air, and she remained unmoved by the attention from the men in the hotel.

"Look, there's no time to discuss all this. I'm going somewhere for an important story." It was as if I was trying to convince myself rather than her.

She appeared not to have heard, and stood there assessing me while the boy looked around with a bored expression, and Joseph and the hotel guests watched us from near the desk. "My fiancé went to the transport operator's house to collect money for my father, did you know that?" she said, not lowering her voice. "My father was Santanu's business partner. He was the one who introduced me to Santanu and wanted me to get married to him. But he began to have second thoughts when Santanu's luck started running out. The government changed, and the politicians who had persuaded him and his friends to surrender were no longer able to give him business contacts. They themselves had been put under investigation about their links to the insurgents. My father, he broke with Santanu just days before he was killed. Do this story for me, please. It's important."

Glaxo tried to catch my eye and winked slowly and emphatically.

"Sounds intriguing, but I have something else to do," I said, feeling stupid and irritated to be arguing with her. If she had come a few days ago, I could have written the piece and got Sarkar off my back for a couple of weeks.

Joseph, standing behind his desk, sensed my impatience and said, "Sir, your bus leaves in fifteen minutes."

I grabbed my bags and began to walk away, ignoring the papers she held out and the expression on her face, now beginning to look threatening. "Why aren't you interested? I thought you wanted to write about what's happening here. So write about me, about my husband, my father. This is what is happening here, this is the story you are looking for."

She started following me. I broke into a jog, feeling angry and irritated, the typewriter case heavy in my right hand. "You won't find anything new where you are going. It's the same old story everywhere." I felt unnerved, conscious at the back of my mind that it was bad luck to leave a place in this fashion, with someone set dead against your departure. "You'll never finish your story, do you understand, you won't get what you're looking for."

I turned back to say something equally sharp, but she was crying, holding out the papers that revealed the business deals between her father and her dead fiancé and the reason for his death. She remained like that, offering me material that I was in no position to receive. "Joseph will give you Robiul's number," I shouted to her, loud enough that the others could hear. "Ask him for Robiul Haq's number. He can help you." There were murmurs among the hotel guests in the lobby as I ran for the bus, already beginning to pull out of its bay.

❖ 3 ❖

my transport to the refinery town was an old diesel monstrosity with narrow, hard seats and windows that didn't shut properly. Streaks of various shades and width ran the length of the faded yellow body, the name of the state transport corporation and its charging rhinoceros logo barely visible beneath the streaks. I jammed myself into the long seat at the back, preferring one of the last two free windows even though the spot at the center of the seat would have allowed me to stretch my legs into the aisle. The other passengers were already frozen in the postures of a long journey, packing themselves tightly into little boxes of space the way people do on buses and planes, robbed of the forgiving sprawl and spill of the train compartment.

The bus nosed its way through the traffic with a harsh grinding of its gears, moving past cycle rickshaws and minibuses furiously circling the vortices of traffic islands festooned with slightly provincial advertisements. *Gwalior Suitings and Shirtings, Come to Centaur Hotel, Charms is the Spirit of Freedom* — the words appeared in bright, cheerful colors over our heads, almost obscuring the skeletal buildings and flyovers that rose behind them with grim determination. As we came out of the marketplace and railway station, the main road of the city appeared like a straight black ribbon in our path, the sandbagged checkpoints retracted for the span of daylight. We stopped at temporary bus shelters to pick up single men, shabby and slight figures who staggered down the aisle with cheap zippered canvas bags and openmouthed jute bags that bore the slogan *Big Shopper* on the side. They quickly picked their traveling companions from the double seats, and I remained on my own at the back.

The cigarette factory came up on the left and Robiul's neighborhood flashed by swiftly, leaving me with a fleeting image of him sitting in his crowded study composing tender applications on his Olivetti for the Marwari trading concern. Gradually, the everyday traffic ceded place to long-distance buses like ours, to overloaded supply trucks and army vehicles that thundered down the watery road, while the closely packed concrete structures of that strange, cloud-covered city gave way to petrol stations and low, wide government bungalows with faded blue signboards in front of them. Three young men rode past on new motorcycles that had no numbers, the transparent plastic sheets that still covered the passenger saddles flapping in the wind.

We were nearly on the highway when we saw a soldier waving at the bus, a woman and boy at his side; the woman looked like an officer's wife accompanied by her husband's orderly. The bus driver didn't stop, but a big pothole forced him to slow down momentarily and we heard shouts and smacks against the exterior of the bus as the soldier ran alongside, struggled with the door, and swung himself in. The driver braked hastily, and the conductor, a middle-aged man whose mouth was red with betel juice, made toward the door as if he had been planning to open it. I could see him breaking into a strained smile, the red juice dribbling from the corners of his mouth, apologizing as the soldier balled his hand into a fist. The point had been made, however, so no blows were struck. The soldier got off the bus to fetch the woman's bags while the conductor hastily ordered a couple of villagers up from the seat near the door, moving their bundles toward the back. The villagers quietly obeyed, settling themselves next to me on the backseat near the other window, while the woman and her son took the just-vacated place at the front. In a final warning, the soldier wagged his finger at the conductor before stepping off the bus.

The highway was cracked and broken, barely wide enough for two lanes of traffic, a shadow of a road pushing its way through the fields and villages. We slowed frequently to let faster vehicles pass, many of them army trucks. Large tin hoardings appeared by the road, but advertisements for soft drinks and cigarettes had given way to signs for seeds, fertilizers, engine oil, and tires. The colors were no longer quite so bright and hopeful, and the lasting impression in my mind was that of an unvarying, faded yellow—much like the color of the bus—a yellow that permeated and stained the landscape with its weary presence. The slogans had been sketched in clunky lettering accompanied by simple illustrations on discolored backgrounds. It was unclear whether the products, some of them from the seventies, were still being sold in this region, or if the companies had simply given up long ago.

The bus rattled on, and the names that appeared sporadically on shopfronts were from the lost pages of a child's school atlas on India—Urubani, Nakhola, Chaparmukh, Misa,

Hatikhuli—the places themselves no more than small settlements on a widening of the road that allowed cars and trucks to be parked along both sides. One petrol pump, two hotels—places for eating in rather than for shelter—an auto repair station, a rudimentary marketplace with a few stalls selling everyday necessities. The people walking by looked smaller than their counterparts in the city, the men appearing almost stunted as they shuffled down the road in baggy polyester shirts and trousers, some of them barely avoiding the bus as it hooted impatiently at them.

We stopped for lunch at one of the bigger halts, with supply trucks massed along the bends in the road, dwarfing the shacks they were parked in front of. Some of the passengers went behind the trucks to relieve themselves, amid drivers and their assistants bathing and carrying out repair work. Others made for the toilets behind the hotels, picking their way across slimy bamboo matting laid over unpaved drains and waterlogged yards, while the hotels hummed with the sound of scurrying, dodging boys rushing from table to table with full plates.

The army officer's wife sat nursing a cup of tea inside one of the hotels, her short haircut and the pastel shade of her sari indicating her social status. She was not the kind of passenger usually to be found on these long-distance buses, and it would have seemed far more natural if she had stepped out of an official car with the driver holding the door, the hotel owner rushing to reserve a separate space for such an important guest. She appeared unaware of the incongruity, however, seemingly content to let her plump, sad-looking son stand by himself on the road, watching the trucks and their drivers. After his interest in them was exhausted, he looked back at his mother and seemed about to return to her side, then changed his mind. He drifted about for some time and came back a few minutes later—unable to divert himself any longer—and approached her cautiously. I drank my tea and watched as she counted out some change for him; she sank back into her reverie as the boy left with the money.

He circulated through the roadside stalls, carefully surveying the contents of the jars in three identical shops before buying some biscuits. An openmouthed bag lay at his mother's feet, and he waved the biscuits above the bag as if he expected something to happen. A nose appeared from the bag, then a pair of eyes, followed by the floppy ears of a Pekingese dog that licked the boy's hand and the biscuits indiscriminately. The boy lifted the dog out of the bag and sat next to his mother, the Pekingese resting quietly on his lap, until the driver blew his horn in long, ominous-sounding blasts that indicated it was time to move on.

THE HIGHWAY BECAME EVEN NARROWER, though this had not seemed possible, and the bus moved like a pen over the flat paper of the district, leaving behind a trail of diesel fume and the discarded detritus of the passengers—banana peels, cigarette packets, newspapers that had been used to wrap food, red splotches of betel-nut juice. Villages appeared in thick banana groves and orchards, and my eye was drawn to the whitewash of community temples and the dull tarred frames of long, flat school buildings raised on stone plinths. Small squares of land were parceled up by thin bamboo fences, clothing of indeterminate shapes and colors drying on them, while amid the rice fields and clumps of water hyacinths, moved the single, solitary figures of cranes.

As we moved further from the city, the occasional tribal villagers appeared in the countryside, conical reed hats on the men, the passing glimpse of brown breasts on a woman as she stooped among the plants. Inside the bus, the passengers now lolled, dulled by the heat and the food in their bellies and the great distance still to be covered. Some new passengers had boarded at our lunch halt and dispersed themselves through the rattling body of the bus; an old priest, the caste marks of the Vaishnavite visible on his forehead like a carefully painted set of extra wrinkles; a rotund government clerk who clearly ran a small business in his home village, judging from the amount of things he was carrying; two young Muslim men, self-conscious and serious in their white pajamas and carefully trimmed beards; a newly married woman, strangely unaccompanied. It felt like a microcosm of the region, indeed of the nation.

In the words of the German editor who had sent me the note, it was exemplary, but how did one communicate this to anyone else? Whatever logic or pattern held the travelers together was invisible to me, and in the absence of that knowledge, I could not be reporter or writer, and was merely one of the many passengers at the mercy of the strange intercourse between bus and land, to the rhythm of the wheels and the answering syncopation of the road that ultimately seemed indifferent to us and our passing presence.

Night fell, and both the country outside and the people inside the bus disappeared, and I had nothing to observe except for the occasional light in a passing hut, or the flaring of a match as the conductor, separated from me by a span of unbridgeable darkness, lit a *bidi*.

The Pekingese dog barked sharply when dawn came, but his young companion did not wake up.

darkness

CHAPTER FOUR

❖ 1 ❖

I had no intention of reading Euan Sutherland's book that night. In fact, when I glanced at it in my flat, it seemed unlikely that I would do anything more than keep it as a memento of my venture into the morgue. The discovery of the photograph had made me suddenly hopeful, and perhaps it was an effect of the fever that made me want to call Herman right away to talk about it. The only thing that stopped me was that the neighborhood phone booth from where I made long-distance calls was closed at this hour, and I flipped through Sutherland's book as a way of diverting my mind before going to bed.

Sutherland's stiff, self-righteous tone dulled my mind more than diverting it, and I gradually began to sink into a stupor. He had written a memoir of the years 1940 to 1946, when he was "acting" editor of the *Imperial*; some complicated politics had involved sacking the previous incumbent without actually removing his name from the paper. Sutherland's account was full of dates and facts and the names of other Englishmen, everything glued together with a dry, earnest analysis of how the Allies had conducted the war on the Burma front and how Sutherland had run the paper during this time. He saw them as campaigns of relatively equal significance, and as the memoir moved back and forth between military affairs and his negotiation of the paper's fortunes, it became quite clear why so many copies of the book had been lying in a disused room for nearly fifty years. (Or perhaps Sutherland had left in a hurry shortly after publication; with millions of riotous natives coming to terms with their dismembered freedom, he may not have had time to pack copies of his book.) The names *Gandhi, Hitler,* and *Mountbatten* cropped up with monotonous regularity, and the last thing I remember thinking of before falling asleep was that Sutherland had spent a whole paragraph complaining about a Chinese man who had vomited down his back on a flight to England.

I slept soundly at first, but at some stage I drifted out of my deep slumber into semiconsciousness, spending what seemed like hours thinking or dreaming of the photograph and the morgue. Only a full bladder forced me out of that suspended state; my body felt stiff and my head throbbed when I got up, and I swallowed a Paracetamol tablet.

After a while, feeling chilly but still wide awake, I turned on the reading lamp and picked up the photograph, studying the woman and the two men guarding her. She would hardly have been capable of going anywhere. The men with the guns were in the picture not for her but for those who might see the photograph, and she was present only to fulfill her role as an object of their power. It could be you, they were saying without speaking a single word; it could be you confined to the chair knowing we may put a bullet in your head when the picture has been taken and our presentation finished—and this image will be all the world will have to remember your final moments by.

The photograph had not been taken by a professional; that much was clear. The man capturing the scene had used a small automatic camera with a built-in flash—a stringer's cheap, simple accessory—that had splashed its weak light on the face of the woman while leaving the men and the rest of the room untouched, as though even the flash had discriminated between prisoner and guards. The wall in the background was pale blue, and a naked light bulb was visible at the top of the picture, suspended from a curved wooden bracket. Partly because of the flash, the woman's complexion appeared much lighter than that of the men, although only their forearms and the area around their eyes were visible. They would naturally be more browned if they lived like guerrillas in the jungle, but the woman's yellowish pallor and her smallness made her seem almost from a different ethnic group.

She was slender, in her early twenties, but she didn't have the kind of face one would expect in someone so young. It should have been unformed yet, still assimilating the experiences of adulthood, but instead it possessed a wariness that concealed something and put her beyond the reach of the photographer or the men who had put her up for display. I was surprised to see an intelligence, even alertness, in the woman's eyes. There was no plea there, no embarrassment, but simply a cautious acceptance of that flash violating her face.

The caption had been scrawled in a blue ballpoint pen over the little oval logos of the film company on the back: "The MORLS leadership today exhibited a porn film actress as an example and warning to the people of the state. They shot her as punishment to impress upon the people the importance of desisting from all corrupt activities encouraged by Indian imperialism. It further exhorted the people to lead a sound moral life as a harbinger of liberation." The writer had been in a hurry, jotting down the caption hastily, perhaps using a formal press statement as a template and finding in it the words "exhorted," "desisting," and "sound moral life." I knew already that the picture had never appeared in the *Sentinel*, and I wondered how swiftly it had passed through a chief sub's sweaty hands, and just how quickly he had judged it unimportant.

The reasons for his rejection of the story were clear enough to me. "Too far," I remembered one of the editors saying to me at lunch when I asked him why we covered the region so poorly; it was the cry of the self-important city-dweller, of a man who had no interest in anything that did not touch him directly, concerned only with the rules of his job and his prospects for promotion and the hierarchy that dictated what was news and what was not.

Too far. It was a phrase I heard echoing from many mouths during my journey along that troubled highway, as if the woman I was looking for was not a person but a place, the very embodiment of an edge over which I could plummet if I didn't maintain the proper distance and disinterest. But my accidental discovery of the photograph that night in the morgue had already closed the gap. Even Sutherland's book—unlikely source though it might have seemed with its fixed moral universe, its stark black-and-white schema, and its rigid colonial hierarchies—would provide an instance of that kind of closing of distance. These things are planned elsewhere.

. . .

I RETURNED TO SUTHERLAND'S BOOK, not really reading it so much as skimming through those sections that seemed most interesting. Sutherland talked a lot about the weather, which he described as abominable, and I found it amusing to think of the *pukka sahib* sweltering in a heat similar to that which I was experiencing, perhaps even suffering from a fever like me. I grew more involved in Sutherland's narrative though, especially when I learned he had lived not in the quarters on the top floor of the *Sentinel* building, as I'd assumed, but at a company flat near Bishop's House, barely twenty minutes from my Bhowanipur residence.

I tried to remember if the building still existed, and from memories of hurried forays through that neighborhood came vague impressions of an old, empty ruin still owned by the *Sentinel*. It had fallen into disuse and was now tied up in litigation because refugees from the Bangladesh War had occupied it in the seventies, and the two big flats on the top floor turned into tenements shared by twenty or more people, their ragged washing spread along verandahs divided by crumbling fluted columns. Sutherland would not have been pleased, because even in the 1940s he had been unhappy about the squalor and debilitating climate of the second city of the Empire.

Then I read about a march through Manipur, and although I was unsure if I was actually reading from the book or simply dreaming I was reading it, the name *Manipur* was a sharp blow to my semiconscious state, bringing the photograph to my mind again. I sat up with a start and the book slipped from my hands. A pale early light, still fresh and cool, was already visible above the treetops near Ashutosh Mukherjee Road, turning the streetlamp across my window into a dull glow. I heard a distant tram—they were always the first to hit the road—and the sound of a shop shutter being opened, and there seemed no point in staying in bed, trying to sleep. I went out to a little *dhaba* near the *gurdwara* for an early morning meal of *jalebis* and tea, and when some of the stiffness seemed to have cleared from the walk there and back, I picked up Sutherland's memoir again. There was no index, so I looked through the pages until I found the word *Manipur,* and then leafed back to the beginning of the chapter.

❖ 2 ❖

A narrow path, barely wider than a forest track, curled around the hill on its way to the guesthouse at the top. Although fresh tire treads marked the passage of cars, the path was untarred, little more than a flat muddy depression in the sloping wild grass. A final turn led to the back of the building, where the track was paved. It was quiet as I approached the guesthouse, with not a sound except for the bleating of a goat. The building looked fairly new from the back, maybe five to ten years old, a surprisingly large concrete structure with two floors of balconies and angled windows looking down on the valley. Some effort had been made to give it the appearance of an expensive hotel, and there would have been a pleasant view from it had it not been for the power station crouching between the guesthouse and the valley.

There was no one near the power station as I passed it. The whole thing looked run-down, with wires and pylons rust-coated behind the crisscross pattern of the fencing, weeds sprouting between the concrete flagstones, but it was clear that it worked, if only because I could hear machines humming and meters ticking away, like a hidden time bomb in that otherwise timeless landscape.

I walked around to the front of the guesthouse, coming across another path leading up from the main road, though this one was merely a series of makeshift steps cut along the slope of the hill. An oil company jeep stood in the driveway. The trees and plants in front of the building were well looked after, the trunks carefully painted white at the base, but there was mildew on the walls of the building and the paint had peeled off in many places. The little desk in the lobby was empty, although off to one side, from what seemed to be a kitchen, there came the sound of a television and the smell of fish being fried. As I looked around for the caretaker, someone, half in shadow, came and stood in the doorway. I stepped forward for a closer look and saw that it was a young woman in a bright yellow sari, her untied hair suggesting that she was not expecting strangers. She was holding a round, naked baby in the crook of one arm and sucking on the thumb of her free hand. She had full lips that turned outward as she sucked her thumb, and the gesture was both infantile and coyly suggestive, her gaze on me unfaltering even when a man appeared hurriedly from behind her. He tried to block the woman from my sight as he approached, and just as I thought he was going to walk right into me, he turned and went to the desk, not looking at me until he was safely behind it.

There was a bound register, a phone, and a big glass paperweight in front of him, and he fidgeted with the paperweight as he waited, not saying a word. He seemed to be in his thirties, although his hair was thinning and the lines around his chin had started losing their firmness. He appeared unremarkable in every way except for his eyes, which gave the impression of caution. This was a man who knew things, such as why this vast building had been built in the middle of nowhere and the kind of guests it attracted—but he wasn't going to give any of those secrets away. His smooth face twitched slightly, almost in a smile.

"I have a room booked," I said.

He looked at me blankly. I pointed at the register. He said nothing.

The woman continued looking at me and sucking her thumb. Only the baby seemed to understand my need for a room, because it made an attempt to move away from the woman toward the desk, but she adjusted it against her arm and held on firmly. Finally, the man opened the register with great effort, as if the cover were made not of cardboard but iron, and made a cursory pretense of looking through the register. When he spoke, it was without voicing the words, in the manner of someone mouthing a phrase for a lip-reader; even words spoken aloud would commit him to an indiscretion, it seemed, but I understood what he was saying.

"No empty rooms."

I pulled the register away from him: it was almost entirely blank, with a few entries at the beginning dating back to three or four years ago, written in a hand that was much too neat and sure in its spellings to be his. I must have looked as if I was about to hit him, because he spoke quickly. One word.

"Chit?"

I realized he wanted a note from the oil company, and I pointed at the phone, mentioning the name of the public relations officer with whom Robiul had arranged my stay. It must have meant something to the man, because he reluctantly opened a drawer and took out a set of very small keys strung around a large rusted ring. Then looking at me sadly, he held out a hand perfunctorily for my bags, and began leading me to my room. The woman lost interest in us and went back to the kitchen with a great swaying of her hips.

As I climbed the wide staircase behind the caretaker, our footsteps echoing in the empty building, the smell of fish reminded me that I was hungry. The caretaker shook his head when I asked him about food, saying he needed to be informed in the morning in order to serve lunch to guests. "No one else staying here?" I asked. He nodded vaguely in response to this question and proceeded along the staircase.

Near the landing on the second floor was a round space with a glass wall encircling it, something like a rough imitation of an atrium, apparently put up by a builder suddenly infected by the knowledge of contemporary Western architecture — but perhaps equally suddenly disillusioned, since the atrium had been left unfinished. There were bricks, wires, sheets of glass, pieces of wood, and long empty tubes that had housed strip lights, all lying abandoned on the floor, as if the workers had departed midway when money for the construction ran out or some superior decided that such innovations were quite unnecessary in this wilderness. I looked around and saw exposed wiring and bare sockets on the walls, and when the caretaker led me to my room at the end of the passageway, the first thing I noticed was the waste basket with a foot pedal, its plastic instruction sheet still pasted to the drum.

The room was small, but there was a coffee table, a two-seater sofa with its back to the window, and a single bed over which a white mosquito net hung like a canopy. Again, I had the impression of a design imported from some vague awareness of hotel rooms in big cities, but the light over the bathroom mirror didn't work and there were no towels or toiletries in the cupboard except for an old, nearly empty tube of Colgate toothpaste, bent in a neat arc by the person who had used it last. The caretaker waited while I looked around the room and the toilet. When I'd finished, he grunted and said, "Dinner? You will be staying for some days?" He relaxed discernibly when I told him I would be leaving the next day; "Nobody comes for long," he replied cheerfully.

I had been wondering where he was from. Even though he was a man of few words, there was something distinct about his accent, a way of speaking that was not local to the region. "When did you come here from Orissa?" I asked casually, hoping to catch him off-guard. He spoke almost like a Bengali, but not quite, and it seemed like a good guess.

"Me?" he said with an exaggerated casualness that included a shrug of the shoulders and a surprised lift of the eyebrows. "I'm from here," he said, pointing at a wall. "But I speak Oriya and many other languages."

"And your wife?" I asked. "She's from here too?" She seemed too dark and tall for the region.

"Yes, yes, from here," he said, moving toward the door. "We are all from here. We have always been locals."

I was puzzled by his speech. He sounded like a Bengali at times, an Oriya at other moments, sometimes even like a Nepali, though he didn't have the typical features or mountain build. The oiled hair and narrow frame spoke of the plains, as did his prominent vowels and sibilants. But since he and his family seemed to have an undisturbed little dominion at the guesthouse—something that would not make him popular in the town—he probably had good reason to be cautious as to his ethnicity.

"Everyone's local out here, everyone," he said. "Outside people, they just can't adjust to life in these parts. This place is not for them." He looked at me and my bags slyly as he spoke, his gaze halting momentarily on the typewriter case, perhaps because he was puzzled by its shape and size.

"And that jeep in the driveway? Does that belong to outsiders or to local people?"

The caretaker gave me another of his shifty glances, said something about buying supplies for dinner, and slipped out of the room. When I went down to the lobby after a bath, I heard his wife singing in a Bengali dialect that suggested the provinces around the rice town of Burdwan, and the mystery of his ethnicity was solved.

❖ 3 ❖

There were indeed other guests in the building, as I found out later. I had gone to the bus station for lunch and returned to sleep through the afternoon. It was hotter than it had been in the city, with less evidence of rain, but the open spaces of the hillside cooled my room down rapidly as evening approached. From my venture to the bus station I had glimpsed the giant oil refinery plant, with high barbed-wire fencing and guard towers set in a large perimeter around squat flotation tanks and pumping machinery. In the past month, insurgents had blown up a nearby pipeline. At the shack where I had lunch, I was told that senior officials had visited recently and that security had been increased.

Oil, in the middle of this nowhere? Not enough oil to quench the thirst of an entire country, but sufficient to justify expensive equipment and staff, and quite enough to create a grievance for the insurgents who claimed, quite rightfully, that all the wealth was taken out of their region with nothing given in return. I suppose I should have gone to meet the company official who had arranged for my stay in the guesthouse, but I had no interest in any inconsequential encounters in a place where I was putting up for merely one night. I had found out from the man at the ticket counter that there was a bus leaving for Dimapur the next day, and that was all I needed to know about the refinery town.

I went out for a short walk in the evening, not venturing beyond the grounds of the guesthouse, watching the twilight as it hung over the countryside, and bats flittered and wheeled through the sky like badly made mechanical birds suspended on pieces of string. When I returned, I heard two male voices further down the passageway from my room. I took out my notebook, the envelope with the photograph of the woman, and the packet Robiul had given me. I was looking through his list of names when I was interrupted by footsteps outside, then a brief murmur of voices followed by a set of very authoritative knocks on the door.

There were two men in the corridor. The one closer to me had a sunburnt face, with a flat nose and small bright eyes under a crew cut. He was wearing a short-sleeved shirt, and his arms were thick and muscular, with brass amulets on both biceps. He had a watch on his left wrist, and an intricate green tattoo of some kind of dancing girl spilled out from under the strap. He looked at me quizzically, appearing almost friendly in spite of the short hair and clothes that announced his profession as clearly as a badge.

The other man I felt less certain about. He was taller and

much older, hanging back a little, but still close enough for me to be struck by the tinge of sourness emanating from him. He wore the expensive clothes and shoes of a business executive, but they sat badly on him. His haircut and mustache had the same regimented air as that of his companion, but his hair had thinned and gone gray, while his muscles had turned into an accumulation of flab near the waist. If you forgot about the discrepancy in height, the two men looked like before and after versions of the same thing, as if I were being shown what would happen to the younger man once age and newly acquired wealth had caught up with him.

"I am Captain Sharma," the one in front said.

"Who are you?" his companion asked.

"Press. Reporter," I said brusquely.

Captain Sharma's small eyes lit up. His companion scowled and said, "Nothing to report here." Then they came inside, as if it had all been arranged between the three of us long ago, and I felt certain that another odd and pointless exchange was about to take place.

The captain sat on the sofa, seemingly friendly and relaxed, while his companion looked around the room uneasily as if he suspected a trap being sprung for him. "That is Mr. Das," the captain said. "Retired policeman now domiciled here." Mr. Das said nothing and watched me from behind cautious eyes and tight lips. When he saw my typewriter case, he picked it up and hefted it in his arms. I sat on the bed and watched indifferently. The captain cleared his throat and said, "I am visiting from training camp of Special Security Bureau in Lakhimpur."

He smiled and looked amiable as he said this. It turned out that he and Das were old friends and had come to the guesthouse to drink, partly because the liquor was provided at subsidized rates by the oil company.

"It is quite the same in the army," the captain said cheerfully. "I could have brought my own bottles. But the view here is soothing and balmy. Also, Mrs. Das is very disapproving of alcohol."

Mr. Das, meanwhile, had taken my typewriter out of its case and turned it upside down.

"Don't do that, Das," the captain said. "The typewriter, it is not a mere machine. It is an instrument of culture."

"Huh," Das said.

"Culture is the highest faculty of mankind. Let us never forget that."

"Bullshit," Das said.

The captain seemed unaffected by his companion's skepticism. He addressed me directly.

"You are, of course, a reporter. But perhaps you also have some interest in the arts? In poetry?"

"No, just newspaper work."

"Which newspaper?" Das asked gruffly. He had put the typewriter down.

"*Sentinel.*"

The captain stood up and looked at me, his hand extended. There was a gleam in his eyes. "The *Sentinel*? The paper from Calcutta with that wonderful Sunday magazine? The paper that covers so much of the arts and culture and gives me unalloyed delight every week?"

He pulled his wallet out hurriedly and presented me with a cheap-looking card, his name and address printed in pink on the white plastic.

"I am, sir, also a writer," he said gravely. "Much interested in conveying the spirit of arts and the culture in the region. Some interest and expertise in medieval carvings. You will therefore furnish me with the name of your Sunday magazine editor."

The captain carefully wrote down the name and address in a little book, while Das flopped down next to him on the sofa, seemingly annoyed at being ignored.

"Writers?" he said. "What writers? I know all about writers."

"He is reporter, Das, not writer," the captain reminded him gently. "The difference is quite vast. We are not blessed with enough fortune to be visited by writers. Here, in the wilderness? Even though the view is soothing and balmy and there are such excellent specimens nearby of sixteenth-century carvings, there is little chance of an uplifting engagement with the font of creativity." He tugged at the amulet on his left arm as he spoke; perhaps it was the font of his creativity.

"I know all about writers," Das repeated. He had a one-track mind. "Locked up writer once. Big writer too."

The captain shook his head at Das.

"You could not have locked up a writer, Das. Writers are important people."

"He was a foreigner. Without an Inner Line permit for visiting this area. So I put him in lockup. When I was posted in border district."

He looked at me with a grim expression as if daring me to challenge his account. The captain watched Das sadly.

"Even so, Das. Writers know no boundaries. They live for the cause of art. You should have been somewhat obliging."

"He may have been spy, not real writer at all."

The captain immediately lost all sympathy for the arrested foreigner.

"And how?" he asked, puffing his lips out.

"English type. Six-one, weight seventy-eight kilos. Distinguishing mark mole on left ear. His name was, his name was . . ." Das's memory failed him momentarily. "Graham. Greene Graham. Put him in lockup for one week. Gave him only regular prison food. Not even boiled water, only water from the tube well," he added viciously.

The captain clucked his tongue disapprovingly.

"Interrogation?" he asked.

"Yes," Das said. "April 1961. No proper papers. Claimed profession of writer and the protection of his British nationality. Self-informed Foreigners Registration Office, who contacted British high commission in Calcutta. Was told to await further instructions. Subject addressed complaint to self about arrest, then about food and sleeping arrangements. Claimed that all papers, including passport, permit, and money, had been stolen by man posing as guide near wildlife sanctuary. Asked him to await confirmation of status of British nationality from high commission. Then subject was brought before self for creating general disturbance in the lockup. Once again, subject complained about food and sleeping arrangements and hygiene, also about the lack of boiled water. Claimed to have suffered from hill dysentery on two previous occasions. Reflected on subject's complaints. Finally, asked subject to demonstrate writing credentials."

"How?" the captain asked, leaning forward with discernible interest.

"Told him to write a story. If it was good, as judged by self, deputy, and block development officer, there would be some minor adjustments to living conditions and food, perhaps with regard to boiled water and latrine arrangements, until further instructions arrived from Calcutta."

"Then?"

"Subject wanted typewriter. Official typewriters not for personal use," Das added sanctimoniously. "Told him to use paper and pen. Complained about right kind of paper and pen. Gave him school exercise book and two pens. Took one whole day to write one story."

"And?"

Das waited, then said with satisfaction, "A very poor story. A complete artistic failure, as agreed upon by self and BDO. Deputy thought writing had merits, but he was outranked. Deputy had some artistic inclinations, but that was not pertinent to the example at hand. We summoned prisoner and I admonished him severely. 'Mr. Greene Graham, you have wasted valuable paper and the official time of important government functionaries and moreover sheltered here under false pretenses. What you have written is not only bad, it is positively hopeless. No moral to your story at the end, in fact quite full of many immorals, and your understanding of human psychology is shockingly poor. The behavior of your characters is unbelievable, Mr. Graham, and we who are experienced in such matters refuse to believe that your characters could have acted in the way you say they did. As for events in the story, the best that can be said for them is that they would not be out of place in a children's story, in a fairy tale. You have failed the test. Mr. Greene Graham, I have never heard of you before your detention, but I am quite assured that you are not a writer. In fact, I suspect that you may not even be Greene Graham, whoever he is.'"

"So?"

"Punishment. Hazri-babu, my attendance clerk, absent for days. Write out all attendance entries in register, doing so cleanly and neatly. Then take exercise book bought for purposes of demonstrating writerly credentials, and fill remaining pages with following sentence written in clear capital letters, 'I shall not claim to be writer anymore.'"

The captain frowned. He didn't like this part. Das chuckled and began cleaning his teeth with a toothpick he had extracted from his sleeve, looking at me as if to say that he could put me to the test too. Then he took the toothpick out of his mouth and said, "The photograph? What is that?"

"Something I am working on," I said cautiously. I had left it on the bed when they came in, and I hadn't noticed him looking at it.

"Evidence in criminal case?"

"Not that I know of."

The captain reached out and picked up the photograph, turned it over to read the caption, and then passed it on to Das. He looked at me with surprise and said, "Ultras?"

Das, who had finished scrutinizing it, said, "Not our ultras, Sharma. Manipur ultras, of no concern of ours."

The captain looked dubious and said, "You are doing story on Manipur ultras?"

"I'm looking for that woman." I saw him frown, and added quickly, "Human interest story."

He nodded as if he finally understood.

"Victim of circumstance, yes?"

He was interrupted by a gentle knock on the door. The caretaker was outside, holding a tray with bottle and glasses, managing to look obsequious and annoyed at the same time.

"You will join us for drinks?"

The captain seemed eager to continue our conversation, but I declined. He shook my hand vigorously, saying that he would be grateful if I personally recommended him to the Sunday magazine editor.

I did not see the pair during my solitary dinner, but the caretaker's careful manner and his reluctance to accept a tip indicated that something had changed in his eyes. As I signed a couple of bills for him, he said that Das was security chief for the oil refinery. "Powerful gentleman," he said with some admiration, but when I asked him if Das was from Orissa, his flow of speech ceased as abruptly as it had begun.

A SILENT CHILL DESCENDED on the guesthouse that night as I holed up in the room with my papers. Occasionally, I heard the captain and Das laughing, and if I listened very carefully, I could make out the faint noise of a Hindi film playing on the caretaker's television. There were no lights at the back of the guesthouse, and an almost complete darkness covered the hills until it ran into a pale milky glow on the horizon that must have been from floodlights on the refinery grounds. Had it not been for those indistinct voices and the distant light, it would have felt like nowhere, and even the solidity of the objects in my room would have been mere props in a dream, powerless against the overwhelming absence—of light, of sound, of people, of purpose—that lurked everywhere.

I turned to the photograph, concentrating on the woman's inscrutable face. She appeared to be returning my gaze, but when I examined her closely, her eyes fell on something else, something behind my shoulder, or perhaps slightly ahead. I was seeing her the way the camera lens had, the way the photographer had seen her through the viewfinder—that photographer who would also have been aware of other things: the voices of people from the local press, the presence of the insurgent leaders, perhaps the murmur of guards posted as lookouts.

Who was the photographer? I wondered. And then it struck me that Thoiba had taken the picture, Thoiba who was dead from a road accident, and I felt a sense of unease as I realized that I was looking at what a dead man had seen and locked into frame before pressing the shutter, and that the reason the woman did not meet my gaze was because she was really looking at the invisible specter of Thoiba hovering somewhere, occasionally behind my shoulder, at other times slightly in front of me.

Two beams of light appeared at the back of the guesthouse, and I heard the jeep as it followed the path its headlights had hacked through the darkness. Shortly after, there was a muffled knock on the door. The captain looked mildly embarrassed as I opened the door. "Das has gone home," he said. "I stay here tonight. Tomorrow a visit to local ruins to scrutinize specimens of sixteenth-century carvings. Something I would like to tell you before then." He was wearing a white singlet and navy blue shorts, which, along with his hairless legs and unwrinkled face, gave him the air of an eager schoolboy. "That woman you are looking for," he said. "Perhaps you are going in the wrong direction if you want to find her." He pointed with his thumb behind his shoulder. "To Delhi," I heard him say, "You should go to Delhi."

CHAPTER FIVE

❖ 1 ❖

I sometimes wonder if I would have read that chapter of Sutherland's at all if the name *Manipur* had not caught my eye during the semiconscious state caused by the viral fever. Once I had read the chapter, however, the story told in its pages could not be forgotten. It would come back to me at odd times during my journey in the region, resurfacing with utter clarity even when the rest of the book had faded completely from memory. It was a fragment different from the whole, a jagged shard that struck some nerve in my body with its recurrence of sonorous place names that reached into my present as I struggled up Highway 39 and saw the names on dusty hoardings, faded signboards, and memorials.

Sutherland's narrative opened the door to a time long past, to people very different from me or from the strangers I met during my journey, but I later had occasion to wonder if there was not something uncanny about his tale and the circumstances of my encounter with it. But here it is; let the Englishman speak in his own words.

❖   ❖   ❖

I have mentioned earlier in passing that I had turned my flat near Bishop's House at the South End of Chowringhee into a kind of billet for uniformed guests. It happened on the spur of the moment, but it seemed the right thing to do when I found out that the colonial families in Calcutta were considerably squeamish about taking in non-commissioned men. They would host officers with grace and, in fact, plotted quite furiously for the honour, but a long stay in these tropical climes had created in them an almost native sense of hierarchy that was quite perplexing to the sturdy and cheerful national service men turning up here in the winter of 41.

A strange place, a new climate, with either the prospect or experience of the devilish Jap at close quarters in the jungles of Burma, and then this business of having no place they could think of as home before they were sent off to fight. I was a bachelor. Moreover, a newspaper-man does not fit easily into the intricate caste-system of the colonials, so that my practice of having half a dozen or more service men stay over with me did not create grave scandal or mass outrage among the memsahibs of Alipore.

The arrangement turned out well, and for the next four years or so a splendid cast of men, mostly NCOs and RAF flight-sergeants, streamed through my flat and kept me entertained and my Indian servants busy. Some of them appeared more than once, but there were many who died in an obscure part of the world so that civilization might be saved from the menace swarming in from the

East, and these unfortunates never had the opportunity of return. By the end of 44, when it became clear that the Jap was finally beaten and on the run, I felt as if we had all been through it together, from inevitable disaster to glorious triumph.

If one man sticks out in my mind from amid that host of cheerful, personable faces, it must be because his was the oddest experience among all those men, who encountered a range of horrors from Jap ack-ack to blackwater fever. I have no doubt that I shall remember him even when I have ceased to live at this flat on the South End of Chowringhee, when Chowringhee and Calcutta themselves are no more than distant Eastern memories. That time will not be long in the coming.

The man whose curious account so bothered me came to stay with me in 42, the survivor of a particularly rough passage from the Salween through the jungles of Burma and base hospitals in Assam. I shall call him Jim, because although I intend to honour his most intimate confidences and have nothing to present that could sully a good man's name, it seems best to conceal his identity out of proper regard to the memory of the man.

Jim appeared for the first time through a recommendation from the clergy at Bishop's House, a splendid physical specimen in spite of the things he had gone through recently. He was a tall man, with a torso shaped like a barrel, and he had a way of looking at one with something so direct and frank in his blue eyes that I was moved to both pity and fear for him. There was a terrible innocence in him that one thought the jungles and the war should have by rights taken away, and it was only in his terse manner that one sensed his youthfulness struggling desperately to retain its equinamity in the face of the unspeakable horrors of war.

My heart warmed to him instantly as he stood in the living-room with his kit bag, towering over Abdul and Gunga as they hurried to make this new sahib comfortable. The only other guests at the time were a Blenheim crew, a cheerful bunch of fellows who, in spite of narrowly averting a nasty spot of engine trouble just a few days before, were up and about taking in the sights and sounds of the second city of the Empire.

I would have felt goodwill towards Jim even if I hadn't been told that things were in a bad way inside his head. Jim had been sent to me by Brierly, an odd chap at Bishop's House known as the Red Priest because of a dust-up he'd had with Mosley's men some years ago during a demonstration in London. Brierly told me that although Jim looked sound enough, they had only let him out of the base hospital in Tezpur because of the shortage in beds. He also said that Jim should under no circumstances be allowed to wander around alone in the Calcutta sun and that I ought to be somewhat careful about his sleeping arrangements.

Jim himself vouchsafed not a single word except to say he was grateful for my hospitality and there was nothing wrong with him any longer. What about trouble sleeping, I asked, and he went red, saying he thought it would be best if he could sleep alone. He hadn't realized how communal the arrangements were here, and didn't know if he could share a room with someone else. The trouble was he had these awful nightmares, he said, and although he remembered not a thing when he woke up, he was quite violent in his sleep; he'd busted up a nurse in the hospital quite badly and was terrified of falling asleep if there were people around.

Well, one had to do something about it so the poor chap wouldn't wander around Calcutta or try to stay up all night, and rather than shack him up with the tired airmen, I thought of getting one of those Indian string beds put into my room. The heat was terrible and I had just had the company provide me with a cooling machine for the bedroom. Without that and the regular yoga sessions with Bishtoo Ghosh, I doubt I would have survived the abominable weather. I had the thought that the cooling machine might help calm Jim's nerves down. I didn't like to imagine what might happen if the nightmares got hold of him during his sleep, because he was the kind of chap one would want on one's side in a scrape.

I had to stay late to work that day because of a spot of bother with the army about a letter we had recently published, giving the opinions of an "unknown" soldier about certain withdrawal tactics, and when I came home I was too tired to worry about being set upon as I slept. Jim had sheepishly agreed to bed down in my room, and he was lying like a log when I went in. The night passed without incident for me, though I seem to remember a strange dream where my editorial predecessor Rowe admonished me— quite unreasonably I thought—for changing the paper's political line from support for the cause of Indian self-government to a position that was quite critical of that possibility. When I saw Jim in the morning he said he couldn't remember when he had last slept so soundly.

I returned home the next evening in a relaxed state of mind. Not only had I reason to feel satisfied that Jim's problem had been solved in so efficient and practical a manner, but I had also managed to put the army fellows in their proper place. With many vague references to wartime regulations, they'd demanded the name and unit of the "unknown" soldier, but they backed down quickly when I said that nothing less than a search warrant could force me into turning over details of official correspondence.

Jim was out when I returned, and this worried me until Abdul said that the sahib had gone for a walk by the river, and I thought it likely that the evening breeze of the Hoogly would have quite a soothing effect on his nerves. I had also been toying with the idea of suggesting to Jim that he take up yoga while he was staying with me, but I quite forgot about that during dinner. The Blenheim chaps were leaving the next day, so Gunga had rustled up a special dinner as a send-off, and we were all having a good time without thinking too much about Jim. There had been a thunderstorm earlier, but no one noticed it during the dinner, and it was not until Jim returned sopping wet that I realized it had rained.

He went off to change directly after he came in, and I noticed nothing untoward in the behaviour of the airmen. Shortly after, I went into another room to take a call from the office—the army was apparently still making a fuss about the letter, with Wavell's secretary having got into the act now—and I did not return to the living-room until a good twenty minutes later. I have no idea what happened while I was out of the room, but I remember being struck by Jim's posture when I returned. He was listening to

Moore, one of the crewmen, and his head was lowered like a bull's, the veins on the back of his thick neck standing out as if ready to burst. I heard Moore say, "Some of us here would have never sunk so low," and then he turned his back on Jim even as the latter took a step forward, his fist clenched. None of them said a word when I came in.

The evening wound up soon after, but I noticed that neither the airmen nor Jim once addressed each other, not even when it became time for us to retire for the night and wish the crew good luck with where they were going on to next.

I was up for much of the night. Jim thrashed around in his bed, speaking constantly in his sleep. At one point he yelled out loud and sat up straight on his bed, knocking over the glass of water next to it. It was a disturbing situation, and the next day I sat in my office and considered opening the company quarters upstairs so that I could sleep there. Although the air crew had left, I knew there were some more men coming in that day. I could hardly let Jim not have the cooling machine if he was sick, but on the other hand, there was always the question of how violent he might get. Although I am a six-footer and was in good shape because of the regular sessions of yoga, he was a great deal younger than I and looked capable of snapping me in two in his fits. Noblesse oblige! I stayed put and the next two nights proceeded in the same manner, with Jim's constantly disturbed sleep, his sitting up in the middle of the night screaming and flailing around violently, and his incessant talk about the things that he'd witnessed.

What I gathered, partly from Jim's ramblings and partly from what Brierly later told me, was this: He'd been with a sort of commando unit, and they had been dropped behind Jap lines sometime in November 41 to link up with Chinese troops in the Shan hills above the Salween. In February, they withdrew according to orders, and were moved to Central Burma. Jim received a blow to his scalp and a bayonet wound in his arm in a scrap and was then taken prisoner along with half a dozen other men. From his incoherent account, I got the impression that he saw some of his companions being tied up by the Japs and being butchered with bayonets. He somehow managed to escape, though I wasn't sure how, since the rest of the story was confused.

He seemed to have become a sort of freebooter then, making his way back to India either via Kalewa or Ledo. It wasn't clear which route he'd taken, but it was during this time that something had happened—or he'd done something—which disturbed him. The particular crisis he came back to repeatedly in his nightmares involved joining up with two other soldiers who had also dodged the Japs, and how during their escape from the Jap advance they began operating like armed thugs rather than soldiers trying to get back to their own lines. Among everything else they did, it seems that they attacked a Eurasian family of refugees also trying to make it into India. No one had been killed, as far as I could make out, but one of Jim's companions may have done something to the woman. They also seemed to have seized their pack mule and all their supplies, and effectively left the family to starve to death in the middle of the jungle. This is probably what the

Blenheim chaps knew about, and it is significant that Jim started sleeping badly only after they reminded him of it.

Rumours like that circulated a great deal during the war; it was the temper of the times, and only the best of us can say that he wouldn't have done a similar thing if he was facing the prospect of Jap bayonets or starvation. I saw no reason to judge, especially since I was not in possession of the facts, and in the daylight Jim looked as innocent as when he had first arrived on my doorstep. After three nights of thrashing around—in which no attack was made on me—he received his orders and left. He hadn't mixed with the other men in the meantime, but he appeared genuinely thankful for my hospitality and quite moved as he took my leave. That was the end of Jim's story as far as I was concerned.

* 2 *

The captain sat near the window, tapping out cigarette ash as he talked, the smoke around his face giving him the appearance of a gentle genie. I was no doubt aware, he said, that his organization conducted training courses in counterinsurgency techniques, and that as a result he met people from the army and intelligence and police officers on special deputation. It was from one such person that he had heard something about the ultras connected with the photograph.

"I will tell you what I know," he said gravely. "This will be a token of my appreciation at having met a person quite so fine as yourself. What I will not tell you is not worth knowing." He paused, I waited, and the breeze that had been circulating in the room died. We heard faint singing outside and the sound of someone urinating in the bushes. The captain looked out and smiled. "The caretaker has drunk the remainder of the second bottle while cleaning up. He is a happy man now." The singing faded away as the caretaker returned to his quarters near the kitchen.

The captain started his story. The deeper he got into it, the more intent he became, and yet I couldn't help feeling that he was amusing himself in some perverse way. He had seemed like a cheerful, friendly fellow when he first appeared with Das, but he was less reassuring when encountered alone. "The MORLS ultras were a minor group a few years ago, no more than a nuisance," he said. "Not long after its inception, and following a few hit-and-run raids, the leader and his deputy came to blows. Government agencies were at hand to exploit the situation. Some ultras were eliminated, many surrendered, and the small hard-core element still underground was thought to be of no consequence. That is background information. Now, earlier this year an important plan was set in motion in the states bordering Burma, in Manipur and Nagaland. This involved neutralizing the main ultra groups in the two states, consisting essentially of one Meitei outfit in Manipur and the Naga rebel army, which operates in both Manipur and Nagaland, since the Naga population unfortunately tends to be dispersed across the two states.

"The program drawn up to tackle the major ultras was a total plan, and it consisted of three components: political, military, and tactical." He seemed to have taken a class in the subject rather than discovered the information in the course of casual conversations. "As part of political move, secret cease-fire offers were dangled before all major groups. That was the carrot. The stick came in the form of military pressure, first by arming and instigating the Kukis, who are a deadly rival tribe of the Nagas, and then by conducting hush-hush joint operations with Burmese military. That was Operation Vajrang, 'hush-hush' because we have no official diplomatic relations with Burma." He stuck his hands out and squeezed the air with both fists. The tattoo appeared in greater detail below his watch strap, the pelvis of the dancing girl finally attached to her legs, although her head had now disappeared.

"It consisted of simultaneous raids on ultra camps on both sides of border. Operation Vajrang was thundering success, sir. This was only natural consequence of the action, because large brains had been involved in drawing up the total plan, large and unconventional brains that almost neared the dazzling genius of artistic vision. The military triumph naturally opened up space for tactical moves, because both Indian and Burmese forces were now able to block smuggling routes of ultras. No more moving guns or drugs or Burma timber, and no more war funds. Together, the three components brought ultras to negotiating table for possible cease-fire.

"Then a snag was hit." The captain gestured with his square, scarred chin toward the photograph. "The MORLS ultras, long thought to be defunct, reappeared on the scene and carried out a series of minor but successful operations. In the normal course of things, these ops would be no more than irritants, but not when the forces of order and chaos were locked in such delicate balance. MORLS was apparently quite unaffected by the carefully planned components that had been put into place and seemed to have no problems whatsoever with war funds. In fact, intelligence reports indicated that outfit was as awash in money as if they were minting it.

"One group. Just one group threatened to bring entire process to a halt. It had become a question of face, a matter of honor, you see. How was it possible now for the bigger ultra groups to negotiate, if there was still one outfit carrying out raids against government property and life? So much I know for certain. The rest is speculation.

"When everything was quite likely to be spoiled by MORLS, they took one further step that sent them over the precipice. This was holding the press conference where this woman was exhibited. A bad move. Overconfidence, anxiety, or pressure to keep up successes? Who knows, but it created an outcry that turned public opinion in Manipur quite against MORLS. And it gave the big ultras the opening they were looking for. They accused MORLS of being mere vigilantes and not people's soldiers, pathologically committed to violence against the very victims of Indian imperialism instead of providing necessary succor to them. MORLS was naturally forced to backtrack. They denied they had ever held the press conference and swiftly attributed all blame to Indian intelligence agencies, but for the time being they were forced to lie low, allowing other groups to proceed with negotiations. So the picture was released at a most opportune moment, turning the tide of the negotiations our way again. Very well done, no?" The captain paused and looked at me thoughtfully.

"Now, sir, you will agree with me that the scenario claimed by MORLS, while far-fetched and a knee-jerk reaction to their own momentous tactical blunder, could after all be correct. If you understand the principles along which events proceed in the region—which may be hard, since your excellent papers in Calcutta and Delhi report nothing of the events here and would be unable to find the region on a map of the country—then it is not unlikely that said press conference was indeed staged by government agencies. I am not categorically saying that government agencies would do such a thing, but consider, if you will. Hire a few men from the former ultras who are now on government payroll as informers, get a woman to play victim, and set up press conference. How do reporters know it is not MORLS holding the press conference? A phone call with instructions, reporters taken blindfolded to the inside of some residence, men in masks, a statement, a show of weapons. You and I could do it, sir; you and I could do it.

"You see what I am saying then, that it is possible that the woman is not only not porn-film actress, and therefore unlikely to be a victim of circumstances, but that she may be intelligence operative, perhaps originally from the region, selected to play aforesaid role. If so, and this is all speculation, she would of course be in region no longer. As a friend and admirer of yours, I might suggest that she is in Delhi. If not, she could be anywhere. It is a big country, sir, this wonderfully verdant land of ours, and where would you begin your quest for her? But the principal ethical point I wish to raise with you, the dilemma that brought me into your room once again in the dead of the night as an unbidden guest, is that if she is not victim of circumstance but rather agent in creating specific circumstance, should you still be looking for her?

"It is not my task, sir, to presume to give you advice, but I hope you will reconsider. You are interested in the truth, and yet the very object of your quest for truth is possibly composed of lies. Moreover, if the photograph is fake, people will not want it to be known as fake. That is the nature of the counterfeit and the untrue—its true nature can never be revealed. Otherwise, it ceases to be what it is."

I must have looked skeptical about all this, because the captain smiled and rose lightly to his feet, moving like a cat. "I will illustrate what I mean, sir, with a small example. Of course an example is not the thing itself, but what is at hand will have to do. You see the guesthouse, sir, built with oil company money, inaugurated with fanfare, capable of housing one hundred guests in the luxurious metropolitan manner such guests are presumably used to?" I nodded. "Follow me, then."

He stepped out into the corridor. We went down to the lobby, and out from the kitchen, as if he had been expecting us all along, appeared the caretaker. He swayed slightly from the whiskey he had drunk, but was sobering up rapidly enough for a look of fear to creep into his face. "Keys, torch," the captain said sharply. The caretaker hurriedly fetched both. The captain turned and led me toward the rooms on the ground floor, tapping the walls proprietorially with his knuckle. "Feels sound enough. After all, they were built under the supervision of a talented engineer. A man with grand designs that went quite wrong. Open the rooms." The last statement was addressed to the caretaker, who, I realized, was trembling.

He unlocked the door, and the captain took the torch from him, carefully directing the light along the length of the room. It was completely bare. No sofa, no bed, no table, no bulbs in the sockets or curtains in the window, nothing apart from walls and ceiling and floor. The captain stepped in and shone the beam around the interior of the attached bathroom. The bedroom simply looked unfurnished, but what had really happened became clear only in the bathroom. There was no mirror on the wall, the washbasin and faucets had been removed, but you could see where they'd stood from the lengths of blocked pipes and the square outline of the basin. Even the tiles in the shower area had been prized away from the walls.

The captain looked satisfied and stepped out of the room. We continued along the corridor, the caretaker opening room after room as if trying to satisfy extremely fussy guests, and each time I saw the same results. The building was like a place picked clean by termites, an empty shell that gave the illusion of solidity but was hollow within, ready to collapse at any moment like a house of cards. The captain stopped and faced me. "He has four functioning rooms in the entire guesthouse, and he gets very nervous if he has more than two guests at a time. He never does. If he was upset when you landed up, that was because you brought things too close to the safety margin for his liking."

He looked at the caretaker, for whom it was not hard to feel some sympathy. The captain reached out toward the caretaker and lifted his head. "Where does it all go?" The caretaker said nothing and stared fearfully at us. He began to stutter and his legs shook. The captain looked benevolent, one hand swinging the torch, its light swaying back and forth along that corridor of stripped rooms, his other hand on the caretaker's chin, in the manner of a studio photographer adjusting his subject's face. The caretaker brought his palms together in a plea and looked as if he was going to collapse. The captain let go of the man's chin and stepped back. "Your wife's brother runs a little business not too far from here, selling furniture and building supplies. And you and your family will leave any day now, isn't that so?" He leaned toward me a little and said under his breath, "Of course Das knows. He gets a big cut out of it."

We returned to the lobby, where the wife was visible, peering out from the kitchen, but with no sign of fear or consternation on her face. The captain appraised her with a professional eye. Then he chuckled and looked at me. "The example was educational, sir? In parting then, one word of friendly advice. People travel slowly in this region, but information moves swiftly. Tread carefully where you go, and beware of appearances. That much counterinsurgency training teaches one." His talk was over, and he seemed to be glowing with goodwill and camaraderie. He shook hands vigorously, thanked me for the editor's contact information, and then walked up to his room. I didn't see him in the morning when I cleared out of the guesthouse on the way to Dimapur.

• 3 •

A Khasi teenage girl and her mother sat in front of me in the bus, both of them in the distinctive tartan checks brought to their people by Welsh missionaries over a century ago. It was a reminder of the influences that were still playing themselves out in the region, the ideas of civilization brought by missionaries, colonial officials, and Indian civil servants. In this case, at least, the result hadn't been violent. They had made the pattern their own, I thought, but then my interest in tribal mores gave way to irritation. Their seat was hard against my legs, and every time the teenager leaned back, I felt the metal pressing further against my knees. When she initially turned around to look at me, I gave her what I hoped was a ferocious stare so she would ease her weight a little, but the only reaction I got was a series of giggles and whispered comments to her mother.

The captain's words rang through my mind during the bus ride to Dimapur. I was going the wrong way, he had said, and the road seemed to offer little to challenge his view. Another state bus looking and smelling much the same as the one before, another narrow road called a highway, with the little agricultural plots and the bent, shrunken people looking no different from what I had seen on my previous ride.

The section after lunch brought some change as the uneven contours of the foothills we had been traversing until that point gave way to flat and open ground. Then, shortly after we had come upon the flatlands, we saw the first sign of floods: a glassy surface that stretched out on both sides below the highway, erasing fields, huts, and animals, and leaving only sloping roofs and treetops visible above the water. Once, when we passed very close to a partially submerged concrete building, I could make out human figures on the roof, accompanied by pots and pans and poultry, with clothes and rags strung out on a washing line and the faint blue smoke of an earthen stove curling upward like a dying distress signal. The bloated belly of a cow—no more than a flash of animal skin amid that plane of illusion—appeared occasionally, followed by clumps of water hyacinths that had broken free, and above it all was a distinct smell of rot that rose from the water and drifted into the bus through the open windows. Even when we reached an area where the waters had subsided, the smell remained.

The highway was on raised ground, as were the railway tracks running along a parallel embankment. The frontier rail had suspended the one train it operated along this line, and the tents and shacks of villagers who had found refuge on the embankment rose at intervals from the tracks. The camps were quite different from each other—or perhaps it was I who felt different with each successive camp I passed. Some looked like old ruins, others resembled the temporary settlement of a mysterious group of nomads or the camp of a road gang, and the largest brought to mind the shantytowns at the edge of a great metropolis, so that I found myself looking for the skyline of a city. But nothing returned my gaze save for that unrelenting spread of water, and it was hard to prevent the thought that what I was seeing was more momentous than a seasonal flood and was, in fact, the apocalyptic end of the world.

The end of the world, or the beginning; a divine or infernal churning of chaos to bring the world into being.

Hour after hour went by, one hour spent dozing followed by another watching the water, and the silence inside the bus and the discomfort on the faces of passengers made it seem as if the epidemic wafting in through the windows had already laid claim to us all. The photograph, regardless of whether it captured a fake situation or a real one, seemed a trivial thing in such circumstances, not only unexemplary but unimportant. The insurgents, the government forces, the plots, and the conspiracies, these had all been reduced to a trifle by that bus painfully making its way across the flooded land, where nothing existed except bubbles breaking the surface and waves rippling outward in long, slow cycles.

The bus made almost no stops now because it had become crowded with villagers who had haggled with the conductor before flopping down along the aisle. They looked battered and dirty as they clutched ferociously at the remnants of their possessions; an elderly man sitting by the door stared on without blinking at some distant point on the horizon, as if he still saw the water flooding his fields and hut.

The small, bald man across the aisle from the apple-cheeked Khasi women had told me with authority that army helicopters were making supply drops for the flooded villagers. "Yes? Food?" he asked a villager sitting near his feet. He pointed at the sky. The villager looked at him expressionlessly, raised his right shoulder in a gesture that could mean that he didn't know or didn't care or that they had indeed dropped food packets but it didn't matter any longer.

As we neared those small settlements where the water had subsided, we came to a railway crossing, its painted barrier raised to the sky and the signalman's post abandoned. The floods had retreated only recently from this part of the district, and the road had been almost washed away; as the bus climbed onto the tracks, it tilted awkwardly to the left, its rear wheel caught in a deep hole. The regular passengers chattered at this delay while the villagers sat without reacting. The driver stepped hard on the accelerator, the engine whined, and the wheel turned in its spot without traction. He tried again, this time choosing short little bursts, hoping to tease the wheel into some purchase before he attempted a lurch that would get us out. Someone laughed, saying how lucky we were the train wasn't running.

The tracks began vibrating, and everyone fell silent momentarily as they tried to figure out the source of the sound. It was a steady throbbing, rising gradually in intensity, and the passengers began exchanging uneasy glances. Some leaned toward the driver as if trying to shift the distribution of weight in the bus, and even the villagers began looking up from the floor to the passengers in their seats. The vibration grew more distinct, but it was impossible to tell where the sound was coming from with the bus tilted at an angle, its engine straining as the driver struggled to get the vehicle released. Then, out of the thick mist, dispelling any doubts that the tremors we were feeling were nothing more than a collective delusion, came the clear, piercing sound of a train whistle. Later we would learn it was a relief train dispatched with supplies and workers to the point where the embankment had collapsed, but at that moment it came at us like a ghost train summoned by our sins, determined to crush us even as people screamed and hid their faces and the driver cursed and gunned the engine again. The villagers looked around wildly, one man throwing his arms around my legs in an embrace, and only the old man at the door held his unwavering gaze, the one being among fifty or sixty of us whose mind had room for no more disasters. The bus broke free with a jolt, bouncing so hard on the track that I thought we had broken an axle, but it cleared the track and came to a halt on the road. Behind us, I heard the uneven, staccato clanking of the train wheels as they locked against the brakes.

The fields along the highway began to give way to huts and cottages and warehouses—the horns of auto-rickshaws and cars, the crowds on the streets, a jarring reminder of everyday life after our recent proximity to disaster. There were more horns and shouts as we came across the army checkpoints that kept their barriers lowered resolutely, a steady accretion of stimuli that signaled we were in Dimapur. There were more Mongoloid faces here among the drivers waiting to pick up fares for Kohima, more jeans and boots and pullovers and jackets on the bodies of the passengers. This was the end of the plains; the road ahead went up to the mountains.

CHAPTER SIX

❧ 1 ❧

The end of Jim's story, however, was still a long time in the coming. It took some years to present itself properly, with a premature conclusion thrown in along the way when a very drunk sapper I ran into near Hogg's Market one evening told me that the poor fellow had been killed in the siege of Kohima. At least he had gone bravely and honorably, I thought, so that it was something of a surprise when Jim turned up at my doorstep one Sunday afternoon in 44 like a ghost soldier. He was thinner and lighter on his feet, with the stubble on his face giving him a melancholy air, but otherwise the years seemed to have made a man of him. The shyness was gone, and he asked me very directly if I could put him up for a day or two while he waited for the boat home.

Well, he'd certainly picked a quiet time to appear, during a period when there was an unusual gap in the flow of visitors, and I would have been glad of the company even if it had been someone other than Jim.

The weather was mild, or as mild as it ever gets in Calcutta, and I had Abdul put out chairs on the roof so we could sit there in the evening and enjoy the river breeze coming in from across the Maidan. I must confess that the rumours about Jim and the episode with the Blenheim crew did cross my mind as we made ourselves comfortable, but I was nevertheless taken aback when he said he wished to make a clean breast of things he had only alluded to during his previous stay. Not a word was necessary, I assured him, emphasizing that in my mind he stood untainted by any association with ugly talk. "It wasn't just talk, though," he said. "I feel you should hear it all because you're likely to understand." He fell silent and stared at the skyline. It was an impressive view, too, with the green expanse of the Maidan, the lights over Fort William to our left, and the *Imperial* office building appearing directly ahead next to the Nakhoda mosque. I meant to point out to him that the Americans had put up a new bridge over the Hoogly since he had been here last, their tanks being far too heavy for the old pontoon bridge; but I doubt Jim noticed a thing as he sat there, telling me what had happened since we last met.

Ostensibly staring at Calcutta, he was in fact peering into some invisible terrain that was tangible to me only from the feverish pitch of his words, and I must admit that, in spite of subsequent attempts, I have been able to do scant justice to the intensity of his impressions. More than once the thought struck me then, and it has struck me while writing this account, that the poor fellow was not quite well, and I did not know if these were actual experiences being recounted to me or some kind of fever of a weary spirit that had reached the limits of its exhaustion.

Three years is a long time to forget something one has done, Jim said, especially when those years are torn by war, full of impressions and events that make no sense at all, nightmare displacing nightmare from one's brain. He did not want to excuse himself concerning what had happened, but it had been hard to know where they were going and the position of the enemy during the confused trek back to their own lines. The Japs were all over the place, moving at a furious pace with their light equipment and rations, and the three of them had to be careful not to run into any patrols. They were also uncertain about the loyalties of the Burmese and the Kukis—they had heard stories of villagers handing escaping soldiers over to the Japs—so they operated like a commando team, taking what they could from quick raids on isolated villagers and living off the land. In this manner they gradually made their way towards India and the retreating lines of the Allied troops, bypassing the town of Tamu with its stately pagodas to approach the river lying between Tamu and Moreh.

It was hard to explain to strangers, Jim said slowly, the exact nature of the bond that was formed when one was on the run, and how one often went along with the others out of sheer camaraderie in the face of certain death. That was not an explanation, of course, and there ultimately could be no explanation for the matter, but he had thought he was finally done with that sick episode by the time the tide of war turned against the Japs. It was not a question of evading responsibility for the incident near the river; if others had heard of what had taken place, they gave no sign of it beyond the occasional whispered comment behind his back; no officer questioned him or asked him to give an account of what he had done during those weeks in the jungle, not when there was a messy retreat going on and the Japs kept coming through the hills and valleys, taking one position after another as they raced for the heart of India.

So Jim had thought, letting the incident drift away from him like smoke from a campfire—that evening when he stood guard over the man kneeling next to the pack mule while the woman cried out from the bushes and the sun set over the flooded river Jim and the other men planned to cross on their way into Moreh.

His companions on that journey back had long since disappeared, swallowed up by the war, and as he awaited the outcome of the battle of Kohima, he had a palpable sense of relief, of being free of the past. He had distinguished himself in the war since that event, taken some blows and returned more. He had been sent home for training, picking up enough Japanese to be assigned to interrogation duties with his new unit. He had liked this business of languages, finding himself gifted with a good ear, and he had begun reading and thinking hard about what he was seeing in the course of the war.

My own Hindoostani was quite impeccable, I informed Jim. It was astonishing how some men found themselves in possession of unexpected talents when in new lands, just as there were those who tended to lose all sense of proportion. Rowe, our disgraced editor, came to mind as an example of the latter kind, agitating for Indian self-government while lacking the faintest knowledge of the conditions and the people in spite of decades spent here. Possessing a foreign language gives one a window into the native mind, I told Jim, and it is especially useful if the native in question is Asiatic.

"I hope you're right," Jim said. "That is why I had to see you. Felt an editor might understand things a common soldier can't make sense of."

Three years had gone by, the same territory, and only the order of battle had been reversed. They reached Kohima after the road from Dimapur had been cleared. The Jap advance had been broken, and although they did not know it then, the outcome of the war had been determined during the battle across the Deputy Commissioner's tennis court in Kohima when the Japs failed to dislodge Allied troops and take the town. It was their final effort; unable to capture enemy supplies, their own lines stretched thin, and with reinforcements arriving for the Allies, the Japs had no options left except defeat. There were still counter-attacks though, so Jim's unit pushed on cautiously, over tree trunks mangled by artillery barrages and boulders that had been dislodged from the mountainside, past corpses and equipment lying discarded in the monsoon mud. Only after they had left Kohima behind and were on the road to Imphal did it become clear that the orderly re-treat of the Japs had become something of a rout. Oh, they still fought hard, even after their bunkers had been relent-lessly pounded by artillery and Hurricane bombers. There were snipers and traps and jitter parties and ambushes, and the first few units Jim encountered fought to the last man, bayonets and swords drawn when they ran out of ammunition. No prisoners were taken from that lot, Jim said, and there was little in the way of interrogating to be done with them, only a methodical going through their meagre belongings, a slow sifting of the remains of the dead for the reports to be filed with divisional headquarters.

The resistance became more sporadic as they got closer to Imphal. The bombing had created craters everywhere, and the monsoons had turned those craters into giant lakes the men had to wade through. It was an endless trudging in an endless rain, past tanks and 150 mm guns abandoned by the Japs, their brown trucks visible among the trees growing at the bottom of sharp precipices. The Japs had started running out of food and ammunition by this time, only occasionally mustering up ambushes from the remnants of courage or desperation. Jim spoke passionately of the disarray of the Jap retreat, and how he began to come across more and more suicides now, the men blowing themselves up with a final grenade they had saved as a guarantee against dishonour, the officers using their swords. There were others who gave themselves up, starving, half-naked figures emerging from abandoned machine-gun nests, babbling in a tongue that was no longer Japanese or anything remotely human.

They were taking more prisoners now, rounding up shrunken men with bandaged feet and matted hair who screamed and cried like children, but Jim felt a sense of calm accomplishment as he saw to their needs and interrogated those who could still communicate something. They found more corpses as they came into the Imphal Valley, and it was when he saw the man who had died at the edge of the river, where he had dragged himself for a final drink, that Jim remembered everything once again. The river, the bushes, the woman, the pack mule, and it came to him as suddenly as a tropical fever hollowing out a man, until he could barely stand.

It got worse as they progressed, as he began to see the dead mules with their bloated bellies everywhere. It was as if the terrain itself were fiercely determined to bring it all back to him in the sharpest detail, and he became certain that he would not last till they reached Tamu. But there was no turning back, not from what had happened, and not from the progress of the victorious army of which Jim was a part. He couldn't concentrate on his work as the Jap positions were cleared and the prisoners rounded up; all he seemed capable of seeing was the face of the woman as the other two took her into the trees, and the husband and the children as they knelt next to their pack mule. He had managed to forget the children earlier, but how could he have done that, because now he remembered clearly that there had been two of them, Eurasian boys with large eyes who clung to their father without saying a word?

Jim paused for breath and looked out over the ledge. He had a tiny paper parcel with him, which he had been fingering obsessively. He put the parcel down and stared at the road where a red-turbaned policeman was directing traffic. "How orderly everything is in your second city of the Empire," he said bitterly. "Wonderfully arranged, all straight lines and precise rules and stiff spines, and how all that becomes a big lie when you move to the edge of the Empire and run loose in the jungle with guns and knives."

I was taken aback at his vehemence. I didn't know what to say. "Things would collapse without order, and without us, dear chap," I said. "You mustn't take what happens during war as an aspect of everything we stand for." Below us, the policeman blew his whistle furiously. A cart approaching from the direction of the Maidan had tried to sneak past while the policeman's back had been turned. Naturally, it had run into another cart, creating an ungodly mess just as the sun was setting peacefully over the Maidan. "Look there," I cried. "These fellows couldn't manage traffic without our rules and the will to impose them."

"I know," Jim said gloomily, and lapsed into silence. Then he began speaking again, but with a doubtful note in his voice as if I was incapable of understanding the things he was talking about.

He had begun having nightmares again, he said, his arm lashing out in the dark and knocking over chairs and tables as if he could drive away the images in his head with a blow of the fist, while his waking moments were possessed by the knowledge of how close he was getting to the place by the river where he had failed so completely, each mile accomplished by his unit taking him nearer to his shrine of shame.

I hastened to interrupt him. "It is the time, the war," I said. "The best of men could go mad in such a place as you were in."

"So others told me, but I do not think it was the place, except that it stripped us of the layers of civilization we go cloaked in when we are in our safe, orderly homes. No, what I found there when running away from the Japanese was my true nature, my true self. That is my despair, and perhaps also my only hope for redemption of some sort, because I like to think I uncovered a better part of me when I returned to that same region three years after the incident."

He nodded to himself, and hugging his knees closely as though he were cold, he continued. They had reached Imphal and were huddled in camps in the pouring rain, waiting while the Fourteenth Army prepared itself for a final devastating thrust into Burma. It rained throughout the day. The mornings were as dark and gloomy as the nights, making it seem that the sun would never rise over the scenes of carnage. Sitting in his tent, drinking tepid tea, and scribbling in his diary, Jim felt neither the thrill nor fear of battle. To him, it was as if a final war was being fought, and he wished he could be certain of right and wrong because all of it seemed muddled in his mind. When the wind blew out his candle, he sat in the dark listening to the soldiers outside, to the Africans from the highlands and the Indians and the Yorkshire lads, feeling with a sense of incredible urgency that he had to make sense of things before his opportunity for comprehension ran out.

After he had finally relit the candle, he began looking through some of the diaries and papers he had found on the Japs—even their common soldiers tended to store a few personal papers in their helmets, usually letters or postcards or photographs, often written with a lyrical tenderness that shocked Jim's fellow officers when little bits were read out to them. Most of the British officers didn't understand how killers and fanatics could be writing things like that to their families. Jim didn't understand either, or hadn't at first, although he'd been baffled rather than shocked or outraged. But as he recalled his own patch of darkness, he thought he glimpsed the spirit that went into the writing of those notes and diaries. Anything to keep the horror at bay, anything to have some light and warmth to remind oneself of the part that was yet human, that still struggled to free itself from the irreversible acts committed by the rest of the self.

That evening he began doing something that surprised him, especially as it came from no conscious decision. He began copying the papers into his own journal, translating them into English. Sorting them out into separate piles, each pile representing a dead soldier, he began with the first letter—a sergeant and former student of economics writing to his sweetheart. Jim's copying was a slow, painstaking process because his command of the language was still fairly rudimentary. Often, he did not have an adequate vocabulary or understanding of the context to carry out an accurate translation. But he did not let himself become disheartened by his limitations, telling himself that he grasped the sensibility behind the words perfectly. There were many speakers and many different moods, some sad and melancholy, others funny and light-hearted, but he scribbled on slowly as if the papers were merely talismans and what he was really doing was acting as an amanuensis for the spirits of dead enemy soldiers.

When he woke in the morning, he knew what the rest of his war would consist of. He rode in the jeep like a different man as the convoy headed for Moreh, almost unheeding now of the corpses and prisoners and the ruined buildings being bulldozed to one side as the road was cleared. He waited impatiently for night to fall, that monsoon night so indistinguishable from the day, and when the unit had stopped and it was evening, he retired to his tent to continue his copying.

Jim paused and picked up the package he had placed by his chair. "I'll show you all of it later, everything I copied out, because there's something I want to do with it. I thought you might know how I can do that, being an editor and so on, but that can wait. There's not very much here, not as much as I wanted to copy, but I could recite it all to you from memory. Not sure you would want to listen, but let me tell you just this part from a diary I found on a dead gunner near Moreh. He'd run out of ammo long ago, and anyway there wasn't much he could have done with the bombs coming from above. We found him with his fingers around the pen, the diary open to the page he'd been writing on. Everyone knew what he would have been noting down, sitting as he was in stinking clothes in a hole in the ground filled with water with bombs tearing up the hills all around him. Death, defeat, pain. What else was there for him to write about? What else has there ever been to write about?"

But what Jim found in the gunner's diary had nothing about bombs or starvation or dishonour. He'd been looking at the journal along with an intelligence officer who had just joined his unit. "The sorry bugger was writing poetry," the intelligence officer said. Jim was not so sure. "The gunner was describing what he saw around him, and he had written how peaceful everything was. He said that he looked out over the ridge, and he saw cherry blossom trees glowing in the dusk, and that under the clear sky, with a gentle wind blowing, he could hear the temple bells of the shrine near his home, and although he was sleepy he felt that he had to get up now and take a few steps so that he could see the old men sitting outside the shrine."

But Jim's fellow-officers did not understand. The intelligence officer laughed. "Fellow went mad," he said to Jim. "Was pouring rain and bombs around him. Clear skies and gentle winds indeed." The other men agreed, because they had seen similar sights evoked in some of the previous letters, where Japanese soldiers described the forests of India and Burma as if they were home already, evoking their neighbourhoods and friends and families. "Malnutrition, fear, disease, and the little fanatic just couldn't take it any more," the intelligence officer explained and turned away.

Jim didn't agree. He didn't believe it was madness to be writing about the Yasukuni shrine while dying amid bombs and shells in an unknown place. He understood, he said, and if he held the diary and closed his eyes and concentrated, he could make the mules and river and corpses disappear, and he too could believe that he was standing near the shrine with cherry blossoms falling softly on the roof.

When they reached Moreh, Jim saw that a detention centre had been set up near the divisional headquarters, a row of wire cages strung out by the side of the road. The cages were packed with prisoners who had been brought from the forward area to be interrogated and processed. Jim was busy the next day, sharing his duties with Wright, the intelligence officer. It was a disheartening business, he said, interviewing the starving men, limping from Beri-

Beri, some of them barely able to sit while questions were asked of them.

Wright pretended to be bored while interrogating the prisoners, although he was clearly fascinated by them in a grotesque sort of way. Jim had begun to think that he was not a very good intelligence officer; he was too prone to outbursts of aggression, much too interested in acquiring mementoes that could be found in the chaos everywhere, especially map cases and Japanese ceremonial swords.

It was nearly the end of the day and they were both very tired when a final prisoner was brought in. The prisoner was a young man, limping, accompanied by a Sikh soldier who towered over him. He stumbled as he entered and the Sikh had to hold him up. Wright didn't say anything, just yawned and stretched and played with his matches, and Jim impatiently ordered the Sikh to set the prisoner down on the chair.

"Shall I make him cry?" Wright asked. "Funny how that's always the first thing they do."

Jim knew Wright was upset. There had been an incident the previous day when Wright had been out with a patrol. Kicking open the door of a hut, he had surprised two Jap soldiers hiding inside. He had got them both with a burst of his Tommy gun without any chance of return fire, but a new map case in the hut had been ruined by his own bullets.

Jim thought it strange that a man should let something like a map case play on his mind so much, but he was determined to do his bit and get back to his tent and the papers as soon as possible. The prisoner shivered, and Jim asked him if he would like some tea. The tea was brought in, and as the prisoner sipped it slowly, holding the cup with both hands, Jim asked his questions gently but firmly. He wanted to know what the prisoner had been doing before the war, but although the man spoke a particular word over and over again, Jim could not understand what it meant. He looked to Wright for help, but Wright had risen from his chair and was pacing around impatiently, ignoring both Jim and the prisoner.

The prisoner wanted Jim to understand, and, putting down the cup, he leaned forward and made a screwing motion with his hands, producing a buzzing sound with his tongue. "Zzzzz, Zzzzz," it sounded to Jim, and he watched carefully, feeling that every act of interpretation was important to him now, as if only by deciphering the sound of this sick and defeated man would he be able to make sense of his own life. "I've got it," Jim said to Wright. "Rivets, that's what he's showing us. He was some kind of mechanic. He's showing us what he did before the war." Jim raised his hands and made the same circular motion, producing a similar sound from his mouth. The prisoner smiled with delight, his tongue sticking out with exhaustion and fulfillment, and Jim heard Wright stop pacing around and slam his hand on the table.

"Have you quite finished?" Wright said.

Jim looked at him in silence. The prisoner's smile had vanished.

"Now that you have the intelligence that is going to win us the war, perhaps we can proceed with this business my way."

He looked at the prisoner and went around the desk very slowly, approaching the prisoner in a manner quite different from the disinterest he usually affected in the beginning. The man stiffened and shrank in his chair, looked at Jim, and then turned to Wright hopefully and smiled, extending his hands to display the riveting action once again. Wright grabbed the prisoner's hands—he could have circled the man's biceps with one hand—and shook him in fury. "Cry, you Jap scum, cry. That's the way to begin."

Although he hadn't understood a word, the prisoner began crying.

Jim tried to look away. He got up from his chair, intending to do what Wright had done—to pace around in the room and let his fellow officer interrogate the prisoner according to his own methods. When he hit Wright, he still didn't realize that that had been his intention from the very moment he rose from the chair, and that he had finished with his translations and his war for good. He looked at the room, at the prisoner sobbing in his chair, at Wright with one hand clapped to his mouth, at the Sikh guard who stood unblinking and impassive behind the prisoner's chair as if he hadn't seen a thing.

Wright was bleeding, but the words he spoke at that moment were distinctly clear to Jim. "Filthy little bugger, at least we didn't go around raping women and killing our own civilians."

Later that evening, Jim went to the enclosure. The askari on guard saluted and let him in. The riveter hobbled to his feet and bowed, and Jim had an orderly bring a lantern and two cups of tea. He had no official business being there, he said, but he was past caring. Outside, the campfires flickered, and the song of the Sikh soldiers came from one of the fires, a plaintive song filled with a yearning that Jim felt he understood perfectly. The prisoner listened too, and they sat there without exchanging any words. He left camp the next day and made his way towards Calcutta.

Jim finished his narration, looking out into the darkness that had engulfed the city, leaving me with a lingering sense of unease. "You don't mean to say," I said hesitantly to him and then stopped, not knowing how to proceed. "Surely you didn't leave without approval, without even knowing if Wright reported the incident to the authorities?" The thought that I was sheltering a deserter was awkward, and the afternoon when his arrival had filled me with such pleasure seemed very distant indeed. Jim didn't say anything. He handed me the packet. "Both the translations and the originals are here. If there's some way of sending the original letters back to Japan, when all this is over, you would be the right man to do it."

I didn't see Jim in the morning. Abdul said he was still sleeping, and I left for work with an uneasy conscience, pondering over my divided duties to Jim and the army authorities who should certainly be notified of his presence.

There was an almighty fuss waiting for me at the office, though. I knew that Rowe had journeyed from England in a personal capacity, but it was most awkward that someone officially still the editor of the newspaper should be hobnobbing with Mr. Gandhi and his crowd of Congresswallahs. Rowe had sent us a report of a conference he had attended in Bombay and he wanted us to carry it in the next day's edition. In a note to me, he said he was most perturbed about the line we had taken with regard to the

Hindu-Muslim question, that we had no idea of the kind of passions we were stoking and the price that would be paid by the natives for our mistakes.

I spent the better part of the afternoon on the phone with members of the board, pressing upon them the urgency of the situation and the delicate handling it required. There was no question of allowing the piece to appear in its current form, but we could not censor the writings of our own editor. When the board's decision was communicated to me, I was both gratified by the faith they had shown in me and painfully aware of the enormity of the decisions facing me. I had been making such decisions for four years, but from that day they would bear the official weight of the editor of the most influential newspaper India has ever seen.

I was pondering over the course of action before me, the manner in which I should notify Rowe of the termination of his employment with the paper. The position had been largely symbolic for the previous four years, but an institution like the *Imperial* imparts dignity even to such symbols.

When the phone call came from the police headquarters, I was quite unprepared for what followed. It was Peters, a man I had met a few times at the club, and he was good enough to tell me that there was a bit of a nasty business involving one of my guests. I thought Jim had got into another one of his interminable brawls. "Seems like an accident," Peters said. The body had not yet been transferred to the morgue and was still at Princep Ghat. A couple of eyewitnesses, both natives, were being held at the spot and he was going there directly to question them. Would I be so good as to come along and identify the body?

Postponing the task of informing Rowe that he was no longer connected with the paper, although of course we would be happy to consider anything he cared to offer us on a freelance basis, I left the office to meet Peters. It was a quick ride, the ghat being not far from the office, and Peters filled me in on what he had found out so far. Jim's body had been fished out of the river, and from the account of the eyewitnesses, there was no reason to believe foul play was involved.

The ghat was busy at that time of the day, and we had to make our way through the crowds to where the constables had covered the body with a sheet, the eyewitnesses standing to one side looking overawed by the situation. Peters realized that there were pressing tasks awaiting my attention at the office, and all he wanted was a quick identification. There was no need to look too long to recognize Jim's face. I told Peters that I understood the deceased to have deserted from his unit, and Peters said I shouldn't worry. It was a clear instance of suicide, and I had only been trying to help a disturbed man.

One of the eyewitnesses, a porter, had no English, but the other was a babu eager to display his acquaintance with the language. Both, however, agreed that they had seen Jim jump. He hadn't struggled in the water at all. Peters said Jim's tunic had been weighed down with rocks, and repeated that there seemed little doubt it was an open-and-shut case of suicide. The babu, a large, dark fellow in a dhoti, nodded in agreement. He had apparently heard the sahib talking to himself; the sahib had been pacing the ghat for a while before he jumped into the water. "And what does that prove?" I asked, slightly annoyed by his su-

perior manner. "The gentleman was quite mad, sir," the
babu replied with a devious smirk on his face. "He looked
at that neem tree there and declaimed aloud that he was
viewing the cheery blossoms of England."

It was a tragic episode with which to mark the beginning of my career as the last British editor of the *Imperial*.

❖ 2 ❖

Dimapur looked like a smaller, narrower version of Robiul's
city, with an underlying frantic tone to its otherwise
provincial air. The bus terminus and the area around it was
busy with people and their belongings, the bulky olive holdalls
of soldiers and the amorphous bundles of civilians being
loaded hurriedly onto the roofs of buses in preparation for the
day's final exodus. Those with less luggage climbed into
Maruti vans that would make the run to Kohima with five or
six passengers sharing the fare. A jumble of shops, mostly
warehouses and agencies for traders coming down from Kohima, gave the place the appearance of a small North Indian
town, and only the empty and deserted railway station
sounded a discordant note.

Robiul had given me the name of a hotel not far from the
bus terminus. Called the Great Eastern (in imitation of a five-
star in Calcutta), it loomed over the street, and the sight of it
was not comforting. It seemed to be a hotel purely by virtue of
being the tallest building on the street, its half-dozen floors
joined by a narrow staircase and a creaking lift. As I surveyed
the narrow concrete structure squeezed between a tiny petrol
pump and one of those ubiquitous all-purpose stores, I found it

hard to tell what color paint had been used for the walls. Its small windows were caked in dirt, as if they had never been opened, and the building showed no signs of life apart from a line of washing on the balcony of the topmost floor.

The man at the reception had thick, curly hair and a goatee. His face was soft and fleshy, and he wore a tie that reminded me of the pharmaceutical salesmen I had encountered earlier. Although he spoke little, he had the air of a man who had fallen from better things, and a business magazine laid facedown on the reception counter (a new publication from Delhi that was usually full of glossy pictures of corporate executives leaning back on dark leather chairs) indicated that he hadn't stopped hoping for better things, although the hotel seemed to be the last outpost on a downward route.

A thin, toothless man in a uniform of khaki shorts and shirt, his feet bare, led me—up the stairs and along a corridor so narrow that I could touch both walls if I stuck out my elbows—to a vacant room on the third floor.

The window looked onto a backyard filled with junk: a bucket, broken earthen pots, newspapers, rags, the remnants of a broom made with bamboo strips, a can for Castrol engine oil, wrappers, used condoms, and broken whiskey bottles, all of it arranged around the rusting frame of an old jeep, its tires and steering wheel and seats stripped off. The sheets smelt of sweat and the whole room had the distinct, sweet odor of marijuana. The old man had waited after letting me in. When I gave him a tip, he said he could bring me food or tea from the restaurant across the street if I wanted something to eat; the hotel didn't have a kitchen.

It did however have a telephone in the office behind the front desk—a red rotary phone with a small lock on it, next to a little plastic statue of Ganesh—which the man at the reception pointed out to me when I asked him if I could make a long-distance call. Breathing heavily as he wrestled with his belt, belly, and trouser pocket before extracting the key to unlock the phone, he stayed in the office as I dialed the number, leaning against the wall while I waited nearly five minutes for Robiul to answer. When I gave up and said I would try later, he nodded placidly, the expression on his face indicating that he had expected no other result.

I went to eat at a *dhaba* that served truckers and drivers. The food was bad, and the naked bulbs over the trestle tables cast a dim yellow light that made my eyes feel as if everything were slightly out of focus or being viewed through a tinted screen. I found out later that it was like that in the entire town, and indeed all the way to Imphal, because the power grid in the region couldn't generate enough voltage. It was to make the evenings unbearable. My eyes could never quite adjust to the yellow tinge, and it always felt like the onset of a fever, a sickness from which there was no relief except in complete darkness or in daylight.

In the yellow light, I could see that the *dhaba* wasn't crowded; the last convoy of trucks had already headed out, accompanied by a police escort. The few drivers eating here were either turning back toward the flooded plains or waiting to load up before climbing toward the hills; there was a tired impatience on their craggy faces as they chewed on their rotis. One man stood out from the rest of the clientele, a small, prim-looking character at the table across from me who kept staring in my direction but looking away whenever I raised my head. What I caught of his look before he turned away was a measuring, assessing glance. He wore glasses, and his ironed clothes and well-polished shoes were out of place in that rough-and-ready *dhaba*, yet he showed no signs of being conscious of his incongruousness.

There was no food on his table, only a black zippered folder of fake leather with a thong at one end. The words "Twenty-Ninth Conference of Assistant Bank Managers, Jabalpur 1991" were stenciled across the folder. After I had finished my meal, I asked for a glass of tea and spread my map out on the table, hoping to study the rest of my route. The stranger leaned forward a little, as if he wanted to take a look too. There was curiosity in his face, but also a patronizing air that annoyed me. I ignored him, wanting to avoid another uninitiated conversation.

I had finished more than half my journey, and was at most three or four days from Imphal. The road snaked down southward on the map, although I would be going up into the northeastern hills to reach Kohima, the highway continuing along the spine of the hills before it descended into the Imphal Valley in Manipur. The space looked intimate on paper, an area thick with lines and dots and strange names, but when I followed Highway 39 beyond Imphal to the border town of Moreh, the map changed character. Across the border, in Burma, it was all blankness.

Back in the hotel room, I tried the fluorescent lamp and gave up after suffering its incessant flickering for a couple of minutes; there just wasn't enough electricity to help it close the circuit. I leafed through the contents of Robiul's envelope in the yellow light of the regular bulb, transferring some of the names and numbers to my notebook; then I went down to try to call him one more time. The receptionist was not behind the counter, and a folding metal grille had been extended across the front door and bolted at the bottom. Through the windows, past the heavy red curtains layered with dust, I could see the market was already deserted. There were few streetlights, and the shops were closed, although it was not yet seven. One last shopkeeper locked the pull-down shutters of his store, adding the finishing touches to this security arrangement by waving a flaming roll of paper at it, a kind of barrier of holy fire to add to the metal. Finally done, he stamped out the embers and left, and out of the darkness, as if shadows were becoming solid, appeared a paramilitary patrol. They settled into a waiting position in front of the shop, their sticks and cane shields and helmets a sinister parody of a cricket team's gear.

Inside the office, there was a light on, and the overweight receptionist appeared when I knocked, the fringes of his goatee stained with dal. He held up a large hand smeared with food in explanation and nodded affably when I asked if I could use the phone; the desk with the phone was crowded with little earthen pots of vegetables and dal, while a pile of rapidly hardening nans lay on a newspaper, next to a black zippered folder that announced its owner as having been a delegate at a conference of bank managers in Jabalpur. I looked at the man, sitting with a plate on his lap, and as he nodded, I realized he had been waiting at the *dhaba* to pick up the food.

The receptionist had already returned to his meal, gesturing briefly at the phone. The man from the *dhaba* smiled—it seemed to me he was smiling to himself rather than me—and fished the key out of his pocket. The receptionist put his plate down, took the key, and unlocked the phone. They both waited while I tried Robiul and listened to the answering ring from his phone, although by this time I was beginning to think that his line had been disconnected and I was getting what people called a false ring.

When I gave up, the receptionist locked the phone and handed the key back to the man from the *dhaba*. He was not very old, but there was a withered watchfulness to him I associated usually with traders and politicians and bureaucrats, people who made a success of their lives through the observation and exploitation of the weaknesses and fallibilities of others. He was the kind of man who would watch you stumble on a pavement and wonder who had the contract for paving it, and how much he had made from it. I didn't know much about him, but even so there were telltale signs that marked him out as a man with a malign influence on the receptionist, from the key in his pocket and the way the receptionist stopped eating when he did to the very manner in which he held himself, a small man occupying a large, self-important space.

He asked me to sit while the old man in shorts brought us tea. All he said of himself was that he was manager of the local branch of Bank Republic, a large national bank, and that he lived in the hotel. Then he casually brought up the map and asked what kind of work I did, looking mildly interested when I told him I was going to Manipur. "Rajan here"—he gestured at the receptionist—"worked in Manipur for a while. In Moreh, border town near Burma gate." Rajan looked nervously at us. "Full of thugs, but also many interesting business opportunities. That is the way here, with money always to be made in such places," the manager said. "Rajan will tell you why he left."

I disliked his way of speaking for Rajan, but the receptionist seemed quite used to it. Rajan's voice became reflective as he spoke, and although from the substance of his story there was no doubt that he had been unhappy and scared to death in Moreh, and quite relieved to leave finally, there was also a touch of regret in his tone, as if he had let go of a freedom without quite realizing it at the time. He had been a bank officer too, an assistant manager for the Moreh branch of the Bank Republic. Moreh was a rough place, Rajan said, because of the insurgents and the smuggling. The groups were divided along ethnic lines: Nagas, Kukis, Burmese, and Tamilians descended from laborers imported by the British from southern India to work the rubber plantations of Burma. Frequent turf wars broke out over the smuggling business, and just before Rajan was sent to Moreh there had been a gun battle at the Morning Market because Naga insurgents had picked up a Tamil boy suspected of working as an informer for their Kuki rivals.

Rajan kept a low profile in Moreh—there wasn't much to do in the town, nothing in fact except for buying smuggled goods from the Morning Market or getting drunk—and he was getting by until two men came into his bank one Saturday. The bank closed at twelve and the men walked in when the tellers were already packing up for the day. The two were army officers, one an Indian and the other a Burmese officer in the uniform of their border guard, his eyes covered by reflector sunglasses. They had a canvas bag with fifty thousand rupees in it, and wanted Rajan to make out a bank draft for the cash. The normal procedure would have been to ask them to fill out the requisite forms and return after three to pick up the draft; since the bank was about to close, he should have told the men to come back on Monday. They wanted the draft then and there, however, and Rajan was scared. Only the Indian officer spoke to him, and Rajan guessed that he was from the north somewhere, a man who seemed intimidating in spite of his jolly, relaxed manner. The Burmese didn't say a word, but stood there the entire time without taking off his sunglasses, holding the canvas bag while the Indian filled out the forms, writing down the name of a company in Meerut in Uttar Pradesh as the recipient. Rajan knew there was a big army cantonment there, so he didn't suspect anything; when he asked the officer if the company was a supplier, the officer replied that it sold bagpipes to the army.

Bagpipes? This was absurd, I felt compelled to say, but Rajan was adamant that the Indian officer had mentioned bagpipes, and moreover, hadn't seemed to think there was anything wrong with making out a bank draft for fifty thousand rupees for a bagpipe supplier on the other side of the country. He'd agreed to draw up the draft, even though it would be bending rules, and the men didn't object when he said he had to take the bag of money to his office to count it.

Once he was in his office, Rajan had closed the door and, following the standard procedure for banks in the region, compared the numbers on the notes against two sheets pasted on the wall. These listed the series numbers of banknotes stolen by insurgent groups, but the codes on the notes didn't match those on the sheets, and Rajan felt relieved. Because it was such a large amount, he decided to do a final check. He opened his drawer and referred to a recent circular about spotting counterfeit notes floating around in the region. He read the instructions, took a couple of samples from the bag, rubbing them against his fingers. They matched in every particular.

He remembered hearing a quarrel on the road outside the window, the sound of curses in Tamil, and thinking that it seemed to be happening very far from him even though the window was just a few feet away. It was a hot time of the year, and Rajan was sweating profusely. It was a while before he realized that he hadn't turned the ceiling fan on. He moved slowly toward the switch, and all sorts of unrelated thoughts occurred to him, such as a sore on his foot that had been bothering him for a long time; he'd been thinking of going to Imphal to have a skin specialist look at it. The one thing that seemed strangely unreal to him, an assistant manager who had handled stacks of notes in his first few years of work, was that he was in such close proximity to a canvas bag full of counterfeit currency.

It was as if the entire nature of his existence had been called into question, Rajan explained, just to know that such things really existed and that he was in the middle of a transaction involving false currency. It felt almost like the loss of religion, he said, as if some mad iconoclast had shown him how easy it was to dress up a doll or a book and genuflect to it and bombard it with empty rituals. He checked some more of the notes in order to be absolutely sure, feeling desperate as each one turned out to be counterfeit. They weren't amazingly good fakes either, but they would not have been spotted in small batches in regular transactions unless the receiver became suspicious of how new and crisp the notes looked: there weren't too many fresh notes in the region, and anything that wasn't torn and patched-up was always in demand.

Rajan didn't know what to do. If he accepted the money and made out the draft, he would lose his job and go to prison. But the two men were waiting outside, the Burmese man had a gun in his holster, and both the tellers had left by then. The bank guard was still there, a retired Nepali soldier with an old rifle, but he was standing outside the main door.

Rajan decided to play for time. He went back with the bag

and, summoning the bland officiousness that was part of his job, said he could not issue the draft that day. It was out-of-state and there were special procedures, he said in a bored tone. The draft would not be valid unless it was countersigned by the manager, who was not present. There was, of course, no manager in that tiny branch in a border town, but Rajan was saved by the fact that his office door said "Assistant Manager," giving the impression that there *was* a manager somewhere, a mysterious higher authority whose office was not visible to the public. The Indian said they would return the following week, and in a sudden spurt of bravery, Rajan asked them if they would like to leave the money in the meantime. He had a momentary vision of helping the government arrest the men, of being recognized and rewarded for his efforts, perhaps even being promoted out of Moreh. The Indian looked at Rajan calmly, smiled at him, and said they would take the money with them. They picked up the bag and left.

Rajan wiped his throat with a handkerchief and loosened his tie. They never came back, but he subsequently received a series of phone calls. No one spoke, but he heard the sound of a knife being sharpened at the other end of the line and knew it was a message to him not to reveal what had happened. One day soon afterward, as he was taking a walk, he nearly got run over by a military truck speeding through the crowded main street of Moreh. He wanted to get out, but the bank wouldn't consider a transfer before the year was up. He wrote a resignation letter, packed his stuff, and boarded a bus to Imphal. Then he left Manipur and drifted around for a while, moving from town to town, until, beginning to run out of money and having difficulty getting work, he found himself in Dimapur.

Rajan opened his palms to gesture at his surroundings. He

didn't have to say where he had ended up. The little man had been listening attentively. Now he nodded and looked at me. "I rescued Rajan," he said in a chirpy tone, with a slight shake of his head toward his companion. "We were colleagues once. Batchmates during training. Now Rajan is in my employ." Then, just in case I hadn't understood, he added proudly, "I own the hotel. It is my own private enterprise. There are excellent opportunities here for private enterprise if you have the knack. You should keep your eyes open as well."

Rajan began collecting the empty glasses of tea.

• 3 •

Perhaps it was the doing of the guardian spirit of the hotel, but neither buses nor taxis were running to Kohima the next morning. The vans I had seen lining the approach to the bus station were gone, and pedestrians went about their business slowly, stopping at tea stalls to gather around newspapers. It was hard to pick out facts from the rumors, but a violent incident of some sort had apparently taken place in Kohima.

The incident took on greater definition as I approached the *dhaba* where the truck drivers were getting their morning tea. An army convoy was said to have opened fire on people in a busy marketplace, mistaking a bursting tire as evidence of an ambush. There was a strike in Kohima, the drivers said, so there was no point trying to get there. But, as always, there were other stories on offer, and one of the drivers, an old Sikh, told me in confidence that the highway had been blocked further ahead by truckers protesting against the increased taxes imposed by the insurgents.

Whatever the ostensible reason for the delay, centered around uncertain events up in the mountains, this outpost in the foothills had started withdrawing into itself in anticipation of trouble. The frantic pace I had seen when I arrived yesterday had been blunted; shops were open, but the owners projected an air of alert indolence as they read the small, leafletlike local newspaper, having taken care to keep their wares inside so that they could close at a moment's notice if necessary. I had expected a mob of disappointed passengers at the terminus, but only small groups of porters were present, leaning against silent, empty buses that reeked of diesel, holding *bidis* and cups of tea and looking as if they too would disappear at the first sign of trouble.

There was no one at the counter to answer questions, but a handwritten sign announcing an indefinite suspension of the bus service had been pasted over the counter. At the edge of the terminus, however, stood an ancient jeep with a canvas top, a relic that bore an uncanny resemblance to the wreck behind my hotel room. This was apparently the one vehicle willing to risk the trip to Kohima, although both jeep and driver were of such indeterminate character that I paused momentarily to reconsider. I wasn't in a great hurry to get to Kohima; a day or two would make no difference to my purpose in Imphal, but the thought of facing the hotel owner and Rajan again made me approach the driver cautiously.

He was tall and skeletally thin, with long, stringy hair reaching down to his neck in a ponytail. An old black suit was draped around him, and this, along with the stonelike reserve of his face, gave him a larger-than-life aspect, an almost symbolic quality, as if he represented time, or death, or some such thing. He leaned against the jeep as a woman—presumably another prospective passenger—bargained in a monotone. There was no way of telling what he thought of her or the price, but it was unusual for a woman to be going anywhere on her own, and especially so on a day like this. The driver loomed over her even while slouching, his hand lazily rising and falling as he smoked a rolled-up *biði*. The woman didn't once look at him, her glance directed somewhere vaguely toward the bonnet of the jeep as she enunciated her words as carefully as if she were speaking to a child.

The man turned toward me as I approached. "That price all right for you?" he asked. Then, without another word, he leapt into the front seat and started the rattling engine. The vehicle shook violently, followed by a series of explosions from the exhaust, and the woman climbed into the back hurriedly, looking at me cautiously as I followed with my bags. "I have lost much time already," she said, apparently addressing me, but it was the driver who answered. He jerked the gearshift and, locking her eyes in the rearview mirror, said, "We'll make up all your lost time, don't you worry. I'm your boatman." Then he laughed to himself and lit what smelt like a joint.

He drove steadily enough at first, going at a cautious pace as we passed troops and policemen. We saw a line of people forced to squat on the ground by soldiers, holding their ears. The driver smiled wryly, and I saw him studying me thoughtfully in the mirror. I fiddled with my glasses and beard in what I hoped was a benign, professorial gesture, and he seemed to lose interest in me after that.

We climbed rapidly, taking the hairpin bends so sharply that my companion's lips grew ever tighter, but the driver slowed down appreciably as soon as his sharp eyes spotted the olive of the military. An army truck appeared parked to our right, where the land fell away steeply into a ravine. Half a dozen soldiers were strung out in a loose line, pissing into the steep drop. Some of them turned and watched us sullenly as we passed, doing their flies, their swarthy faces and thick mustaches speaking of a terrain very different from the one they'd ended up in. It was not a sight to make a Naga happy.

The highway was still narrow, but better maintained, with freshly painted milestones and cheerful little rhyming slogans on them. The landscape was different too, the alluvial soil of the flood plains having given way to the red loamy earth of the hills. As we rose toward the body of mist hanging around the mountaintops, there were almost no signs of human habitation. Tin-roofed bungalows appeared in occasional clusters of two or three, standing in little patches cleared from the thick lines of conifers everywhere, while rows of buckets stood below mountain springs that had been channeled into pipes made out of bamboo trunks sliced in half.

There was something quite different about the drive up to Kohima in an old jeep with just one other passenger. I was insulated from the everyday crowds, and after the flooded plains and the thick press of bodies in the state transport buses, a melancholy, reflective note characterized this ascent. The craggy cliffs, dark trees, and drifting mists accentuated the mood, and I slid into a reverie that was unbroken by either the woman or the driver, the latter having settled into the relaxed alertness that the experienced ganja smoker rides on.

The air was cleaner and colder, so clear that the red and purple of the rhododendrons and orchids and even the dull olive of the army patrols appeared as flashes of startlingly vivid color in the watery landscape that made it seem as if I were traveling to the source of all my dreams. A light rain began to fall, tapping slowly but insistently on the body of the jeep, and the woman shivered. She drew her shawl tightly around herself and spoke out, her profile framed against the window and dissolving into translucent streaks.

"Will there be a curfew when we get to Kohima?"

"Quite possible," the driver said. "What difference does it make? Things shut down after three even on normal days, hey?"

"It never seems to end. How do people manage to live here?"

"Oh, like they do everywhere else. You take one step at a time. So what brings you here?"

"I'm going on to Imphal from Kohima. My husband will be waiting for me there. You see, he's running a project near Imphal—he's the director. How it's grown! He began with a small office, showing local people how to combine their traditional craftsmanship with modern equipment and designs, and now it's a massive development project, touching every aspect of these people's lives. I work on the Delhi end of the project, with the grant givers and donor agencies and everything. We don't get to see each other so much." She hesitated, then added quickly, "But we're a team."

"You didn't go straight from Delhi? This is kind of roundabout way, you know. You could get stuck; if there are landslides or something, then it takes long time for highway to be cleared."

"I know, but I found out a friend of mine was here and I just had to meet her. She's all alone, and because I was coming to the region anyway, I decided to see that she's all right."

"Something wrong?" the driver asked.

The woman thought for a little bit and decided to take us into her confidence.

"She's in Dimapur with her son, staying with her brother before she goes back home to the south. Her husband is in the army. She's left him."

She waited, as if we would see that the connection was quite obvious. It was the driver who responded.

"Sleepin' around and all that?"

"Of course," she said with outrage. "And he gave her something as well. Something he picked up from his sleeping around. Poor Parvati with her son and her dog, quite alone, trying to start her life all over again."

The driver listened gravely to her rant. In spite of his wry humor and disconcerting love for fat joints of grass, there was a gallantry in his behavior toward her that I thought to be an expression of the culture of the hills. But she was too preoccupied to notice his manners, shifting around on the seat as if there was much more on her mind than her troubled friend or the state of affairs in Kohima.

She was a small woman, but her smallness was not a comfortable petiteness. It was the wound-up state of a tightly coiled spring. Her hair was gathered in a bun, and she sat with her narrow shoulders sloped forward, one hand clenched around her bag, the other holding on to the back of the driver's seat. Earlier, her lips had been pursed in a whistling gesture, as if her thoughts were rushing out like sharply expelled breath; now her gaze flickered restlessly as she spoke to us, never settling on me or the driver or the road—and only her hands were still.

"I'm luckier than Parvati. I live alone too, but because my husband is involved in something grand. It's so much harder for him, being here on his own trying to achieve something in the middle of all this violence. He doesn't mind the curfews or shootouts or threats. He talks to everybody, to the insurgents and the army, trying to convince them of the need for change. They listen to him, and I've heard that they even admire him."

She spoke of her husband with a cautious pride at first, as if uncertain of our response. Gradually, talking about a familiar person seemed to calm her down. "For me, though, coming here, making this trip because he wanted me to, it's very hard. I don't know how he does it, staying here year after year, doing the grassroots work."

"Like I said, ma'am, he does it same way as everybody else. Even the army buggers do it that way."

A small group of soldiers was trudging through the rain, some of them very young, and one, carrying a rocket launcher, no more than a boy.

"Look. Left, right, left, right, all the way to Kohima."

In her newly relaxed state, she laughed. "Even when I met him, he was different, you know. So full of energy. You want to hear about it. How I met him?"

"I love romance stories," the driver said. "But you'll have to make it real quick. We're not so far from the town."

"It made me believe in something, the way I met him. I think of it every day in Delhi when I feel he is far away in the region, sitting by himself in a bungalow reading a book, with the wilderness all around him. I tell myself that my being on my own is nothing, nothing at all compared to what he is going through, and that he is doing something great. I turn off the lights in my flat and lie in the darkness and try to imagine what it is like around him and how he feels, and then I start drifting back to when I first saw him. The monsoons had just broken in Delhi and a friend of mine had been knocked down by a bus. Another friend and I went to AIIMS to find her, and we were running around in that crazy hospital trying to find someone who would help us, someone who could tell us which ward she might be in, when this junior doctor appeared in the corridor, asking if he could help. My husband's not a very big man, not quite as tall as either of you, but my friend later told me that she had this impression of a giant bearing down upon us with incredible force. She was struck by his eyes, she said, there was something odd about them, the way his pupils dilated, and she was transfixed, hopeful, and afraid, all at the same time."

"And you, what did you think?"

"I wasn't thinking anything. I was too surprised and confused, because I remembered suddenly that I had dreamed this very scene the night before, right down to the exact detail of his face looming before me and asking if he could help while a hospital gurney passed in the background, and I kept wondering how it was possible that a dream could merge into reality."

"Shit, you said romance, not horror," the driver protested. "I don't like horror."

The woman frowned and leaned forward.

"It was very strange, especially because I got the feeling he knew why I was so uncomfortable around him. He gave me this smile that seemed to say, 'Of course, you dreamed of this last night. That is the way things happen occasionally, when the distinction between dreams and reality disappears. You can call it magic or hallucination or madness if you want to, but what you call it doesn't really matter.' My mind was in a blur with the shock of the accident and seeing his face and recognizing it from the dream, but he didn't say anything to me. He helped us find our friend, being very kind and authoritative at the same time. He made sure she was all right, gave us his number, and found an auto-rickshaw that would take us home without charging us a lot of extra money."

"He was a medical resident at the AIIMS? A doctor?" I asked, some of the pieces falling into place for me.

"He didn't stay as a resident at AIIMS for long. Soon after we met he quit, never practicing as a doctor. We didn't get together until a few years after that first strange meeting. By that time he was already into the nonprofit work, planning something special in the region."

"You think he could have stayed a doctor and still done good work here," the driver said. "There's a big quota of diseases here, from cerebral malaria to AIDS. People need medicines and doctors all the time."

"Oh, but his vision was so much larger than that," she said. "He wanted to change lives from beginning to end. Whatever you may think, he's done it, as you would know if you visited his project. Everything you could ask for, school, AIDS clinic, rehabilitation center, fishery project, all of it working in complete harmony. Almost a new society, something beyond the quarrel of the government and the insurgents. Because, you must understand, he's a man of action and also a thinker. His ideas, if only you two could hear them. It's very sad that he's still unknown in India, but his fame is spreading abroad, I am sure of that. In Europe, in the Scandinavian countries, in America, they have begun talking about his work and his ideas, and I have to struggle to meet all the donor agencies waiting in line with their grants.

"What's really amazing about him is his ability to learn new ideas, to adapt to different circumstances. When he began his work in the region, he said that he had made the mistake of starting out in a conventional way. The first project was a disaster. They were in a river island trying to help the villagers stop the erosion of the banks, but a local group of insurgents didn't like it. They kidnapped some of the coworkers and one man was killed. My husband escaped because he wasn't on the island that day, but the project had to be shut down and the army moved in. I thought he would be shattered when he came back to Delhi after that, but he was invigorated. He thought for a long time, staying by himself in a little room he had rented in the outskirts of the city, without a phone or anything, trying to get deep into himself. Then he said that the problem in the first place had been in going there with fixed ideas about development, and he was determined that when he returned, he would just slip into the region, become one with it, in perfect harmony with the environment. He is destined for great things," she concluded fiercely.

Out of nowhere, there came to my mind the clear image of a college examination paper flapping about on the floor of Robiul's house. I'd picked it up and handed it to him with no more than a quick glance, yet I could recall one of the questions as clearly as if it had been etched into my brain: "Thomas Carlyle in *On Heroes and Hero Worship* says, 'No sadder proof can be given by a man of his own littleness than disbelief in great men.' Discuss, with reference to the context." I was sure that the woman's idea of her husband's greatness would not have met the standards of the examiners: there was too much faith in the proposition, and not nearly enough context. The idea of his selfless efficiency was thrilling, especially after some of the people I'd met recently, but I was afraid it would not be sustained if subjected to close examination.

The cynicism of a journalist, I thought, of a man who has

seen feet of clay on far too many occasions, but then I noticed that the driver was looking at me with a somber expression. My eyes met his, and he shook his head slightly and gestured ahead, to where a large patch had been cleared in the forest and fenced off with wooden posts and barbed wire. In the middle of the enclosure stood a blue signboard, and the driver slowed as we passed so I could read it. The board was old, its paint peeling in many places, the exposed metal rusted, and there was a date on it announcing the inauguration of the site for a development project sponsored by the World Bank. The words faded as we approached a bend, but I had seen enough to feel it evoked not so much an inauguration as a hasty, untimely burial. The driver's eyes met mine, and he nodded quickly again and took a drag on his joint, his sallow face melancholy and thoughtful.

Another sharp turn, with the houses blooming thickly on the hillsides, a few villagers with wood on their backs heading toward the town. A sloping meadow ran to our left with a row of neat gravestones, their crosses at attention like soldiers. "The Kohima war cemetery," the driver announced, as he killed the engine and began coasting downhill.

light

CHAPTER SEVEN

❖ 1 ❖

There are certain people who make you reveal aspects and attributes of yourself that usually lie hidden, and perhaps there are places that do the same. I got into Kohima intending to spend no more than a day or two there, but something kept me in that hill town with its pine-scented outskirts and tribal villages perched like birds' nests on the surrounding mountains. On the surface, I was held up by news of landslides on the road to Imphal, this delay serving as a final faltering over the purpose of my quest, a stumble at the threshold of the story. Yet what happened in the town was more than an inconvenient, prolonged stopover. There was a kind of unspooling of the threads wound tightly inside me, a process that was both uncomfortable and clarifying, and it ensured that the search for the woman would from that point on possess a different timbre.

Even the town left me feeling more ambivalent than any place I had seen so far. In a way, Kohima was what I had expected, as taut with violence, anger, and bitterness as everyone had said it would be. Two parallel governments held sway over it, with the administration of the Indian republic giving way to the rule of the Naga rebels after dark, but Kohima offered me more than that dual state of terror.

The twilights were long there—a sort of twilight quite unknown in the plains—and there was a strange peace to the clouds brilliantly colored by the light of the setting sun. Watching that extended twilight from my hotel room, I could feel a similar pause in myself, a suspension between entrapment and freedom where I became aware of my inner state of being. I found this strangely new, this contact with impulses and regrets and anxieties that had been buried deep for many years. It did not always feel pleasant, but it was a form of release, allowing me to see both outside and inside of myself with greater accuracy.

There were external reasons for all my reflection and navel-gazing. People reacted differently to my presence in the streets—my height, complexion, and beard singling me out as a possible member of what many of them considered an occupying force—and it was often difficult to convince hostile, fearful strangers that I wasn't a government official or a soldier. You would think they would have known better; I hadn't cut my hair in months, my untrimmed beard had flecks of gray in it, and my shoes were falling apart. But even soldiers and policemen became confused and deliberated for long moments about whether or not to challenge me when I approached their barriers and outposts, and the constant scrutiny made me study my features with great attention when I was alone in my hotel room.

With the townspeople I tried the absentminded indifference that had prompted the driver to become friendly, while for the soldiers I allowed my Hindi, my bearing, and my big northern face to do the job of representing me. In some ways, I had always been like this, adjusting myself to local predispositions and inflections; it came from my mixed parentage, from growing up with a spinster aunt in a city far from the region of Punjab that my forefathers called home, and from the boarding school in the North Bengal hills where I had been sent at the age of twelve. I'd done pretty much the same thing in Calcutta too, when I projected myself as a genial, Bengali-speaking northerner to the prickly clerks at the municipal office; so this business of adjusting my speech and posture wasn't a new experience.

But then a small piece of news reached me quite accidentally one afternoon, casting my shifting identity into an even greater state of doubt. An editorial written in the *Nagaland Post* by someone with a local-sounding name had caught my eye, and I called the editor to find out if I could talk to the writer. The article was about the manner in which the traditional independence of the hill women had been eroded by the violence of the government and the insurgents, and there was a paragraph about a woman in neighboring Manipur that intrigued me. I told the editor I was with the *Sentinel*, and he readily agreed to arrange a meeting with his writer the next day.

It was a clear day with a slight chill in the air as I set out for the newspaper office, and I enjoyed the walk through the sloping, winding roads, with bungalows set along terraces, the church tower in the background playing hide-and-seek among the hills and the buildings. There was one particular spot from where I could see both the spire and the giant sculptured horns that formed the archway of the entrance to the old Kohima village, and the view left me with enough of a sense of mystery and awe to make me want to come back to Kohima someday.

I had time on hand as I made for the newspaper office, and the roundabout route I had chosen took me past the graveyard of British soldiers killed during the war, a site scrupulously maintained with money from England even now. The Japanese had less luck with their bodies, as I knew all too well from Sutherland's story. They were the defeated army, after all, and only winners can afford memorials of stone. A reconciliation ceremony of some sort had taken place a few years previously, incorporating Shinto rites into a Christian service for the two groups of veterans who had flown in, but it had been a fleeting, invisible peace—the war lingered on, past merging indistinctly into present as the soldiers waited behind their barricades and insurgents slipped in at night to take out an informer or put up a poster commemorating their latest martyr.

The streets became more crowded as I approached the town center, with alleyways twisting off from the main avenue. As I entered the passage leading to the newspaper office, a tall soldier from a Jat Regiment ran after me, crying, "Rajinder, Rajinder," with a boyish enthusiasm that was quite unexpected in such a large, ferocious-looking man. I stopped, and he trailed off as he saw my face and realized his mistake, then turned away without a word.

Inside the gray, nondescript building where the newspaper was housed, a young man with a handheld metal detector sat behind a counter next to the stairway, but he waved me through without asking for identification. The office itself consisted of a long room occupying the second floor, with a glass screen at one end partitioning off the editor's cubicle. It was a rudimentary setup, but the men gathered around a dummy news sheet looked up and smiled at me as I passed, and I felt a wave of longing for this intimate setting, so different from the empty, echoing corridors of the *Sentinel*. Sema, the editor, made me feel otherwise, though. He was friendly enough, close to me in age, but there was a jumpiness about him that I found disconcerting. He'd left his passport lying on his desk, and fingered it occasionally as he spoke, reaching out at other moments for a much-folded paper whose yellowed print and heavily condensed Times Roman typeface told me that it was a copy of the *Sentinel*.

Sema called for tea and said Maria, the writer of the article, was on her way. I asked him casually how old the copy of the *Sentinel* was. "Is there crucial news I've missed? Has the government in Delhi fallen? Are there national scandals I should know about?" I said the words jokingly, but I had not thought of national events for over a month now, all of that subordinated by my journey to the edge of the republic. Sema stroked his wispy Ho Chi Minh beard in reply, looking troubled. Then he opened the paper to the classifieds on page two and pointed out a boxed announcement. I glanced at it with a blasé air I thought would not be unbecoming in a big-city reporter who knows all the secrets of his paper, but the words took away my insouciance in a second: "The Management of the *Sentinel* wishes to inform all concerned parties that Mr. Amrit Singh no longer represents the *Sentinel* in any capacity, pending a departmental enquiry. The management assumes no liability for any actions or agreements he may enter into in his individual capacity. Signed Rana Sarkar, General Manager."

That Sarkar had been made general manager from an acting editor position was news to me, but then so was this departmental inquiry and suspension order. "The *Sentinel* does not have a wide circulation here," Sema said quietly, gesturing at the tea that had arrived. "Still, Mr. Singh, you may not want to depend too much on your affiliation with the paper until this matter has been cleared up with them."

I didn't say anything for a while. I felt humiliated. Beneath that, and keeping pace with my pounding heart and becoming stronger by the minute, was a sense of disgust for feeling so vulnerable. After all, I had disappeared and cut all ties of my own accord; I had broken ranks to find freedom, and was by no means expecting to be welcomed back by the paper when I returned to Calcutta. But the feeling of failure bubbling up in me was real in spite of all that, building into rage at Sarkar — and I would have hit him had he been in front of me.

Sema stared at me with a puzzled look on his face, and I tried to compose my features, wondering what to expect from him. He spoke first. "It wouldn't really matter to me very much. Even if I had not received a call from Robiul Haq vouching for you, I know only too well that honest men are often disenfranchised by institutions." He pointed at the passport. "I just got that back, Mr. Singh. My papers were taken away by Indian soldiers at a checkpoint last night. It happens all the time. You get invited to drink with the commanding officers where they are very hearty and slap you on the back. Then you're out on the streets and you revert to being just another potential troublemaker with slanted eyes, keeping your hands in the air as the soldiers curse you and pat you down."

"It sounds like we understand each other," I said.

He nodded gravely.

"Robiul called?"

"He will call again at the hotel. He said he had news."

Sema tossed the *Sentinel* into the wastepaper basket at his feet. He waved his hand at the journalists on the other side of the glass screen, and a young man with a Pentax poked his head round and said, "The picture will be better against a blank wall."

"If you go with him, he will take a passport picture. Tomorrow an identity card will be delivered to your hotel showing that you are a special correspondent for the *Nagaland Post*. It won't help you at every checkpoint or with slow-thinking militants, but it will provide a little insurance. That's the least I can do for Robiul. Please, Maria is here."

Maria looked on with an amused expression on her face as I stood in front of the wall and lifted my head according to the photographer's instructions. The picture session took only a couple of minutes, but somehow seemed to happen very slowly, the explosion of the flash and Maria's banter with the men creating a background noise to the onrush of thoughts inside my head. I saw her nose ring glinting as she turned to face the editor stepping out of his cubicle, I caught the indulgent look on the photographer's face as he told me I'd blinked and he would have to take another shot, and I was aware that I couldn't understand what the editor and Maria were saying to each other because I didn't know the language they were speaking. Somewhere far in the back of my head I heard Herman the German laughing. "I promised you freedom, Amrit," he said. "Here you go. Free at last from the *Sentinel* to begin a new life."

I didn't realize that the photographer had finished until Maria stepped forward and stuck out her hand. She was a small woman, just over five feet in height, dressed in jeans and a white shirt, with no jewelry other than the nose ring. I nodded in agreement when she said we should go to a nearby Chinese restaurant to discuss her article, and Sema raised his hand in a parting wave as we walked out of the office.

I couldn't get the *Sentinel* announcement out of my head, and I looked at the town with resentment and anger, as if the place was to blame for what had happened, barely hearing Maria's words. She was completely unself-conscious, and even though I would have rather been alone, I was grateful that she continued talking without much in the way of responses from me.

"So, Amrit, you're surprised to find a Goan woman at the other end of the country, especially when you saw a local name on the article."

"Quite a bit. But your real name's Maria?"

"It is. When I first moved here, without knowing what my life would be like after I had left everything behind, my husband suggested a new name. He thought it would make me less of a stranger to the people here, and the more I thought about it, the more the idea appealed to me. I was shedding an old skin and taking on a new one by moving here. Of course, they call me Maria all the same, even though they don't think of me as a stranger anymore. But I got what I needed, a new identity, a fresh start, maybe even a new life. It brought me luck."

We were out of the alleyway and in the marketplace. The soldier who had run after me was standing there with his friends, and he leered as we passed. "Rajinder, Rajinder, where did you pick up the woman from?" he shouted as we approached the restaurant, but Maria didn't react to him at all.

* 2 *

my interaction with Maria was really a long, extended conversation with many pauses, taking place over five or six days. It began quite unremarkably, even unpromisingly, at the little Chinese restaurant off the main road, her bright chatter contrasting with my slightly jaded questions about her article and whether she knew anything about the Manipuri woman she had mentioned in passing. But we decided to meet again the next day, and that encounter led to others. They took place mostly at the hotel (and on one occasion at her house) and provided me with enough new facts and rumors to alert me to what I would find at the end of my journey—had I stopped to think about it. But I didn't think too much about it then, caught up as I was in analyzing my life and speculating about Maria's situation.

Her husband had been away for some time when I met her. He was spending a year in Geneva on some kind of human rights program, and Sema had given me the impression he was a former militant who had turned his back on violence and decided to engage with the state in a different way. This information was interesting, but I found Maria's attitude toward his absence far more puzzling. She talked of missing him and seemed proud of him, showing me an interview he had conducted in Geneva with rebel leaders who had gone there for peace negotiations with the Indian government. Yet there was a completeness to her life without him that seemed suspect to me, the way she spent her days writing for the paper, doing some vague nonprofit work with an organization for village women, and—while I was there—talking to me endlessly about my article for Herman's magazine.

I realized Maria was an independent, self-reliant woman, but it seemed reasonable to expect some signs of rupture in her life, some vital absence that characterized her state of being while he was away. Yet I found none of that in her; she lived in an old bungalow, and the house was gloomy and dusty, giving me a glimpse of innumerable rooms and passageways from which aged servants appeared unexpectedly to hold me in long, appraising stares. There wasn't a single picture of Maria's husband in the drawing room. The furnishings, the stuffed antler heads on the walls, and even the books in the drawing room were at least fifty or sixty years old, and Maria herself looked like a spoiled guest rather than a resident as she lounged on the sofa with a shawl wrapped around her. She told me that her mother-in-law lived upstairs, and I left quickly because I got the impression that the mother-in-law did not welcome visitors.

It was possible that my own expectations were skewed because I had no experience of living with anyone, but even the subject of Maria's husband's absence came up only in a roundabout way: two or three days into our acquaintance, I asked Maria if there was something wrong with her phone because whenever I called her, there was a delay and faint click before it rang that struck me as odd.

"Oh, it's because of my husband," she said, trying to be understated about it, although it was transparently clear that she was delighted I had noticed this phenomenon. "It's his old insurgent links, and the interview he did from Geneva for the *Nagaland Post* about the seccessionist point of view has escalated matters a little more. The phone's been tapped ever since he left, and the intelligence folks listen in on everything. That's why we have to hold face-to-face talks if we want to discuss important things." She surveyed the hotel lobby, a big room with crossed spears and colorful tapestries on the walls. "Anyway, I like coming here, Amrit. It's elegant." It was also empty, and although there were well-tended gardens and lawns, I could see the fence and metal gate that was locked twenty minutes before the curfew began. "It has the best coffee in town. Sometimes one misses the big cities, Amrit."

The big cities she told me about that evening included Calcutta. She had grown up there, she said over sips of Nescafé, and her first marriage came to an end there when she walked out on her husband one night; she had slept on the city's streets after running away from him, but I was never sure how she got out of that situation and ended up in Kohima. I had come to expect such surprises from Maria by this time, the nonchalance with which she revealed personal details while being extremely closed about matters that appeared quite commonplace. She had talked to me at length about her article during our initial meeting, growing quite animated as I showed her the photograph, but she wouldn't say anything about the work she did for the women's organization.

This erratic pattern of confidences and withheld information didn't bother me too much. Maria had become a trustworthy ally in my search for the woman in the picture; she had indeed heard about the press conference and even referred to it in passing in her article, and she said she was honor-bound as a feminist to help me with my story. That may have been so. The fact that I was dependent on her must have given her a sense of power, but I felt there was also a wild romantic streak in her that the story appealed to. Although she would never have admitted it, the potential mystery of the photograph probably meant as much to her as its obvious connection to violence against women, and it wasn't difficult to sense her enthusiasm as she went about uncovering that mystery for me, digging around for information in the local network with far greater efficiency than I could have achieved, and bringing me her findings with pleasure even if she was reticent about her sources. For the first time since I had set foot in the region, the picture slowly became part of a whole whose outlines were visible, and the truth as Maria discovered it was both simple and disturbing.

I knew something was up when she called me early one afternoon, sounding very pleased with herself. She said she would come over right away if I was free. The curfew was due to begin around five that evening, earlier than usual because of a large demonstration the previous day, in response to a man being beaten up by the paramilitary. I agreed we should meet as soon as possible; after finding myself locked out of the hotel one evening for an hour or so, I had learned to respect the pattern imposed upon one by the curfew. One could read the level of violence in the town and surrounding areas with unerring accuracy from the hour when the curfew began. Usually it was six, although if it was summer and things were quiet, the government let people stay out till seven. If something happened, though, jeeps with loudspeakers immediately circled the town, asking people to be home by a certain hour. A five o'clock curfew was mildly serious, three was bad, meaning a soldier or civilian or insurgent had been killed, while twelve or one meant that multiple deaths had occurred.

Maria came to the hotel in the pouring rain, dropped off on a motorcycle by one of a posse of local young men who seemed to be at her beck and call. She was clutching an envelope in her left hand and holding out her right palm in a gesture that indicated I would have to pay dearly for the information. We went to my room, and I had coffee sent up for us while she dried her hair in the bathroom before coming back and spreading out the contents of the envelope on the bed. I found it hard to concentrate: the drops of water Maria had missed gleamed on the back of her brown neck, and the atmosphere in the room was thick with her scent. She flung her hair in my direction, and I told myself it wasn't an innocent gesture.

"Shall we concentrate on my finds for a minute?" she asked, and I bent to the objects she had distributed. There were some typed sheets, what looked like a poorly produced brochure, and a set of postcard-sized photographs. "Where's yours? Show me," she said impatiently. I gave her the photograph and she arranged it among her pictures, inserting that unhappy, menacing image into an unremarkable assortment of exterior and interior shots showing a jumble of buildings and vehicles and people inside offices that would have indicated nothing to me had it not been for the sign appearing repeatedly in many of the pictures.

This, finally, was the Prosperity Project. It seemed commonplace to me, projecting that typical mixture of goodwill and smugness that characterizes so much of nonprofit work. As I looked more closely, though, I was struck by the man who dominated almost all of the photographs, the center of gravity for whatever activity was being recorded, a vanishing point toward which the eye was drawn naturally. His build and skin color distinguished him from the local faces, and his was such an expansive and magnetic presence that many of the other people captured in the photographs were glancing at him.

The more I looked at him, the more the random nature of the photographs gave way to something like a carefully constructed narrative. He was showing me around his project: uncovering the project signboard and inaugurating an AIDS clinic, sitting at the wheel of a jeep that had the project name painted on the side, writing with chalk on a blackboard, addressing a crowd of young men from a dais, putting a reassuring hand on the shoulder of a plump man operating what looked like a printing press. It looked impressive when one gave one's attention to the pictures, with the faces of the people so happy and admiring that I wanted for a moment to believe wholeheartedly in what I had heard of Malik and his project.

"What are you thinking of?" Maria said with irritation. "Don't you see her?" She snatched the photographs out of my hand, rearranged them, and pointed at a young woman who appeared in some pictures taken inside an office. It was a somber face, and she often had a notebook and pen in her hand. It was possible to imagine her in that long traditional skirt sitting between two men with guns, but I wasn't sure.

"You think it's her? How do you know?"

"Don't tell me she looks like any other Manipuri woman, Amrit. I'm not prepared to hear that from you."

"Just put it down to a reporter's skepticism, to the need to be certain. It looks like her, but what else do we know?"

"Amrit, what you are looking at are pictures from what has been called the most successful development project in the entire region, an alternative community that was started five or six years ago near the Moirang Lake. It's talked about everywhere in the region, how it has been spectacularly effective in dealing with AIDS patients and drug addicts, how it takes in disturbed young men and women and reintegrates them into the surrounding community and introduces local fishermen to modern techniques. All this has been achieved without money from the government or interference from the insurgents. We have heard much about how well organized the project is, and that there's a lot of money coming in from abroad to support it because it's so successful. The man in the middle is Malik, the director, the creator of the project, and your fairy princess is—well, was—his personal assistant at the Imphal office of the project."

I looked at the assortment of images again, separating out the project pictures from those of the Imphal office. The composition of the people in the second group changed constantly, with a local politician or bureaucrat appearing occasionally, but Malik and the woman were present in most of them. There was a blackboard in one of the pictures, and the people had arranged themselves carefully so that the writing on the board was visible: "Remember those ten famous two-letter words. If It Is To Be, It Is Up To Me."

"Like to know her name?" Maria said.

"That's one step toward verifying that she is indeed the woman in my photograph."

"You sound like one of those pompous bureaucrats in some of the pictures. Of course she is," Maria said impatiently, rolling her eyes. "You know, even when I wrote about the incident, about MORLS and the press conference, I didn't bother to find out who the accused girl really was. I assumed she had the usual victim profile, some college-age girl who had never been anywhere, someone with a deadbeat boyfriend involved in a weird racket and being forced into it gradually. But Leela, she was a smart girl who went to a great college in Delhi on a scholarship, someone who was very much a part of the success that is the Prosperity Project. I've spoken to people who knew her in Imphal, and they say she was much more than an assistant, really more like Malik's right hand."

"How old is she?"

Maria consulted her notes.

"Twenty-four, twenty-five, something like that."

"So what went wrong?" I asked. "Do you think the accusation was true?"

"No, how could it be, when even MORLS denied holding a conference soon after? But she disappeared from Imphal, that much is certain. Look, everyone thinks it was a setup of some sort, that MORLS did it to discredit Malik and the Prosperity Project. No one ever found a porn film; it was only their word for it. Malik was treading on their turf and he has a history of upsetting groups like this. It happened elsewhere in the region during his first project. A couple of his colleagues were taken at gunpoint and pushed off a cliff. See, if he had been corrupt and siphoning off money, they would just take a cut and wouldn't care too much. But a successful project like this erodes their support base among the villagers and exposes them as useless, just thugs running around with rifles."

"How do you know it is a successful project, though? Have you seen it?"

"Come on, look at these pictures. The project office, the AIDS clinic, the rehab center, the greenhouse, the adult literacy classroom, you won't find all these things anywhere else in the region, and let alone functioning properly. It's a miracle, Amrit, what has been achieved at the Prosperity Project."

"But it's the miracle part that bothers me, Maria, because the miracle always seems to have been seen by someone else, never directly. It's like the Great Indian Rope Trick all over again."

"I thought you would be happy about what I found. The pictures aren't enough for you?"

"I suppose they are, and they have given me a lot to go on. But I wish I could speak to someone who has seen the project. Even Malik's wife, who rode in the jeep with me from Dimapur, was going there for the first time. You know, Maria, when I asked you what your husband thought about the big cities you miss occasionally, you told me he was rooted to this region in a way that you and I would never be — to any place. He has a history here, you said, a history of his own people, his own culture, while you and I are just strangers passing through. Maybe you're right. I don't understand why everyone who talks of the Prosperity Project has never been there to see it if it's such a model of how things ought to be done. How far is it from here? Two days' travel? Three?"

Maria had begun to lose her patience with me. I think she was hurt and offended that I was being cynical about what had been an excellent reporting job, and I sensed too late that she wanted some validation from the man who had come from the big-city paper. I wanted to explain to her why I was asking these questions, but she'd turned away and walked to the window. When I joined her, I could see the deserted garden, with water collecting in little pools on the blue plastic that had been draped over the chairs. It was like a calendar picture of a very pretty hotel, but an incomplete picture, waiting for human figures to animate it. Cars hissed by on the street, spraying the occasional pedestrian huddled up against the cold and the rain.

"Amrit, my friend, you still don't understand that the Prosperity Project is a very long way from here. It's in a different state, where Kukis and Meiteis dominate. The Nagas and the Kukis have been fighting battles and burning each other's villages all summer long. The Meiteis in the Imphal Valley are resentful and hostile against the Nagas because they're not getting supplies of essential things, and they are also worried that an independent Naga nation will include a big chunk of Manipur. Two separate dreams threatening to meet at a crossroads, you see. In this kind of atmosphere, people don't travel far unless they are forced to. They stay in their own villages, with their own communities, because every journey is potentially a farewell. So the Prosperity Project is something we're all content to know about. We don't ask for more than that. It's enough just to be aware that somewhere things have changed for the better, so we can hold it close to ourselves like a wonderful dream during our long nights. Somewhere, people are getting cured and not being left to die in the streets. There is a place in the region where the lakes and forests are tended instead of being torn apart by chainsaws and where young men and women like Leela are involved with their lives and not merely with failure and despair. Who wants to look closer and find out that it's not true?"

"I suppose it's not all that important to me, either. All I need to do is find Leela and get back."

"Amrit, there's this incredible Manipuri story I've been meaning to tell you before you leave for Imphal. Just listen, and do your convoluted thinking later. I've never met a *sardar* like you, turning the simplest of things into complicated puzzles no one can ever figure out."

"The story," I said tersely, sounding like the driver of the jeep who had brought me to Kohima.

. . .

"A LONG TIME AGO, when the world was a far better place than it is now, there was a divine couple, a god and a goddess deeply in love with each other. Their love was so perfect that a quarrel broke out between the two about who loved the other more. Even the court of the gods couldn't settle the dispute, so the two agreed to put their love to the test by being born in human form. The challenge was to see who would recognize the other first. They would have no knowledge of their heavenly past, being in possession of nothing more than average human memories of their human lives.

"They are born in different corners of the kingdom of Manipur, she as a princess, he as a commoner. The years of their childhood pass in ignorance of each other, without a single encounter. Then the commoner comes to the court from the village one day, and they meet accidentally in the palace, and they recognize each other in the same instant. Their love is still without imperfection, still equal, but just then a battle breaks out between factions in the court and both are killed in the fighting. The dispute is unresolved.

"So they take birth as human beings again, and again, and again, and each time the same thing happens. They meet as adults, recognize each other instantaneously, the kingdom is pitched into a war, and they die in the ensuing battle. People in Manipur believe that when things are very bad in our human world, when it is a time of war, it means that the two are around in human form, slowly drifting toward each other. Each is looking for the other without really knowing it, attracted toward the partner by the force of their divine love, and the terrible battle of our times will coincide with their mutual discovery."

"Like the present time."

"Yes," Maria said. "But there's more. This is the part I treasure the most. Their coming together in the human world with death following immediately is a sign of the perfection of their love and how it can't be contained within the imperfection of our world. But there will be a time when they meet and admit that it is a draw, that they love each other equally, and that there is no more or less for either of them. They will see, they will recognize their love for each other, and they will not die. When that happens and their contest is over, our world will end in the final apocalypse."

We sat for a little while without speaking, the street outside emptied of pedestrians, the last cars speeding to beat the curfew or traveling on official business with escorts and flashing red lights.

"The curfew begins soon."

"So?" Maria said.

"Well, if we were divine beings, we would take that as a premonition. But we're only human, so it doesn't matter."

I felt happy and light for a moment, and even in the heat of the moment I knew that I would remember the sound of the papers and pictures falling to the floor as we brushed them away impatiently from the bed, unconcerned for the moment with the story they had to tell.

❧ 3 ❧

That I should have learned so much about the photograph the very same evening I made love to Maria did not surprise me. It was part of the pattern I had seen develop through my journey, this simultaneous explosion of separate events that illuminated—and occasionally obscured—each other. I knew it would take me a long time to fully comprehend why things had turned out this way in Kohima and nowhere else, and why it had left a cast of memories very different in quality to those of other places on my route, but for that moment I accepted my relationship to the photograph had changed.

I had changed as well; the new identity card, the surprisingly spontaneous intimacy with Maria, the fresh way of looking at the photograph was part of this transformation. I found myself able to think more clearly, relaxing enough to get my hair cut and beard trimmed, joking with the smart Naga salesman at a shoe store as he helped me pick out a new pair.

When I examined the photograph now, I did so with the knowledge that I had a name at last, along with some hints of personality with which to animate the two-dimensional figure I had stared at for so long. But it wasn't information alone that ruptured the web I'd been spinning around the photograph. There was also an awareness of my own predilections, things that made me think of Leela and the whole episode in a particular way.

Perhaps I had been relieved, without ever admitting it, when the captain at the refinery guesthouse suggested that it was a put-up job. So much the simpler for me when it was framed in that manner, with the entire event being constructed out of a cat-and-mouse game between insurgents and intelligence agencies. It meant that I didn't have to scrounge around for a porn tape or figure out the clandestine history of sordid films made in little hideouts with the help of blackmail and threats or promises of film roles. The captain's version had made it easy for me to remain a distant observer of the tale, without having to step into the world of exploited young women whom I would never understand fully, no matter how hard I tried.

The fact was I didn't understand women, and I had given up on any efforts to do so at a certain point in my life. It had been a relief to me when I left behind my stilted attempts at relationships and took my pleasures from the occasional sexual encounter. There was nothing in my past and its shallow liaisons that could illuminate Leela for me. It is said that you never forget the women you have loved, but I could stare at a former girlfriend in a restaurant and only feel a vague sense of familiarity, not realizing until she avoided my glance or spoke to me that she was someone with whom I shared a past. All that remained from these things was a residue of physical desire and a yearning brought to life at unexpected moments, as when I passed a strange couple on the street and saw the woman touching her partner to adjust his hair or his clothes.

I didn't see myself as a predator for my lack of emotions, but I knew it had closed off an entire realm of experience for me; I had thought it made me unsuitable to explore the nuances of the story behind the woman in the photograph. Could I ever feel anything other than contempt, lust, or pity for a porn actress? Could she react to me with anything but fear?

If I felt differently now, that had much to do with Maria and my relationship to her. It seemed complete in itself; it had no past or future because we both knew our intimacy would end the moment I continued for Imphal, but it didn't feel shallow or purely instrumental in spite of that. Maria worried about my going to Manipur, even though she didn't express this very often. She opened up in other ways as well, and it became clear to me that she really loved her husband. The fact that I had slept with her made it possible for her to talk about him in a way she had found difficult before, and she filled out his story gradually.

The son of a well-known family of tribal chieftains who had distinguished themselves in wars with the British, he was not particularly militant himself; a childhood limp meant he'd been unable to participate in raids during his tenure underground, and had instead worked for the publicity and administrative cells of the insurgents. His mother found his physical weakness distasteful, and thought his quitting the insurgency movement and marrying a woman from a different part of the country were further instances of his unmanliness. He was trying to prove himself, Maria said, preparing for his return so that he could take up the cause of his people again. Her role was to wait and to move aside if she became a liability. She was good at waiting, she said.

I was good at waiting too. I began writing up what I had discovered so far, occasionally calling people in Imphal for some of the background on the Prosperity Project and MORLS. For the first time since I had set out from Calcutta, I soaked myself in the soothing rhythm of the typewriter, watching the outline of a story emerge, feeling Leela herself appear from the shadows in a way that was both reassuring and disturbing. Now when I looked at the picture of her sitting between the masked men, I compared it to other pictures of her. I scrutinized her face and her eyes and her body, examining her slim ankles and small breasts, wondering how long it had taken Malik before he had put his hands on her.

Although I did not want to write it in my draft, I knew for certain that Malik had been her lover. Had she worn a different expression for him, I wondered, one less serious, more open and welcoming? Had Malik found some kind of freedom in her, in playing the time-worn role of a man far from his wife taking on a local lover? Did his sad, neurotic wife, anxious to reach Imphal, yet nervous of the strange region in which she found herself, know about Leela? The heart of the story was nothing like the tale the captain had spun at the guesthouse, with intelligence agents and insurgents, but just a familiar old triangle, a Bollywood family drama set in a somewhat unfamiliar region—in which case my sympathies were with Leela. She was recuperating somewhere from gunshot wounds and would still be in hiding when Malik and his wife were reunited. It wouldn't be difficult for them; they could return to Delhi together if things became too messy around the Prosperity Project, but what would Leela do with the rest of her life?

Maria had been unable to trace Leela's family. There had been some suggestions from people in Imphal that her parents were devout Krishna worshippers who'd retired many years ago to a religious commune in Mathura, and that Leela herself had been whisked away by people at the Prosperity Project following the press conference. I wasn't too troubled by this, because it seemed that I still had a story that could be filled out by local voices. Once I reached Imphal, I would pick up her traces, at least enough of them to bring the story to a resolution, even if she had gone into hiding somewhere in the vast wilderness of the border.

On the one hand this new way of thinking about Leela and her complication with Malik bothered me, as if I was being too quick to put her into a ready-made slot, but I also welcomed the reality she had taken on for me. She was no longer an ambiguous face with an unclear story, but someone of flesh and blood, an attractive young woman who had become involved with a man with unclear intentions and motivations. The German magazine had wanted an exemplary story, and what could be more exemplary than this story of a small-town girl with big ambitions trapped by the turbulence of local politics and a bad decision in her choice of partner?

But the Prosperity Project still bothered me, especially because it seemed so closely intertwined with Leela's story. They didn't have phones at the project site, and no one answered whenever I rang the office in Imphal; Maria's network and that of the *Nagaland Post* could uncover details from the period leading up to the press conference, but little information about the present. There was a great state of unrest in the Manipur Valley, very different from the uneasy calm and shifting curfews that had become characteristic of Kohima. The clashes between Kukis and Nagas continued in a sporadic manner in the valley, but I was impatient to move on, eager to bring the assignment to a conclusion.

ALMOST WITHOUT DISCUSSING IT, Maria and I decided not to meet on the last couple of days I spent in Kohima. We talked briefly, guardedly, on the phone, trying to keep our voices as normal as possible. On Sunday afternoon I went for a long walk in the town, stopping at the graveyard to read the names of soldiers on the tombstones. A memorial in the graveyard pronounced the great sacrifice made half a century ago in jingling doggerel, but I didn't hang around for too long. The dark, overcast sky made the church tower seem gloomy and foreboding, and it felt too much like I was being admonished for intruding on the Sunday services.

At the hotel for dinner, I didn't object when a new guest

asked if he could join me. His name was Ganesan, and he introduced himself as a geology professor at the regional university, the many stones decorating his heavily ringed fingers a small geology lesson in themselves. Professor Ganesan was a southerner, but he wore a shiny black *salwar kameez* more common in the north. Since he was also bald and had gold-rimmed glasses, he positively gleamed in that quiet little dining room, functioning as a source of light that outshone the dull yellow glow of the overhead lamps.

As soon as dinner was finished, Professor Ganesan asked me if I would do him the favor of allowing him to study the lines on my palm. There was something childlike in this request made by such a large, middle-aged man, so I held out my hand. The professor adjusted his glasses, pushed his eyebrows together, and bent low. His look of benign, abstract concentration did not once change as he traced the lines on my palm, and he surprised me when he said, "A childhood without parents for the most part, but not without love." I thought of my aunt Harpreet when he said this, of her carrying out her role as a guardian while my dapper father went around the world as a merchant navy sailor, sending occasional postcards and parcels from ports with glamorous names.

They were very similar in nature, brother and sister, outspoken and independent, but my aunt had put herself to a lot of trouble for my sake. My father had had no such compulsions; when his marriage broke up and my mother said she didn't want custody, he deposited me in my aunt's care and took off for Singapore. Until the disaster in the Bay of Biscay, when I was around ten, he dropped in for only occasional visits, taking us to expensive restaurants where all the women would stop eating momentarily as this tall, strikingly handsome man entered, accompanied by a fat woman and a small, silent boy.

My mother, meanwhile, had remarried soon after her divorce, and it was not until I was fourteen or fifteen that I learned I had seen her almost every day; she was the carefully made-up woman who read the English news on Doordarshan three or four days a week. My aunt sighed as she told me this, shifting her heavy frame on the sofa.

No, I owed nothing to my parents—but I never heard a word of reproach from my aunt about either of them. She put up with me till I was twelve, remaining loyal and supportive even when she decided I would be better off in a boarding school. It was well after I had finished both school and college, after I had spent a number of years drifting around in Delhi, that she decided she no longer needed to stay on in Calcutta for my sake. I had come back to the city to work for the *Sentinel* by this time, and she handed me the keys and the papers to her flat, triumphantly exhibiting a big Air India envelope in her other hand.

She was taking off to indulge her two deferred loves, travel and cricket. She had saved enough money to go around the world, and she was going to do just that, following the Indian cricket team in their tours abroad from the West Indies to Sharjah. (Even now, when I catch a game on television, I find myself unconsciously scanning the crowd for her face, wondering if she likes Durban or Perth, and if she is abusing the daylights out of the Indian batsmen when they play and miss outside the off stump or look uncomfortable against short-pitched deliveries.) She was worth more to me than my parents put together.

Professor Ganesan released my hand and looked up at me. "I have such respect for you, sir. I was not misled by my instincts in asking to see your lines. What a hand, what a hand, with character from beginning to end. An unusual childhood, a troubled youth, and an adventurous life moving from place to place, with a disaster narrowly averted just very recently. The gods smile upon you, sir. I see great ambition, not fulfilled so far, but Jupiter will not be kept squeezed on the periphery for long. A minor recommendation, however."

"If I believed in palmistry," I said, sounding harsher than I intended to.

Professor Ganesan was not put off in the slightest.

"But of course, as I said, there is character everywhere. You are not the one to rush for a stone to improve your fortune."

"Maybe there is less of my character in this hand than you think, Professor Ganesan."

"There is one stone that might prevent a future mishap, and it is nothing expensive. Any small jeweler can provide it. It is known as the cat's eye and is recommended for those whose dominant planets happen to fall in the third quadrant. The planet Saturn has a baleful influence at certain times, and the stone would deflect a significant blow, I feel."

I smiled and rose from the table, and Professor Ganesan rose with me, looking rather Saturnine in his dark clothes and his gold-framed glasses, the rings on his fingers like satellites in orbit around him. He had not told me what he was doing in a Kohima hotel dressed in a *salwar kameez*, but I was too absorbed with my memories to think too much about that. I did not feel in the least surprised that an amateur palmist should have been accurate in some of his guesses. It was the nature of the place, not the science of palmistry, that had once again brought up the question of who I was and who I had been and what I would become. After all, Sema had given me a new identity card in Kohima. Perhaps prolonged self-scrutiny was the price one paid for the freedom of a new identity.

CHAPTER EIGHT

❖ 1 ❖

was writing up my notes when I came across a sheet of paper Robiul had included in his envelope. It was a breakdown of the insurgent groups operating along Highway 39, a
list with a strong resemblance to a Bradshaw's railway
timetable and equally incomprehensible. He had made a note
of towns along the highway and the key insurgent groups in
each area, and it looked as if the insurgents were running a
complicated relay race.

Ref. Town: ULFA
Gght: Karbis
Dmp: NSCN (I-M)
Koh: NSCN (I-M)
Mao: NSCN (I-M)
Kargh: NSCN (I-M)
Kkpi: KNF, PLA, UNLF, MORLS, etc.
Pal: NSCN (K)
Tnp: KDF, MORLS

Mor: KNA
Pal-Mor: 1 Army, Assam Rifles, BSF, Customs,
Manipur Rifles, Manipur Police, Manipur Excise

For the final stage of the highway from Palel to Moreh, Robiul had also helpfully included the government security forces I might run into. When I looked at the number of entries, it was really a wonder that all I had encountered so far were floods, fleeing villagers, and solitary strangers with a desperate edge to their stories.

His list in front of me, my thoughts turned to Robiul and why he hadn't called after telling Sema he would be in touch. I'd have liked to share the progress of my story with him, but his phone still rang on without an answer whenever I called. I lay back on the bed thinking of the people who had helped me with the story so far, their faces floating in and out along with snippets of conversation, and I felt as if they too had been running a relay race of sorts, passing me along like a baton that might explode at any moment.

My thoughts were interrupted by the receptionist. "Minister Vimedo to see you, sir," he said. I wasn't expecting any Minister Vimedo, but went down anyway. The receptionist stood nervously behind his desk, watching a stocky man in a charcoal gray suit as he paced to and fro through the lobby, his path a straight, unwavering line that led from the entrance to the elevator and back again. I had taken the stairs, and my arrival went unnoticed until the receptionist coughed and gestured at me with his head.

The minister focused on me as I approached, apparently pushing away the thoughts troubling him, squaring his wrestler's shoulders and extending a firm grip. He was well over sixty, this old lion, his manner direct as he told me we should go to the empty restaurant because he had something important to tell me. I learned later that he had ceased to be a minister a few years ago, when he was deposed in the state elections by a much younger rival whose long hair and rock-star looks had found greater favor with the constituency. But having served in three Congress ministries and two coalition governments, he remained Minister Vimedo to everybody, a permanent if weathered feature in the landscape of local politics.

The two waiters clearing up hurried to set a table for us as we entered, but Minister Vimedo waved them away in an imperious gesture. Sitting down, he took out a blue notebook, placed it on the table, extracted a fountain pen from his breast pocket, and put that on the notebook. When it looked as if he was ready to interview me instead of the other way around, he said, "So. Prosperity Project. MORLS." He opened his notebook to the middle and leaned forward.

"Questions a good reporter must ask. What is the date of inception of the project? 1989. What is the date when the small insurgent group PKK was reconstituted as MORLS? 1989. Are there links apart from this temporal coincidence? Quite a few. What is MORLS? Movement Organized to Resuscitate the Liberation Struggle. An insurgent group that intends not only to fight the Indian army and paramilitary for the seccessionist cause, but also to control the deviation of older insurgent groups from the liberation struggle. Their words, not mine. In other words, a meta-insurgent group that will, if necessary, practice insurgency tactics against other groups. A wheel within a wheel, a cog that controls other cogs.

"Instance one. May 1990. An order banning women from wearing Western or Indian clothes. Only strictly traditional attire to be allowed. This in a state where women have had significant power, where an entire market is run by a women's cooperative. Negotiations were organized with MORLS leadership to get them to retract order, with the Director of the Prosperity Project as a successful go-between. Why did they listen to the Director?

"Instance two. Location of Prosperity Project. Originally sited in Loktak but moved to Moirang Lake region, falling under area controlled by MORLS. Why did MORLS allow this project to be set up in their area? A guerrilla must swim among his people like a fish in water, according to Mao Tse-tung. Why was MORLS not worried about the possible erosion of their support among the local people with the inception of the Prosperity Project?

"Instance three. Constitution of committee to conduct recent peace negotiations in Nagaland and Manipur. Members include self as well as Director of Prosperity Project, who is a representative of civil society. Preliminary negotiations accepted by all groups except MORLS, with Prosperity Director conveying message from MORLS requesting more time to consider negotiation offer. Why does MORLS only communicate through Director?

"Instance four. Press conference by MORLS accusing Director's assistant of immorality. Certain members of negotiation committee, led by self, recommend immediate military action against recalcitrant MORLS group, but Director objects in favor of gaining trust. Offers own intervention with MORLS leadership at aforesaid press conference as successful example. Please follow carefully. I quote from minutes of meeting."

Minister Vimedo looked at his notes and began reading.

I recommend restraint to the respected committee members because I believe MORLS is close to accepting becoming a party to the peace talks. Even though they appear adamant, there is a way for me to make them see the other point of view, to convince them that it is in their best interests to participate in the negotiations. I have proved myself before, as my fellow members of the committee are aware.

At the press conference held by them where they accused my assistant of taking part in an immoral film, they stated their intention of carrying out harsh punitive measures. My own position was hardly secure at the conference, where all of us, journalists included, had been taken under great secrecy and armed guard. The MORLS leadership present were taking few questions; they were under pressure because of the peace negotiations other groups were participating in. They made it clear that they feared no one, least of all the deviationist groups talking peace with the double-dealing Indian government. The valley was corrupted in every way, they said, and they brought Leela out to offer her as an example of the corruption.

She was blindfolded, so she couldn't see me or the journalists, and she had her hands tied behind her back. I wished there were some way to let Leela know that I was there with her, but, with the reaction of the MORLS leaders in mind, I chose an impassive air instead, as if I were no more than a detached observer of the proceedings. Two of the ultras led her to us, and they removed her blindfold only when they took her to the next room and asked the journalists to come in one by one to take pictures. After the picture session, they would execute her. "Her life is worth nothing, but her death will show the people and the deviationists the rightful way," one of the MORLS leaders said. The journalists around me looked upset and scared; they had not come to participate in the killing of an innocent victim, but no one dared say anything. I spoke up, and I tried not to appear threatening or morally superior in any way. "Will the respected leadership of the movement—?" I began to say, and one of the insurgents raised his gun. The three leaders who were sitting at the central table gestured at him to stop, and one of them said, "We have always looked upon the gentleman present as a friend, even though he does not belong to the valley or subscribe to the principles of the movement. Now we do not feel so sure. The serpent has been found lapping the milk of corruption in the very heart of the Director's project, and we feel rightful anger at the gentleman. Still, he will speak, because the movement has principles of innocence and guilt. Unlike the government, we do not institute kangaroo courts and introduce special laws for military rule, we do not participate in a massacre of the innocents. We are led by the age-old wisdom of the people of our land, and we will allow even the enemy to speak."

I thanked them, and I tried to keep my voice clear and respectful. I knew it was important not to antagonize them or appear threatening in any way. "Will the honored leadership of the Movement Organized to Resuscitate the Liberation Struggle consider that the woman is herself but a victim? Her immorality, which I do not challenge, since the evidence has been laid so succinctly before all present by the leadership, is unquestionable, as is her punishment. What all of us assembled would respectfully request the leadership to consider is if execution is too great a punishment for someone who is, after all, one of the people. She is a daughter led astray, a sister gone wrong, and surely the justice of execution should be reserved for those who corrupted her. We will say no more, having great faith in the wisdom of the leadership."

Everyone was silent. The leaders did not say a word in response, but withdrew to another room to confer. When they came back, we wondered if they would shoot all of us in their anger and confusion. "The wisdom of the movement prevails," one of them said, and my heart sank. "We have considered. She is indeed our sister, our daughter, and a victim to the forces of corruption. We will not execute. However, we will mark her. The harlot will be shot in the legs twice, so that she may never participate again in immoral pleasure without remembering the wrath of the movement. We punish, and we also protect." A cripple, I thought. Alive, but still a cripple. The man spoke again, looking at me from behind his mask. "As a special favor to one we thought had been our friend, the injuries inflicted will not be serious. They will consist of surface flesh wounds. The harlot will have the chance to walk again so that she may find the straight and narrow path she has strayed from." They had, in essence, done everything I wanted, but the decision had appeared to be their own.

Respected fellow members of the committee, that is how we must proceed, with restraint and with cunning, if we are to bring MORLS to this table and usher peace into the region. I have complete faith in your good judgment, and I believe that you will agree with me that now is not the time for military action against MORLS.

Minister Vimedo finished reading and looked at me. "You are impressed?" he asked, knitting his eyebrows together. "Even though you have not met him yet, does this not give you some idea of the Director's presence and his persuasive abilities? Do you not find yourself admiring him for his deft handling of the situation involving the girl, his courage in speaking up?"

The minister waited for a response from me. I remained silent.

"Do you know what the devil is, Mr. Singh? Do you know that Satan is not a creature with horns and cloven feet but a seducer with a silky voice? This man is an impostor, a charlatan among us, playing us all along for his own purposes."

Minister Vimedo was shouting now, and the waiters in the room scurried around anxiously, avoiding looking at the minister directly and yet propelled along by his anger.

"You see how proud he feels at snatching victory from the jaws of defeat? That confidence is misplaced, Mr. Singh, I tell you, if it is confidence and not some ulterior motive. MORLS will not agree to sit at the table for talks. Therefore, the valley remains the problem even while the hills have quietened down.

The insurgents here are coming and beginning to listen to us, even though they have been fighting for a long time. Do not forget that a Naga nation was demanded on August 14, 1947, one day before your Indian republic even existed. Still, they will talk, because they have some commitment to the cause and the suffering they see in the people.

"I am not a sentimental old fool." He looked at his hands. "Almost nine years ago to the day, I was traveling from Dimapur to Kohima. I needed to work on some papers, so I sat in the escort jeep while my wife and sons remained in the official car behind us. The convoy was ambushed outside Kohima by the Naga rebels, but they held their fire and let the lead jeep pass. They were not interested in the bodyguards in front. They wanted me, so they waited until the official Ambassador car and the rest of the convoy was visible before they opened fire. My wife and one son died instantly, the other was in a hospital for three days before he went to the Lord. I did not have a scratch on me.

"His ways are mysterious. Still, I will sit and talk to the people who killed my entire family, just as they will listen to me. But this MORLS and their middleman, the Director, that is an entirely different matter. We will not have peace if they are allowed to go their way. Sooner or later, all groups involved in discussions with us will tire of our special dispensation toward one tiny group with no great record of military action, and they will change their minds and pick up the gun again.

"We cannot let that happen. I do not back away from fights, Mr Singh. College wrestling championship, service with Indian Air Force in '62 and '71. Five assassination attempts. The ambush on the convoy was only one of many. But the chance for peace has never been better, and our window of opportunity is very small."

His voice died away suddenly, and there was a note of doubt and frailty I had not heard in him before.

"Unless his motives are not merely his own, but part of something larger that I don't understand, some strategy I have no awareness of . . ." He trailed off once more, rapping his hand feverishly on the table. "But I cannot believe that," he said. "How can I believe that and still go on? Mr. Singh, if you find links between MORLS and the Director, if you find any reason to believe that he has a vested interest in prolonging the peace negotiations and keeping MORLS out of it, you must let me know." He gave me his card. "Call me regardless of whether it is day or night. Send me word. I will be waiting to hear from you, Mr. Singh."

* 2 *

The early morning wind blowing into the bus was cold enough to sting, and most of the passengers had fallen asleep within an hour of leaving Kohima. The streets had been empty when we left the town—the graveyards, the church tower, and the old villages looking very much like the dioramas of local life displayed at the state museum—and even the soldiers at the checkpoints seemed sleepy as they lifted their barriers to let us pass.

The highway was maintained by the Border Roads Task Force all the way up to Maren, and it seemed in good shape. We were still in the mountains, and the road wound its way along cliffs that rose sharply on one side of us, while on the other the land fell steeply away into a river swollen with rain. As the hours passed, the going became more uncertain, with precarious wooden bridges suspended over the gorges. Twice the bus halted before a bridge, and all passengers except women and the elderly were asked to cross by foot, while the emptied bus advanced inch by inch along the creaking wooden planks worn away by a season of use and inclement weather. Traffic was light, with few signs of human inhabitation except for occasional hamlets and watchtowers that rose over the highway—where soldiers, looking like disgraced figures exiled by the local community, manned machine guns.

We stopped for lunch at one of these small villages, coming to a halt near some open bamboo sheds and a cluster of flies and stray dogs. Children with bloated bellies watched us with curiosity, while wrinkled old men nodded at us over their bamboo pipes as if to say they had seen many travelers like us during their long lifetimes. The heat from the lowlands was beginning to make itself felt now, and when we set off again, the driver's assistant kept the door open and sat dozing on the steps with an enviable ease while the bus curled and bumped its way along the highway.

I had been traveling for half a day now, and felt a mixture of elation and sadness as the sun began its downward arc and a slivered moon appeared in the sky. I thought of Maria and Minister Vimedo and the various things they were waiting for, but I was possessed by a certainty that my own wait was almost over. This bus would let me off in Imphal, and difficult though the situation there might be, I had enough material about Leela to piece things together. Minister Vimedo had added to my unease about the Prosperity Project and Malik, but that seemed like another story altogether. There would be enough for me to create a coherent narrative, and the anticipation of an end to this long journey led me to think of what lay beyond. I had enough money for a plane ticket back to Calcutta, and Sema had suggested that I go from Imphal to Silchar by Highway 53 if direct flights were still suspended; he had heard there was a plane that flew between Silchar and Calcutta twice a week, and I would be able to avoid retracing my overland route if I took it.

I had no idea what lay in wait for me in Calcutta, but perhaps the Germans would like my story enough to toss another bone my way. The flat I didn't have to worry about, but I didn't know if the *Sentinel* would play my suspension order by the rule book and give me half pay while a committee deliberated over the charges against me. These thoughts made me impatient, and the trees and cliffs and streams and watchtowers outside suddenly appeared motionless, the miles to Imphal undiminished as the bus rattled on, still stopping frequently in front of rickety bridges. Our progress became ever slower, and we began to run into mobile army patrols. The first one to direct us to pull over appeared soon after we had crossed a particularly weak bridge; we'd just boarded the bus when the patrol emerged from the trees, and the driver's assistant conveyed the soldiers' instructions to the passengers.

Most knew the routine already: the men climbed off the bus again, leaving their bags behind, their hands empty and faces blank. While the soldiers waited, they formed a loose line, not looking at me as I joined them, still holding my bag. Some of the soldiers carried out a search on the bus itself, poking underneath the seats and pulling cases out from the overhead rack; I hoped they would be gentle with my Hermes in its case. In the meantime, another soldier was patting down the line of male passengers. He approached me slowly, a small compact man from the Garhwal Regiment, and I was taken aback when he started shouting at me. Some of his companions had been covering us from a distance with their guns, and they stiffened immediately, their attention drawn to me while the soldier slapped my hand away from my bag and grabbed it from me.

I felt slightly bewildered as I looked at him, the suspension order from *Sentinel* coming to my mind at that very moment. By now he had backed away a few feet, and was cursing me as he rifled through my possessions. I watched as he withdrew Robiul's envelope and shook its contents over the road, the photograph and the papers scattering on the tarmac.

A couple of the other soldiers laughed, and it was too much for me. He was at least a foot shorter than me, and as he stepped toward me and reached out, I struck his hand away, shouting out, "Where's your officer, soldier?" I was aware that I'd used the you reserved for a subordinate. The soldier looked as if he was about to hit me, but then hesitated, and the moment was lost for him. "Didn't you hear me? Where's your officer?" I snapped, and the inflections of my Hindi combined with the sharpness of my tone pulled him up short. He regarded me cautiously now, ignoring the clothes, the wild beard, the fact that I was traveling on a common state bus, and then gestured with his head at some post in the hills. "He's up there, sir. But not there now."

His companions had taken over searching my fellow passengers and were carefully avoiding the two of us, unsure if there would be trouble from their officers and wanting no part of the blame.

"Have you finished with my bag?"

"Yes sir," he said, picking up the papers and the photograph and replacing them inside the bag. "Routine procedure, sir," he said, in a tone that was partly an apology and partly an explanation, handing everything back. About to ask his officer's name and rank in the same peremptory tone I had used thus far, the anger and frustration faded abruptly, leaving behind a weariness at the pointlessness of the entire exchange: his was a farmer's face no different from that of the small, friendly men I had met so often in the hills of northern Uttar Pradesh. "Major Bhatnagar, sir, commanding officer," he offered without my prompting, and I nodded curtly and turned away from him.

The local passengers avoided me as I boarded, and I felt like a disembodied observer as I returned to my seat. I looked at my nondescript clothes and the old, battered bag I was carrying, and marveled at how these things had been overridden by my features and the Hindi I spoke, which must have reminded the soldiers of countless commanding officers (some who could have been distant cousins of mine, for all I knew) who looked and spoke the same way.

When the next round of searches took place, I complied with a detached air, not reacting to anything at all—not even when they took a young man aside and made him pull down his pants, laughing as fear and the cold air caused his skin to break out in gooseflesh.

There was evidence of recent landslides as we drove on, with great muddy patches on the hillsides denuded of trees, and mounds of rocks, branches, and dirt next to the highway. Around four, the bus pulled over for a tea break at a spot where a single shack overlooked a steep gorge, the waters below red with mud that had swept down from the hills. Other buses and cars were parked at the place, and the shack was crowded. It was dark inside, but in the light of the Petromax lamp hanging from the ceiling, I could make out a sign that said "Permit 429, Canteen for BRTF construction gang." It was a rudimentary provisions store with hardware goods piled at the back, and the storekeeper and his helpers were struggling to cope with the sudden demands for food and tea from the throng near the counter. There were two boys tossing packets of biscuits to the storekeeper from the shelves at the back, while a third grimy boy made tea on a pump stove placed on the floor.

Roadside halts like this were often busy, especially when sunset was no more than an hour away, but the passengers gathered here didn't look as if they were in a hurry to hit the road right away. They all wanted food, but the storekeeper only had a selection of Britannia, Krackjack, and Cream Cracker biscuits in stock, and a fight broke out when those at the back thought the supplies might run out. Elbowing my way in, ignoring the dirty looks and protests from the other passengers, I reached the counter, grabbed a glass of tea, and emerged as quickly as I could from the claustrophobic store.

"Why the sudden panic?" I asked the driver's assistant. He grinned and pointed ahead. "Fresh landslide. Two hours to clear. Maybe." When I looked at him skeptically, he told me not to worry. With so much traffic stuck here, we would have to travel in a convoy and the army would provide an escort. "What if they can't clear it tonight?" I asked. "Then everybody sleeps in the bus. Safe. Army posts sentries. Get some biscuits for dinner."

There was a flat, open piece of ground away from the road, looking down at the river, and I sat there with my tea. Up ahead to my right was a metal bridge, new, shiny, and quite unlike the wooden bridges we had traversed so far. A smell of diesel and tar permeated the air, and the sun was sinking rapidly behind the hills on the other side of the river, turning the water bloodred. I was cold, but didn't want to get up to find a pullover among my things in the bus, and so I stayed on, holding on to the tepid glass of tea for warmth. The river was flowing in the opposite direction to the route I was taking, and I felt the certainties I'd gathered in Kohima gradually seep out of my head. The water shimmering below was visible but beyond reach, seemingly without form or substance — much like the image that had driven me forward for the last few weeks. What satisfaction was there in knowing the woman was not really a porn-film actress, or that she had suffered surface wounds rather than been crippled? And what did it mean that nothing of this existed for those who lived beyond this circle of fear, as no doubt it would cease to exist for me upon my return to Calcutta?

Slowly, the darkness of the sky dripped down the hills and trees toward the river. I thought I had gone blind, but then my eyes fixed on some lights near the bridge, and I found my orientation and became myself again, a man squatting on his haunches on a flat piece of ground with a river below me and a shack and vehicles parked behind.

◆ 3 ◆

I slept fitfully through the early part of the night, feeling cramped and cold. The man next to me disappeared sometime in the middle of the night and did not return, so I stretched out gratefully, turning sideways and dangling my legs over the edge of his seat. The windows had been pulled shut because of the cold, and the heavy breathing and snores of the passengers made me think of the bus as some kind of aged, overworked beast. Except for a narrow passageway through the middle, the highway was completely blocked by the vehicles parked around the shack, and without raising my head, I could hear those few restless souls who had been unable to sleep pacing around outside in the dark.

Around two I climbed out to take a piss, stumbling over the legs and arms that had spilled onto the aisle. The shack was still open, but the owner had run out of milk for tea long ago and was now selling glasses of army-issue alcohol at exorbitant prices. Some of the men drinking his liquor had lit a fire on the flat stone I'd been sitting on earlier, and I bought a glass of rum and went to join them. There were a couple of soldiers present, off duty from guarding the workers clearing the landslide, and they said we would be able to move on by seven or eight in the morning.

The tight circle around the fire shifted to make room for me without a word of complaint, and it felt good to be sitting there rather than trying to sleep on the bus. One of the soldiers cleared his throat. The others looked expectantly at him—I had clearly interrupted something—and he peered at the group as if he wanted to see all of us clearly before beginning.

"Rajinder was the one who really got buggered during that hellish spell we had on the border, though Mani came pretty close as well. It began badly, as these things always do, with Rajinder suspended by the new commanding officer for being late reporting for duty. Things had been difficult for him at home, but he was an honest fellow, a bit simple really, and he wasn't to blame for showing up a day late. He was coming back home from his village in Haryana, making his way across the country on the slow Brahmaputra Mail. A day here or there when you are traveling such long distances means nothing; any other officer wouldn't have given it a second thought, but the new man was merciless.

"Okay, we're soldiers, not too smart or given to thinking, and we know that when things are bad, you have to take it. That's what we did, accepted the new officer's command, thinking if he's hard with us, he's no easier on himself. It's winter season, with everything dry and cold, lots of stuff coming across the border because this is a good time of the year to move things. Under our new CO, we are doing patrols almost every night, setting up ambushes, hoping to make more seizures.

"But nothing happens. We're spending entire nights out in the cold, hiding in the bushes, our bladders full, coming back empty-handed while the other units laugh at us. Something is wrong, we can all feel it in our bones, even though we're mostly just matric pass and it's not our business to figure out where to wait for the consignments. That is the CO's responsibility, since he's the one who gets the reports, but as the days go by we have begun to think we're lucky this border isn't mined, or sure enough our CO would march us straight to a mined area.

"This is when Mani gets involved. Mani is different from the rest of us. He can read fluently, to begin with, and he can think. I envied him for this, but then he was from Kerala, where they're all well-read and Marxists. Mani starts keeping his ears to the ground, and when one day he hears something about a consignment coming through, he passes the information on to the CO. The CO doesn't like that at all. Mani's showing initiative, you could say, but a common soldier isn't supposed to have initiative, not when it makes his officer look bad. Moreover, the CO is aware that Mani is smart and knows the rule book like the back of his hand, so it's not easy to give Mani the kind of punishment he can hand out to others. He quietly agrees to set up an ambush at the point Mani is talking about, we wait, nothing happens, and then the CO says some choice things about Mani and his information.

"Then, Rajinder gets more bad news. We thought he had just swallowed his punishment, which he did, but he also wrote home and blamed his wife for asking him to stay an extra couple of days and not leaving him with enough time to get back. The letter that he received from home said his wife was so ashamed that she poured kerosene on herself and set herself on fire."

"Set herself on fire for a suspension order? Why would anyone do a thing like that?"

"Who knows? Which one of us understands women? And who knows why some of us are more affected by shame and honor than others?

"But Rajinder is devastated by his wife's death, blaming himself, blaming the officer, blaming his wife, too stubborn to ask for leave even though we tell him he's not doing much good staying with the unit. Frankly, none of us is doing any good. We've made no arrests, and the CO's temper is getting worse each day. We've heard rumors that he's due for a transfer but it's not going to come through without one really good seizure on his part.

"We're all praying for the general misery to end when the

CO gives us a serious talk one night, just before we're going out. We'll be successful, he says, because he has *pukka* information this time, and all we have to do is follow his instructions carefully before firing. For the first time in weeks, some of us are hopeful, not just that we're going to achieve something, but that the officer will have his transfer if we are successful.

"It's a cold night, but the visibility is good because of the moon and you can look right across the Burma border to the rice fields and the hills there, even see the nice metaled road the Chinese built for them. We wait, and the night gets cold and our bodies become stiff, and I can't relax too much because I've been assigned to be the officer's personal security man. But my mind wanders a little, and I remember the number of times I've sat like this on some border or the other, especially the one occasion in Kashmir when I was guarding an intelligence agent waiting for his informer to come across from Pakistan. I had to wait some distance away because the agent didn't want me to be visible and scare the informer off, and because we were both watching the no-man's-land, neither one of us noticed this fucking giant bear coming up to the agent, sniffing away. The intelligence agent was unarmed, and I didn't dare shoot in the dark because I might hit him and because it would raise too much of a racket and put an end to the informer slipping quietly across the border. Ah, we waited for a minute or two without making a move, and the bear sniffed at the intelligence agent and obviously didn't like the government smell about him and decided to leave, but for those few minutes I thought the agent was a goner and I would be taking his corpse back to the camp.

"This time at least is different, with so many of us alert,

knowing that we can use our guns if we have to. The wind dies and we see a group of men approaching through the jungle. They don't move in the way these guys usually do on their runs across the border. It's a group of twenty, with crates and bags, and they're making so much noise you'd think they're out for a picnic.

"My companions get ready to fire and the officer's voice cuts through the night. 'Listen carefully for my orders.' I'm wondering why he's more or less broadcasting our position on All India Radio, but the guys coming across do a strange thing. They look right at us, as if they know where we are, and they begin dropping a few crates and scattering some of the bags. 'Fire carefully to the left of the group, and aim high,' the officer says. 'This way no one gets hurt.'

"For a moment, everyone's confused. Then we know what's going on and why we've never made a seizure under him. He's been on the take from these guys all along, and we're going to get a haul tonight only in order for him to receive his transfer. A fake encounter, bullets fired in the air, shells to prove it, and a consignment of arms that will make his record look good, except that if anyone ever examines those guns we capture they'll find out that they're all duds. The smugglers drop their load of duds and get to go across with the real stuff, the officer has his transfer, and there's general happiness all around. We've heard of such things happening with other units, but this is a first for us.

"Mani, who hates the officer for everything, but especially because of the whole business with Rajinder and his wife, loses it when he hears this. He takes aim at the column moving toward the village and lets off a burst. There are confused shouts from the group. 'Careful,' someone yells. 'What are you guys playing at?' The officer leaps to his feet and starts screaming at Mani, and Mani, the mad motherfucker, levels his gun on the officer and is about to shoot the officer when Rajinder and I come down on him and get the rifle out of his hands, and the column of gunrunners starts scattering and the rest of the guys go to collect the duds because something's better than nothing."

"And Mani?" an old man huddling by the fire asked.

"The officer wanted to court-martial him. Mani would have had it if that had gone through, but the rest of us indicated that we would have to reveal the whole story if Mani was punished, so he dropped the idea. He got his transfer anyway and moved out, and a new man, a more or less decent fellow, took over. Mani quit the service a year later. The last I heard of him he was running a fishery business in Kerala and I'm happy for him. He was too smart for this business. Rajinder quit as well, but we were told he never went back to his home village and had become an alcoholic. One of our chaps thought he once saw him at the Kohima bus station, but we never did find out what exactly happened to him."

DAWN WAS BREAKING behind the hills. The fire had died away some time ago, dissolving into a heap of ashes, and the more sedate passengers were beginning to stir inside the buses. The shack owner began serving dark red tea, and what had been a mob concentrated in the store the evening before now became an amorphous crowd spilling over onto the highway, a combination of passengers, drivers, construction workers, and soldiers that suggested some momentous upheaval in progress, like the court of a mad emperor struggling toward a wilderness where a new capital was to be established. Around six, the horns began sounding and the engines throbbed as attendants gathered their straying passengers back into the buses: we would push ahead to the blocked spot and wait there for the obstacle to be cleared, and our bus got into the line of vehicles creeping forward.

We approached the bridge, packed from end to end with traffic in the bright light of the morning, its metal girders gleaming. It took an hour for our bus to make it to the other end, and once there the devastation the landslide had wrought was clearly visible: soil cascaded down in vast swaths, with stray pebbles and clods of dirt trickling in their wake like stragglers trying to keep up with the herd, while the river was choked with branches and tree trunks and boulders. The bus came to a halt again, and the driver turned off the engine and waited. The highway ended in a blind curve some distance ahead, and beyond the vehicles in the lead, I could just make out a little pocket of tents and trucks and bulldozers, much of the scene covered by a thick layer of exhaust fumes, the sharp sound of spades and picks and the moan of a bulldozer reverberating through the smog.

A horn sounded behind us, and an army jeep appeared, the shouts of the soldiers and the noise of the horn clearing a way through the melee. I stood next to the bus, watching the progress of the jeep as it drew closer; it was abreast of me when it stopped, and the man sitting next to the driver jumped off smartly. "The pleasures of the road, sir, are as unexpected as its dangers. Fate dictates that we meet again."

It was Captain Sharma, his small eyes twinkling, his hand extended toward me. A couple of the soldiers at the back climbed down and approached us, while the people in my bus watched cautiously—probably recalling my earlier exchange with the mobile patrol.

"They'll fetch your bags," the captain said, gesturing at his flunkies.

"What purpose would that serve?" I asked.

"Why, I am merely offering you a lift." The captain waved contemptuously at the buses. "They will not get through for a long time. We will. I am only going to a camp near Imphal, but my driver will take you all the way."

One of his soldiers appeared from the bus with my typewriter case and bag and began walking toward us. A child began crying from inside the bus, and I saw the passengers looking, wondering what was going on.

"There aren't too many alternatives. You could sit here for an uncertain length of time and enjoy the bracing scenery. You could walk a couple of hours to the other side of the breach and see if there is a bus from the same service willing to turn back toward Imphal. It would depend on how many passengers you could collect from here for the trek through the mud. Or you could simply ride in comfort, without unnecessary delays, and give me the pleasure of your company. It will be an enjoyable ride, sir. I am still grateful for the introduction to the Sunday magazine editor."

I got in next to the captain, and the jeep made its way through the narrow corridor that had been cleared for it. There were more bulldozers pushing earth against the side of the mountain or removing tree trunks from the highway, dredgers scraping the road, tar bubbling in vats over wood fires, and a host of voices shouting and screaming above the noise of the machines. For nearly a quarter of a mile this went on, with the jeep determinedly negotiating machines and workers, and then we saw the first line of buses and cars on the other side, facing us as they waited for the road to be cleared.

"You have been busy," the captain said as the jeep picked up speed on what was finally an empty stretch of highway. "You are close to the object of your quest now."

"How do you know?" I asked.

He smiled shyly, as if I had asked him a personal question. "So she is a victim after all, even if the MORLS ultras simply made an example of her as an immoral type. But how will you find her?"

"Maybe her boss will help," I said. "Everything points to him. He's still around, running the Prosperity Project, even if she has gone underground somewhere."

"Her boss? The Director? Malik will help?" the captain said.

"Why not?"

The captain shook his head. "You are behind with the news, sir. You disappoint me. I thought reporters knew everything, but I see I was wrong. We will stop at a hotel here for some rest and a little food," he said; we were passing a small village, and the jeep had slowed down. The driver leaned out and shouted at a van to move so that he could park in front of a tea shop.

Inside, the captain and I sat together while his men went off to another table. "I have news for you," he said, tossing a copy of the *Nagaland Post* toward me. "Malik will tell you nothing. In fact Malik is unable to tell you anything right now, and I doubt he would tell you the truth even if he were free to do so."

The news he had for me was not hard to find, since it was the main headline. "Director of Prosperity Project Abducted by MORLS." I read the words with growing dismay. There was a picture of the man I had seen smiling melodramatically in so many of the project photographs Maria had collected for me. But he wouldn't have been smiling in this picture, I was sure, even though it was hard to make out his features. He was kneeling, hands tied behind his back, his head weighed down with a week's growth of beard. Two masked men stood on either side of him, and each of them held a pistol against Malik's temple. Around his neck, they had strung the front page of a newspaper so that you would be able to tell the date on which the picture had been taken. Even though the picture had been badly reproduced, I could tell the newspaper they'd chosen was the *Sentinel*. It was almost exactly the same situation as in the picture I had been carrying with me, and only the objects— and targets—in the setup had changed: Leela absent, Malik in her place, and, instead of rifles, pistols in the hands of the two men.

I had felt a sharp antagonism toward Malik through much of my journey, well before I suspected his involvement with Leela. It was partly because of the way the Prosperity Project and Malik entered into every conversation and query, and partly because I didn't want to entangle myself in the complications of his social work. When I'd heard his speech through Minister Vimedo's notes, the confidence and amplitude of the voice had disturbed me. How was it possible that amid the overwhelming failure and the breakdown I saw in the region, there was a man perfectly in control of the situation? But that was then.

Now, staring at the news report, I found it hard to remain ill-willed toward a man who seemed so broken and humiliated, kneeling for his life, completely at the mercy of the people he had argued for so eloquently at the peace negotiations.

"The peace talks?" I asked the captain.

"On the verge of breaking down. MORLS has rejected the offers of negotiation," he said. "They say it was a divide-and-rule strategy. It's complete war now as far as MORLS is concerned. If you read the story, you will see that they have accused the Director of being an Indian intelligence operative. Their leadership council is considering an appropriate punishment for him after they have held a trial."

"Was he? An intelligence operative?"

"How would I know?" the captain said with an amused look on his face. "Poor Malik. He was so interested in photographs and the power of images. Now he has become a picture himself, but an image without any power."

The captain drank down his tea swiftly, turned toward the soldiers, and told them he would be ready in half an hour. There was more he had to tell me. The newspaper flapped in the breeze of the old ceiling fan, obscuring Malik's picture.

CHAPTER NINE

* 1 *

The captain's monologue required more than half an hour in the tea stall, and he continued talking as we drove on toward Imphal. The names of the small towns—Maram, Karong, Kangpokpi—barely registered with me as I listened to him and watched the shadows playing on his childlike face. Densely forested hills rose and fell with unchanging regularity around us, providing occasional glimpses of watchtowers and Burma bridges strung along ravines. When we reached the outskirts of Imphal and the jeep veered off to drop the captain and his retinue at the camp, evening was already setting in and the sloping hills had given way to the still, watery rice fields of the valley.

I am not sure how much I believed of the captain's story, but what struck me later was how commonplace he made everything sound. As for motive—why would he tell these things to a journalist?—I think it was clear to him that I wouldn't be writing anything about this for the *Sentinel*. A canny man, he probably knew about my suspension, and unlike in his earlier, clumsy attempt to deflect me from my journey, this time he simply didn't care. With Malik's abduction, he knew which way things would turn.

"Being rather well informed and a person who deals with words, you are no doubt aware that the situation in this region has been rather unusual for a good number of years. Every decade has brought a half-dozen fresh insurgencies, new demands and tactics, and some years ago it became clear to certain important people that Manipur had become as significant a site for insurgency as Nagaland has been for more than twenty years. In order to deal with this special situation and to maintain some semblance of control, the government introduced the Armed Forces Special Powers Act in the state. The act subordinates civil administration to the military, and specifies that all government funds for development in the valley must be channeled through the army. It sounds harsh, no doubt, but the development sector and the human rights movement have often proved a useful cover for the ultras, and in a situation of insurgency, control is very important. The Army Development Group was set up to oversee the distribution of government funds, to contract out work, and to decide what work should be carried out where. Villages need help; there are wells to be dug, essential supplies to be delivered, medical care to be given, perhaps an access road to be constructed, and all this happened here through the ADG. It was a useful procedure because villagers had to be on good terms with the army or paramilitary units in their area. It was possible to reward, and it was certainly feasible to punish. People who gave us valuable information got something for their village, while places that had records of supporting ultra units received nothing. The carrot and the stick.

"Perhaps this shocks you—or maybe not, after all, you must have relatives in the forces, and I suppose you understand our compulsions—but thinking has to be fluid in an area of such great turmoil. There are many restrictions and situations here that would not be found in mainland India, such as the fact that six Bihari laborers digging a trench for a water pipe can be gunned down at night by ultras. But if there are such problems, then there are also opportunities here that would be equally unthinkable in the mainland. To understand what I am going to tell you, you must accept this, the absence of old rules and the ability to make up new ones as you go along, the feeling almost of being free from gravity. We felt as if we were walking on the moon.

"I had been deputed temporarily to the Army Development Group for a couple of years, and some of us sensed the unusual opportunities available here. As you no doubt anticipate, we seized the openings available in the development funds for our personal enhancement. As a result, my own thinking had already taken a somewhat unorthodox turn when I met the man known as the Director of the Prosperity Project. His reputation preceded him: I had heard of him as a man who got things done, as someone who had the goodwill of the army, the local government, and the ultras, and that alone was a remarkable achievement, indicating a high degree of intelligence and an ability to manipulate opposing forces. Then, one evening, I was introduced to him by a colonel at the Border Roads Task Force who Malik had helped out of some difficulties. The BRTF, you see, is not an armed unit, although they can request an escort from regular units in the army if it's required. Colonel Kaul was a pragmatic man, quite uninterested in protocol, and he was finding it increasingly difficult to retain his laborers because of the security situation. The labor force is entirely civilian, a mixed group comprised of local people and Bihari migrants, and they were vulnerable to attacks by the ultras. Asking for escort slowed down his work without guaranteeing protection. At most it ensured return fire if ultras tried to raid the construction gangs. Malik set up a deal with MORLS, so that in exchange for a certain amount of protection money, they would not only refrain from attacking the laborers but would also guard them from the aggression of other ultra groups. Colonel Kaul, in spite of his pragmatism, was doubtful about such an arrangement at first, but Malik showed him how economically efficient it was. The cost of the payoffs was far less than that of maintaining an escort unit, and it was a much more secure arrangement. This way nobody was injured or killed, important work got done, and Colonel Kaul remained within his budget.

"I was impressed when I heard this story before being introduced to Malik, full of admiration for the clear and unorthodox thinking he had demonstrated. You are aware, I know, that I have great respect for writers and artists, for those who advance the boundaries of our culture and thinking, and the admiration I felt for Malik was not dissimilar in manner. The man was an artist, a genius, and in the confusion of events here, a confusion to which both ultras and government contributed equally, he stood out as the very embodiment of clarity.

"So I listened to him carefully when he told me about a possible operation that was as simple as it was profitable. He had set up a small counterfeiting business, and he needed my help in dispersing the fake money. He'd found a couple of men who had produced counterfeit money some years ago, before they were caught by the authorities as a result of a drunken quarrel. He brought them together after their release and they started afresh under his direction. There was an old Manipuri man who had worked in the Tezpur treasury in the sixties and who had some sources for currency paper, and they had a sophisticated Canon machine that xeroxed in color. Most importantly, and this is where Malik's characteristic brilliance comes in, they had a Burmese man who was an artistic genius and would have been Leonardo da Vinci had he been born in the right time and place. This man could take photographs, he had made films, he had written books, and he played the crucial part in the counterfeiting process. After they had reproduced the money and cut it into individual notes, the Burmese would paint the raised lettering in note by note. The process was slow, as you can imagine, and we had to restrict ourselves to big bills in order to be efficient, but Malik made sure that we never hurried to produce too many notes.

"My role and that of a few others was to mix the counterfeit currency with regular money, to find people to go into banks for us and get the fakes changed into drafts made out to some companies that had been set up on paper, with notional offices far from the region. It worked, sir, it worked, as long as you kept your head and dealt with relatively small amounts at a time. What we were producing was this little stream of cash; if there were any problems, who would know once it had merged into the great river of money produced by our government?"

The captain smiled broadly and waited for some praise or applause from me, some sign that this was indeed an ingenious scheme.

"It was a good business. Everybody loved it, except for the Burmese artist, who got drunk and cried loudly when the other men soiled the notes to make them look more authentic. Yes, I understand what you are thinking. My purely mercenary motives are not hard to fathom, but why did Malik involve himself in such a racket if he was the visionary I say he was? Well, you understand, the counterfeit money was not important in itself so much as for what it represented. I knew that a good amount of the money was going to MORLS. But Malik was an unofficial adviser to the military authorities and a point of contact with the ultras, and I thought he must have had the counterfeit project cleared by someone higher up. It gave him access to the MORLS leadership, it gained him their trust, and in effect he became one of their financiers.

"Think of it. The audacity and the sheer genius of the man. Both the government and the ultras are on their last legs, choking each other to death, and here he comes and opens things up along new lines of thought. Where all the government manages is a sick little administration, with those dirty notes circulating from hand to hand of the poor, benighted people of the region, Malik's fakes are better than the originals. It made me feel good to handle them, and I was almost reluctant to hand them over to the bank managers and tellers. He understood this; everyone underestimated the power of images, he said. What is a banknote? They call it legal tender, but it is a symbol, something that simulates the republic, and those dirty notes you see around here are a good illustration of how the image of the republic is tarnished and corrupted in the region. Malik would change all that. He was restoring luster to that soiled image, and with his fakes he was imparting a degree of authenticity that was not to be found in the originals. This is what he said to me when I asked him why he was involved in such a small operation.

"Some of this confused me—I did not always quite comprehend what Malik was saying—but what I understood without any problems was that he inspired me, and I have no doubt that he inspired the MORLS leaders. He showed us that things could be done here, if only one had the right approach and imagination. He was an artist, and all of us—army officers, criminals, insurgents—we were brought together by him in a belief that far exceeded what the government or the insurgency alone could offer.

"You see, one of the things that struck me about Malik, and no doubt this is true of great writers and artists as well, was how innocent he was, how childlike he seemed in his unbounded imagination. You know how things are when you are small, how big the world seems, and everyone assures you that if you work hard you will find that big world opening itself up for you. All lies, you realize when you become an adult. If the world is a big place, it is so for a chosen few, to the rich, the connected, the corrupt. For you and for me, it is as small a place as it has ever been since childhood, except that now there is no hope of a grown-up life where everything will come good. Malik was the first person I met who had been uncontaminated by that taint of adulthood. For him the world was still a big, wonderful place, and even here in the backwaters he built fairy castles and magical kingdoms, generating ideas like sparks from a wheel. He had such plans; he had even been in touch with a national daily about jointly financing a local edition. I had hoped . . .

"I had hoped, sir, but now the hopes are crushed by the weight of the world. Malik talked about many things that I did not understand, but I was always aware of the degree of their magnitude. A self-made scholar, he had discovered the remnants of a new tribe near the site of the Prosperity Project. Their language, he said, was unrelated to the Mon-Khmer or Tibeto-Burman language groups of their neighboring tribes, and he had visions of inviting scholars to the project. So many works in progress. Such waste.

"Somewhere there was also a plan, I know, to end the violence in the region for once and for all by inserting himself into the parallel structure of the insurgency. He would be the bridge between these two opposed forces of government and insurgents, and both would find him indispensable. But I was not privy to the secrets of his mind, and it is tragic that it should have ended this way. Perhaps the MORLS leaders grew suspicious of Malik, although I think there was too much pressure on him to bring MORLS to the negotiating table right away. Personally, the end of the counterfeit operation leads to a dip in income, but that is not what I wanted to discuss with you. It was the way the imagination and genius of the man was thwarted, crushed by the mundane world we live in. I am an autodidact, and I have been compiling some notes, a few observations on my experience here and about the genius of the man I had the good fortune to work with. Perhaps an editor could be made to take an interest, maybe you could examine what I have so far. I solicit your advice eagerly. I trust your judgment and experience and defer to it. If necessary, even an editorial fee could be provided for."

I indicated that the latter wouldn't be necessary.

"Of course, I knew it," the captain said, slapping me on the arm. "A truly sensitive man understands the importance of reflecting upon and presenting one's experiences. Malik is as good as a dead man, sir, I tell you that well before the newspapers. The least we can do is honor his memory."

When I got into Imphal itself, I had even more reason than before to resent the way Malik had pushed his way into the scene. This hadn't ever been about him, and yet his disappearance cast a long shadow on the valley. He was the big news of the moment, sharing headline space with the current confusion about the peace talks, everyone wondering if other insurgent groups in the valley would still participate in negotiations after MORLS had rejected them so definitively. The local office of the Prosperity Project was closed when I went to find someone I could talk to about Leela, its doors locked and windows curtained, the few people who worked there apparently in hiding. Nevertheless, I pressed on with my phone calls and interviews, determined to do my article and get out, even though the people I spoke to were surprised I was bringing up an old story with so much going on in the immediate present.

I don't know if I could have explained it to them, because the reasons weren't entirely clear even to me. But I tried my best to disengage from the white noise of Malik's abduction, concentrating on finding the traces of the woman who had lived here, looking for Leela's shadow in this town that appeared deceptively simple at first sight, like a sequence of surfaces without depth.

There were moments when I was charmed by the place, when I passed old neighborhoods sequestered behind walls and saw the careful dignity of the people, the women in their intricately embroidered skirts and the old men, such a startling combination of Mongoloid faces and devout Vaishnavite Hindus in their clean white *dhotis*. Elsewhere, the roads ran above small canals clogged by patches of water hyacinth, while in the center of the town stood a fort with thick walls, an old burial ground for the warrior kings who had once ruled the valley.

But when I looked more closely, I saw something of the anger lurking below those apparently calm surfaces. The hotel was in a more modern part of town, on the road leading to the airport. Many of the houses on this route had been left incomplete, iron rods and girders sticking out like exposed ribs, while the shabby stores gave an impression of poverty and squalor with their stock of cheap Chinese goods that had come across the border and were more easily available than things from the Indian mainland. The soiled currency notes people used almost crumbled to the touch, so that it became a game to try and pass the money on to someone else before it disintegrated. Even the grand fort had long since been turned into the headquarters of the paramilitary, and entry across its high walls was forbidden to the public; instead of the spirits of warrior kings, it was patrols that emerged from the fort these days, conducting long and tedious cordon-and-search operations in the town.

I had noticed that the rickshaw drivers in the town, mostly young men, went about with scarves pulled tight around their faces. They didn't take them off even when they had to tell a passenger the fare, and a local official explained that they kept their faces covered because they were ashamed about the menial work. Almost all of them were college graduates, and because Imphal was a small town, they did not want to be recognized by passengers who might be friends or relatives or neighbors. Wouldn't they know anyway, though? Could one disguise oneself so thoroughly with a scarf? That wasn't the point, the man replied impatiently. Of course everyone knew

which neighbor or relative of theirs worked as a rickshaw driver for a living, but it was a gesture, a sign that they wanted
something better in life.

Maybe he was right, but it didn't change my immediate,
visceral response. The sight of masked men in ragged clothes
pedaling rickshaws around the town seemed like an absurd
extension of the photograph that had brought me so far—
suggesting despair beneath the masks when I had expected to
find only aggression.

I had hardly had time to process these impressions when
Malik's wife arrived at the hotel where I was staying. Until
then, the hotel, with its big iron gate, glass-topped wall, and
profusion of shrubbery had been a refuge from the town, a
space separate from the turmoil and confusion outside. Clean
and well-run, it was virtually empty when I checked in, and
the Oriya man and two Manipuri women who seemed to be in
charge spent entire afternoons watching Hindi films on cable
television. They were helpful, friendly people, and I liked the
fact that the hotel had a life of its own, unencumbered by the
whims of passing visitors like me. But Malik's wife changed
that when she came from Kohima, accompanied by a retinue
of officials and journalists who would try to get her husband
released.

I don't know what had held her so long in Kohima—I
vaguely recalled that the highway had been blocked again after the captain got me through the breach—but the signs were
not good by the time she got to Imphal. The MORLS insurgents, initially making noises about the appropriate punishment for Malik, had been silent for a few days. They were
apparently assessing public reaction to the abduction, although it seemed quite clear to me that people in Manipur

weren't happy about it. Malik was a good man, they said, and the important issue was the peace talks. If Meitei insurgents did not participate in that, it was quite possible that the Indian government would make a deal with the Nagas that would take away a large part of Manipur.

Malik's wife appreciated the local support, but I wasn't sure if she quite understood the complex situation in the valley. I met her in the lobby the day she arrived, two young Manipuri women associated with a local development agency accompanying her. She still looked small and frail, but there was a shrill brightness to her voice I found alarming. If I'd thought she was simply trying to keep up a brave front, I wouldn't have worried; but there seemed nothing forced about her optimism as she fixed her gaze on my shoulder and said, "You're here to cover the story? That's so wonderful of you. When he's released, we can all celebrate together." She smiled at the women with her, and they nodded back seriously.

"Everyone has been so kind to me," she said. "It's his personality, you see, his great belief in the goodness of people. It works on people who have known him even when he's not present." I looked past her to the lawn and realized there was quite a crowd outside: policemen, officials holding briefcases, local reporters and photographers, a group of matronly women, even some youth leaders I had met earlier at a place called the Handsome Book House. Malik's wife didn't seem aware of them. "Don't you feel it?" she asked. "His presence? His aura? His voice? Just listen." She held up a finger and cocked her head to one side, and the four of us stood there waiting for Malik's voice to say something through the ether, over and above the confused hum from the garden and the sound of chairs being shifted in the dining room next door.

I heard the faint strains of a song, voices unaccompanied by instruments rising in pitch, some stragglers a beat behind and hurrying to catch up with the group. I couldn't quite make out the words, but indistinct as they were, I realized that they must be singing in the local language. Then the chorus became stronger, and suddenly the song was recognizable. It was "We Shall Overcome," and it was sweet and sad because it wasn't clear what they were singing against: the insurgents, the government, their state of alienation, the absurdity of the present situation, or the map for a greater Nagaland that impinged on their territory. It could have been any or all of these things, but the effect was nevertheless moving. If it was Malik who'd inspired them, this was not the song I would have expected him to have chosen.

The feedback of a microphone cut into the sound, and stray words and phrases rose over the song, amplified and harsh. I caught the name *Malik* a few times, and the phrase "our friend in adversity." The singing faltered and died down. One of the politicians was making an impromptu speech, and as the platitudes began ringing in my ears, I felt Malik had asserted his presence at last.

An official with a self-important air entered hurriedly and addressed Malik's wife. "Shall we begin the press conference now that everyone is here?"

"What shall I do? I don't know what to say. I wanted to make an appeal to the people to have him released, but they're already on my side."

The official looked alarmed. "Madam, you must say something. The ministers are here, the chief secretary and the director general of the police are here, as well as the press and representatives from the local civil society. They will be disappointed if you do not speak. And if you speak, it will exert moral pressure on the ultras to release your husband."

"Yes," she said. "I mustn't disappoint him. I mustn't let him down."

They headed toward the temporary stage set up outside, the policemen clearing a way for the group, and I heard the sound of clapping as Malik's wife became visible to the gathered crowd.

❖ 3 ❖

MORLS hadn't been listening to the applause. The next morning a man with a bad cough made a brief call to the editor of a newspaper and announced that Malik had fallen down a cliff while trying to escape. He had been injured, but medical attention was being provided and the people would be kept informed of developments.

I didn't care for the turn things were taking and headed out of the hotel before the visitors started coming in to empathize with Malik's wife. But if it had been hard to get people to focus on Leela before, it was nearly impossible now. The list of names provided by Robiul and Sema was drying up rapidly, and I tramped from government offices near the fort to the neighborhoods around the old markets trying to resurrect Malik's forgotten assistant from people's memories. I had no luck. The snippets of information that came my way added little to the material I had collected in Kohima—although I did learn that virtually everyone thought the latest announcement from MORLS was bad news.

In the evening, feeling tired and a little despondent, I went to the Handsome Book House at the market near the hotel, passing a row of shops with a bright array of smuggled goods. There was almost a touristy feel about this little stretch, with sneakers and T-shirts and electronic items displayed in the windows, but the Handsome Book House held itself aloof from such tawdry consumerism. It was a dark and gloomy place that served as newsstand and stationery store, its small collection of books limited to paperback thrillers and guides for taking the civil service exams. But it also functioned as an informal meeting place for young men, journalists, unemployed youth, and various student leaders—people who were tuned in to happenings in the valley in a way the officials and older generations weren't.

I had visited before, and although the youth group I met then had given me little information of use, I thought the place worth another look. The student leaders (none of whom were students; it was just an informal label for political activists in their twenties and thirties, some with covert links to the insurgent groups) were especially important; it was they who said something had gone badly wrong with Malik's abduction, something MORLS hadn't anticipated, and I shouldn't be surprised if there was violence in the town within the next few days.

It was dim inside the store, with that regulation low-voltage yellow light of the region, and I drank tea and drifted from conversation to conversation with these young men, surprised at their resilience. It was no different from a gathering of neighborhood youth in Calcutta, with the same levity and in-jokes, even though political work went on in the background as leaflets were xeroxed and stacked next to newspapers, which would print statements from the leaflets in future editions.

None of the men there had ever met Leela, although some would have been the same age as she. It was a small town where people knew each other—as evident from the rickshaw drivers who covered their faces because every other passenger they picked up might be an acquaintance—and yet there seemed to be no network of kinship or circle of friends of which Leela had been a part. I understood that she was no longer in Imphal, but it was as if she had never existed there. The men I spoke to remembered the project office in the town in a vague way, even that one of the women working with the group down at the actual site had been threatened and shot by MORLS, but they could recall nothing else. And although they had different opinions on Malik and his work, none of them had ever visited the Prosperity Project. I felt as if I had covered no ground since starting out, that the distance between me and Leela had not been reduced by so much as an inch.

One of the men in the group, more reticent than the others, came and sat next to me. He was stocky, with a thoughtful cast to his face that was accentuated by his habit of stroking his goatee when he spoke. "It must seem puzzling, this lack of concern, but it's not because nobody cares. If you had come here the week of the MORLS press conference, everyone would have had the information you wanted. But six months? That's like six years, or sixty."

His name was Meghen and he was—he announced with a certain irony—an unemployed engineer. "I even applied for a driver's job with the state department," he said. "The minister called, very apologetic, saying I was much too qualified and shouldn't be applying for jobs like this. I told him that I would do anything, just to avoid sitting around."

"You didn't get the job, I see."

"No, of course not. The embarrassment was genuine, but that didn't mean he was going to give me the job for free when he could get good money from someone willing to pay for the position."

I asked him why he had come back to Imphal after studying engineering outside the region. Surely he could have found something in mainland India, in the big cities. Meghen looked self-conscious. "My parents are old," he said. "They need someone to look after them, to be around for them. You understand?" He looked at his companions and bent toward me, speaking in a lower voice. "But it's more than that. I missed this when I went to engineering school." He gestured at the other men, at the contents of the Handsome Book House, at the street outside beginning to fade into darkness as the shops closed one by one.

"The fact is I couldn't survive in the big cities. I wouldn't know where to begin. This seems hard to you, the abductions, the killings, the soldiers, the strikes and curfews and violence, but that's what I know. That's what I am, in some absurd way. I think about the possibilities elsewhere every day, when I look at the classified ads in the papers that come from Calcutta and Delhi. Everybody comes here for that reason, because they look at the newspapers and magazines and fantasize about what exists out there. Of course, none of us would get these jobs if we applied for them, but that's not all that holds us back. You know, when I ride home after Rajesh has closed the shop, I try to imagine myself having one of these jobs, of becoming one of the many managers or pharmaceutical salesmen or executives or computer trainers they seem to need out there. At first it's nice, to think as you're driving along an empty road that you will take a bus out of Imphal and then a train and arrive in a big city one morning, just like one of those scenes in the movies or in the ads they show all the time on television. I can see myself in new clothes, with a new bike, shaking hands firmly and smiling confidently. I visualize the kind of place I would have in the city, the way I would arrange things in the flat, the girlfriend I might find, and with each step I take in my imagination, I get a little less sure. It starts feeling more and more fake, and just before I park the bike in front of the house, the images give way to a blankness that's so complete it's a relief to get into the house. What I can't see is who I would actually become, and that is what holds so many of us back, this fear of letting go of that which is familiar for things completely unknown."

"Why this distrust of other possibilities?" I asked. "Someone told me exactly the opposite not too long ago. He said there was freedom in this region because there were no rules here, because you could change and become anything you wanted to be. He said it was like walking on the moon."

Meghen shook his head.

"That's just not right. It's dangerous to think like that, to believe that you can do anything you want here because there are no rules. You have to be very cynical to think like that, or very foolish. Because you see, there *are* rules here. Especially for the moon dwellers. To them, the lower gravity doesn't seem like freedom, but a constraint they've always struggled against. I'll tell you something. Why do you think no one wants to talk about Leela? It's not as if they blame her for anything, but I guess if you were able to hear what they were thinking, they'd say she was a little too fast, maybe just much too keen to become somebody else, too eager to push beyond the constraints, to do something beyond what is possible out here at the present time."

"What do you know about her, then?"

Meghen shrugged.

"That she quickly accepted a job with the Prosperity Project, that she had gone to college in Delhi and was very impatient to do things when she came back here. You see, we have a strange attitude toward women, different from the way you people in the plains think. This is a very matriarchal society and women have respect and authority here. You know about the market run by women, I am sure, but there are other things, like the fact that divorce is not a stigma for women here, that falling in love is okay. In fact, it's a big thing here to elope and get married. Even if your parents have no objections to your partner, you still run away and get married. We're such a romantic people, even when there are killings and explosions and abductions all around us. But we also have some other attitudes that are perhaps not so good. I don't want to say it's only because of the influence of Indian mainstream culture, but have you ever been to Ganesh Talkies to see the films they show? The trash, with violence and rape and gunfights. On the one hand, we talk about our matriarchy, but we do not like women to become too big. If Leela had been just the average girl, it would have been easier for people to understand her situation. But she took things into her own hands, heading out of the town with the project people even after the insurgents shot her. People were angry with the MORLS insurgents about the press conference, especially when everyone realized that the whole porn-film angle was a bluff, but Leela disappeared and other things replaced her in their mind."

The young proprietor of Handsome Book House was ready to close shop by this point in the evening. The others were beginning to disperse, and Meghen offered to give me a lift. "You'll see, people will react to what MORLS is doing now. They don't want to be distracted from the main issue, which is the peace talks involving the Nagas." When we reached the hotel Meghen asked me if I had met Malik's wife. "I wish I could see her," he said, looking up at the building from his bike. He looked shy and self-conscious again, taking off his helmet and stroking his goatee. "It's just that she's like a public figure, a celebrity, and I don't get to see too many people like that. It's not as if there are film stars visiting every week."

I looked up with him, over the wall with broken bottles lining the top, to the third floor, where Malik's wife had her room. She wasn't visible, but it was very peaceful as we waited on the road emptied of traffic, and I felt reluctant to move, content to listen to the cicadas in the bushes and the frogs warbling from the canals choked with water hyacinths. "She must be asleep," I said. "But I can introduce you during the day if you want." Meghen agreed to come by in the morning and started his bike, the sound of its motor echoing through the walls and empty street and setting off a volley of barks from a dog somewhere.

Back in the room, I began looking at what I had written so far. There was more than I had thought, but it was a partial, incomplete account of the past couple of months; Maria, Minister Vimedo, the gaunt driver of the jeep, the guesthouse with its stripped rooms, the woman at the cremation had all been left out. By contrast there was much of Malik, and his Prosperity Project had insinuated its way into my notes.

I took out Leela's photograph, concentrating on her face

and trying to recall everything I knew about her. It seemed to me that she would have been the perfect person to have helped with my story, perhaps, with her yearning for something better, the person to have written it. No longer a symbol of the unknown, she now seemed as familiar as a sister, as intimate as a lover, my double waiting for me at the edge of the republic.

I was shaken from my thoughts by the phone. The woman at the other end spoke slow, careful English, identifying herself as an aunt of Leela's. A clerk at the police headquarters had heard about my inquiries and told her about me. If I went to her house the next morning, she would tell me all she knew about Leela's background. I took the address and the directions and went down to the hotel lobby to see if I could find some food. Sanat, the Oriya receptionist, was watching the news along with Malik's wife, the latter bundled up in blankets on the reception sofa, looking like a child. When she saw me, she gave me a bright smile and said, "Don't worry about the false report about the accident. The police have proved that it was a crank caller. He's going to be with us any day now." With this she rose from the sofa and stumbled sleepily toward the stairs.

Sanat waited till she was out of earshot and said, "She'll come back downstairs soon. Finds it hard to be by herself."

"Is what she said about a crank caller true?" I asked Sanat. "You think her husband's safe?"

Sanat began saying something, but stopped when he heard her coming back and shook his head at me. Then, before she came back into view, he placed his forefinger on his temple and closed his eyes while with his lips he mimed the sound of a bullet being fired from a handgun.

fire

CHAPTER TEN

* 1 *

I was glad to have Meghen taking me to the aunt's house because the directions were confusing. It was fairly early when we headed out, around nine in the morning, and the town hadn't yet emerged from its cocoon of sleep. Meghen had peeked around the lobby and the dining room when he came to get me, slightly disappointed there was no trace of Malik's wife, his mind still caught up with what might happen if he spoke to her. "If there's some way I can help, maybe she'll be impressed enough to recommend me to her husband when he's released."

"Is that what you want from it, Meghen? A job?"

He shook his head, smiling wanly as he put on his helmet. "Good fantasy to have, being taken in by the Director of the Prosperity Project himself. But I should think about his poor wife and her troubles instead. I would like to help her anyway." He was embarrassed and I wanted to reassure him.

"I'll introduce you when we get back. But you might be

disappointed, Meghen. I'm not sure she understands what's going on."

"Who does?" he replied. "Maybe it's best that she doesn't understand what's going on."

We had been riding through empty streets, but Meghen had to stop near the battalion headquarters of the Manipur Rifles because a patrol had just returned from the districts. I watched the policemen dismounting from their trucks, stretching and lighting cigarettes. They were young men, almost boys, spilling onto the road in a flood of green, automatic rifles slung on their backs; they had added little colorful touches to their drab uniforms, shiny Ray-Bans hanging out of tunic pockets and baseball caps turned stylishly backward, so that had it not been for the Kalashnikovs and bulky ammunition bags, they would have looked like Boy Scouts or NCC cadets just back from a field trip or a rehearsal.

The streets were unusually quiet even for this time of the day, and we encountered other patrols as we neared the fort. They were heading for the highway leading south in big open trucks with machine guns mounted on the roofs of the cabs, the black bandannas of the soldiers at the back streaming in the wind. These were regular soldiers, bigger and older men intent on their work in a way the boys from Manipur Rifles couldn't have been. "Something's up," Meghen said, steering the bike away from the main streets.

A military garrison appeared ahead of us, with more trucks parked behind the barbed-wire fencing. Meghen veered off from the tarmac, slowing down as he negotiated potholes and stones, the bike bouncing hard on the dirt track. "They're making a move against MORLS," he said, his voice flat. "They know something. We should get back to the hotel soon and try to catch the news."

The clear light of the day was softened by the trees and shrubs around us, the town slowly shading into wilderness and agricultural land, with small houses scattered unevenly amid vegetable gardens and the luxuriant overgrowth of the jungle. Few people were visible, and even the ramshackle school building we rode past was silent, the football field an empty stretch of dust with a pair of sagging bamboo goalposts at two ends. As we rode deeper, me calling out directions, memorials to the martyrs began to appear.

Meghen slowed down so that I could take a look. They were rough stone slabs, most of them unpainted, inscribed with the names of the martyrs who had fallen to the bullets of Indian forces; they reminded me of the carefully engraved tombstones at Kohima but were the memento mori of a much smaller war, with no consequences for the world or civilization. There was a rank, a date, and the name of the insurgent organization the martyr had belonged to, and I couldn't help observing that MORLS was conspicuous by its absence.

Leela's aunt was a middle-aged woman who was spreading out her washing on a nylon line when we arrived. The house was large, but it appeared weather-beaten and gloomy, the thick masses of old fruit trees and the weed-choked garden revealing there were too few hands and too little money to properly maintain the grounds. The aunt stood still as we came into the yard, looking at us for a long time before washing her hands with thorough slowness at a tube well. When she had finished, she led us to the verandah in front of the bungalow. There was something of a peasant's unhurriedness about her, which wasn't quite what I had expected from the phone conversation, but when she spoke to Meghen, her voice sounded throaty and musical, with a hint of the trained timbre that actors or singers possess.

Meghen translated for me as we sat on the verandah. I brought out my photographs, the original picture as well as those Maria had procured for me, and the stolid lines of the aunt's face gave way to a flash of anguish that was quickly replaced by an expression of detached wistfulness. She rose and headed into the house, moving quickly now, returning with an old spiral-bound photo album, its thick gray pages loose and nearly falling out, blue inland letters and picture postcards sticking out at odd angles between the covers. The album contained almost everything she had about Leela, the aunt said.

And so Leela's life was re-created for me in that setting, with the sound of the wind blowing through the fruit trees, the distant squeak of a tube well, and the clucking of poultry from behind the house. One by one the aunt selected the photographs she wanted me to see, mostly black-and-white pictures yellowing with age, each one a fragment of the person Leela had been, while Meghen provided an alert, measured translation that attempted to thread the images and documents together. In his role as interpreter, he was seemingly anxious to leave out no carefully nuanced details and he often paused or corrected himself, the aunt nodding when she thought he had it right, occasionally interrupting, helping out with her own stock of English or Hindi when she felt his version needed to be rephrased.

The account of Leela's past was many times removed from me, just as her life itself had been, but still I saw it all as clearly as if the memories and experiences were my own, as if I had become Leela for that brief span of time, making my way through the uncertain, bewildering world where fulfillment and failure often appeared in the same guise.

THERE WAS A TIME, the aunt said, when Leela had been thought of as a slightly odd child, withdrawn and introverted, so reluctant to speak at school or home that the teachers almost mistook it for muteness. That was at a very early age though, when she had been in the shadow of her elder sister, Radha, living with their parents in a small house on Police Lane. The two sisters were close, and it fell upon Radha to be Leela's defender and guardian, especially since Leela had a habit of confusing people: she was a quiet girl and tended to avoid everyone other than her sister, yet could fall into long conversations with perfect strangers. In the marketplace, on the streets, at the bus station, she would talk to people she had never seen before, carrying on confident conversations that spun into an exchange of careful details. Strangers were disarmed by her frankness and, in that way some adults have with children, agreed to play by the rules of her game, addressing her as familiarly as she addressed them. Except that it wasn't a game for Leela—later, she would say the stranger she had been talking to was a neighbor or a teacher or a colleague of her father's, even when it was perfectly obvious to everyone else that this was not the case at all.

It was as if she needed substitutes for the friends and family she saw around her every day. Somehow it just wasn't possible for her to interact with others except through this strange transposition of the familiar and the unreal. This embarrassed her parents and Radha, especially when some stranger took umbrage at being addressed so familiarly, but they became worried only after an incident that took place when Leela was around eight. The two girls were coming back from school, and Leela began talking to a man with a briefcase who was clearly not from the valley area, perhaps a visiting salesman of some sort in town on business. The man was friendly, and as Radha stood back watching, he and Leela began walking toward the ring of cheap hotels near the bus station. Radha was a brave girl, so she ran up to Leela, grabbed her hand, and dragged her away, speaking loudly to draw the attention of pedestrians to the situation. The man smiled and said it was too bad that both girls couldn't come and have sweets in his room, but that he hoped to see them again.

Leela's parents questioned her a long time about why she had done such a silly thing, walking off with a perfect stranger even though she knew one should never do that, and Leela kept saying that he was the art teacher she'd had in the second grade, the one who went away after a year but had been so nice that even Radha had liked him. "He looked nothing like that art teacher," Radha said.

"I thought he did," Leela said before retreating into her usual silence.

It wasn't all that important, the aunt suddenly said, interrupting Meghen, and she had no idea why she was bringing it up. Perhaps she'd half-thought it had something to do with the way Leela became involved with the man at the Prosperity Project, but that was really not the case, if she stopped to consider. Malik wasn't a stranger, and he had been good to Leela, giving her a job and encouraging her in her work. And Leela's strange mix of shyness and confidence as a child had nothing to do with the adult she'd become. After all, Leela had changed very rapidly when the fortunes of her family took a turn for the worse.

When she was around ten, they had to leave Imphal because of a property dispute between her father and uncle; after dragging on for many years without any sign of resolution, it came to a head one evening. When Leela's father, a rather mild-mannered clerk, discovered his brother had started building on the disputed land, he went to sort things out. This was not a good idea, because the brother, at first nothing more than a layabout, had worked his way into a violent gang of some kind, and was drinking with his friends. It ended with Leela's father being physically evicted from the grounds. The next day the brother called and threatened him; it was so easy to make two little girls disappear in a town where someone always went missing.

The family thought it best to move somewhere else, especially since there were other problems too, one of which involved the smart and outgoing Radha. She had become listless and often had difficulty walking, and the girls' father believed she would get better medical care in Shillong, where he had been offered a clerical job. The letters that came sporadically from Shillong to Leela's aunt after they moved showed that things were getting worse instead of better as far as Radha was concerned. She became completely bedridden, a fourteen-year-old who apparently looked like a child aged ten, wasting away gradually in bed as her younger sister grew taller than her. The family never quite understood what was wrong with her. The doctors in Shillong said it was something to do with needing a bone-marrow transplant, but Radha's parents had become convinced that a curse had been put on her by the uncle.

The family went to Delhi to see if Radha could be cured at

the big medical institute, but it was no use. Maybe it was too late to do anything, or perhaps they didn't have enough money or power to ensure the proper treatment. Radha died at the All India Institute of Medical Sciences, a sixteen-year-old who had frozen in time, a once confident girl who had become mute and silent except when she thought she saw someone familiar walking down the hospital corridor or visiting a patient in a neighboring bed. After her death, Leela's parents decided they would not come back to the region. Mathura was close to Delhi, and they wanted to spend the rest of their days in the birthplace of Krishna, turning their back on life and death and all its accompanying complications. They returned to Manipur just once—to put Leela in her aunt's care. By that time, Leela had grown. In place of the shyness and confusion, there was a confidence and eagerness about the world that came from see-ing new places and things in the course of Radha's sickness.

Leela was a wonderful addition to her life, the aunt said, pointing at the dim, empty rooms of her large house. To her it seemed that those years had flown past, and before she even realized it, Leela was ready to move on, deciding to go back to Delhi, and somehow even winning a scholarship to an elite women's college that would pay all expenses. And so she left, catching a bus that would drop her off at a railway station from where she would board an express train that would take her all the way across the hinterland into the capital of the republic.

The aunt showed me more pictures and postcards, but I saw far more than those words and images, aware of how Leela had experienced the city, venturing out tentatively from her college grounds in South Delhi to Ring Road and Lajpat Nagar and beyond, breathing in the city smog and learning to be careful of the men prowling the streets in search of a lone woman, somehow growing through it all, her zest for life processing even what was ugly and disturbing into something she could feed on. It wouldn't have been easy, not when she looked so different, with her yellowish complexion and almond eyes, when she had little money and no connections, but she had been there all the same, leafing through used paperbacks in the innermost alleys of Connaught Circle, going to the cultural centers near Copernicus Marg to see a play, looking with a wondering eye at the drab buildings along ITO where the newspaper offices flashed their news of election results in Uttar Pradesh and massacres in Kashmir on giant electronic boards.

I asked the aunt for the dates when Leela had been in Delhi. Of course, even the years tallied, so that her feet were constantly retracing the paths I had taken, my footprints erasing hers in that labyrinth of a city, the two of us circling each other without quite ever meeting, creating a pattern whose meaning would have eluded both of us had we ever been aware of it.

Nevertheless, the pattern existed, so that at the very time when I was drifting in and out of Delhi, Leela was working a petty secretarial job at an environmental organization that left her dissatisfied. Her college friends had deserted her for the most part, having rediscovered the family connections they'd been so dismissive of only a few years earlier, taking their predetermined routes into upper-class marriages, corporate jobs, and American universities. "'I am afraid of growing old and dying here,'" she had written to her aunt, Meghen translated from one of the letters. "'There's a bookstore on Connaught Circle I pass by during lunch hour. I feel as if it hasn't changed at all since the fifties, and even though I have never gone inside, I know there must be dust on the shelves at the back. They have good books in the windows, a lot of history books and literature, but I see few customers, perhaps because the store hasn't changed at all. At first, I used to stop and look at the books in the window display, but when I do that recently, it's not the books I find myself looking at but at the reflection of my face. I find myself thinking that I will become like the bookstore, a relic dissolving bit by bit into the city while change flows all around it. I can almost see myself thirty years later still staring at the window, except that my face is stained and marked and dusty as well. I wish there were someone who would help me figure things out, someone who would give me a chance to try my hand at something better, something I am capable of.'"

Her letters became more frequent, in contrast to the postcards that had arrived intermittently through her college years. They were more reflective as well, and I wondered how much of their content had been written for the aunt, and how much for herself.

"'When I find myself going past the AIIMS building, I often wonder what it would have been like for me if Radha had lived. Would we have been friends, sharing a place in Delhi, or would we have gone back to Imphal and somehow remained content with that small-town life? In some ways, it makes sense to me that Radha died here. Don't get upset about what I say, though; it's not that I think of these things all the time. But they're sometimes on my mind, and it seems to me that I notice the things and people nobody else does, the decrepit and the defeated and the solitary, perhaps because I identify with these aspects so closely.

"'At the corner of the pavement near Janpath, there's a Russian woman dressed in black who stands holding shiny watches, washed up here the way my parents, Radha, and I came here from Shillong. Her face is hard, but I know what must be behind the hardness as she stands in the cold holding her watches, while the men passing by say she's a prostitute and discuss how much she would cost. Some of them crowd around her pretending to look at the watches and try to touch her, so that she has to stand with her arms straight out even if they hurt. Why do I see these things and nurse them and take them home with me when I have gone back to the flat after fighting with the auto-rickshaw drivers or having warded off the hands trying to grope me on a bus? I sit with the lights off in my room, and wonder what I am doing with my life and why the things I looked forward to during college never happened.

"'I've become mean, I think. I sit in the 620, looking out of the window as the bus loops around the buildings of the inner circle, imagining that I am in a little boat that is going around a giant ship, thinking that there are cabins up there instead of flats and offices, that there's an engine room somewhere, funnels blowing out smoke if I look up high enough, and that we are moving across the ocean all around us, and not tied to this desert city where only the sky is free. One evening I was sitting by the window looking out at the ship when a pleasant-looking young man with an English or American girlfriend asked me if I would let them have my window seat. I was so ashamed of myself later, but I said no because I was thinking what right do they have to think that I will sacrifice my pleasure for theirs, what right do they have to be happy when I am miserable every day? I must leave Delhi.'"

SO SHE MADE ANOTHER train journey across the country, this time in the opposite direction, her mind stumbling for a moment on images of Radha, of her parents gravely leaving her at her aunt's house, of her aborted attempt to grasp the larger world. She had given her aunt few details about returning to Imphal, but apparently she had a job. No one had heard of the Prosperity Project in those days, the aunt said. She only knew that Leela did some kind of office work, assisting a man who was setting up a social service organization, a man known to her until recently only as the Director. She had expected Leela to be unhappy after her life in a big city, but that didn't seem to be the case. Leela appeared content, involved in her work, working in the small office as the Prosperity Project began to be noticed as a miracle in this wasteland of violence, as the Director's name appeared more frequently in the local papers. There was even a trip to Delhi at some point, from which Leela returned with enthusiasm, giving the aunt the sense that Leela's life was opening up once again. It was that way for a year or so, she said, and it reminded her of the earlier period when Leela had come to stay with her, a time of fulfillment in spite of the clashes and strikes and curfews.

When things changed, they did so bit by bit, almost imperceptibly at first. Leela had been talking for a while about moving out of the Imphal office and staying at the project site at Moirang Lake. She was excited at the possibility because she wanted to be a part of the actual work happening there, and perhaps there was also a kind of naive belief that things were better out in the country. The aunt shook her head. It was easy to forget, she said, that Leela wasn't a local girl; she didn't have the extended stretch of experience of growing up here that would have dispelled such illusions.

She had hesitated to say this at the time, but Leela's expectations of what there was in the countryside and what could be done showed she was still a city girl, more from Delhi than around here. And she had been disappointed when the Director hadn't lived up to his promise of giving her work at the Prosperity Project; where someone else would have been relieved, Leela had been so upset about not being sent there that she began staying away from the Imphal office. She had never even seen the site, she said to her aunt with some bitterness, and she was thinking of going back to Delhi once again.

But the Director came to take her to the Prosperity Project finally, driving up to the house in a jeep early in the morning one day. Malik didn't come inside, the aunt said, using his name for the first time. In fact, she barely saw what he looked like, so that when she saw his picture in the newspaper now, she couldn't associate the face of the captive with the man who had given Leela a job and then driven away with her. There were a couple of other men, local men, she said, and they waited outside while Leela got her things, excited and happy to be going to the project site at last. All she remembered of Malik were glimpses: the flash of sunglasses, his white teeth revealed in a laugh, a swiveling of his head as he surveyed her grounds that reminded her of military men, and his arms stretched wide as he explained something to his companions. A short man, she had thought, but with such long arms, stretching so wide that he easily spanned her little bamboo gate. That was all she remembered, and the jeep driving away with Leela smiling and waving at her from the window.

The next time she had heard of Leela, it was from the newspapers.

❖ 2 ❖

The towns I had traveled through in the past month or so had taught me many things, but no place imparted its lesson quite so well as Imphal. What I learned here was that disappearance is not an unusual thing at all. It can happen to anyone, at any point, and not just to a young woman getting into a jeep to visit a place that has become so intertwined with her dreams, hopes, and fears that its existence is in some ways inseparable from her own.

Somebody or other went missing every few days in Imphal. Often enough it would be a young man taken away at night by men who were dressed in ordinary civilian clothes but hadn't bothered to disguise the number plates of their Gypsy van, yet no one had a monopoly over disappearance. If young men suspected of links to the insurgents disappeared, so did fat traders and nervous bank officials and middle-aged tax commissioners. And if MORLS had made the Director of the Prosperity Project vanish in the most dramatic incident of recent times, who could say with certainty that the same wouldn't eventually happen to individual members of the group as they were picked off one by one?

On our return from the aunt's house, Meghen and I found out that Malik's absence was likely to be a permanent, final one. We watched Malik's wife being moved out of the hotel. Sanat came up to my room and joined us, peering out from the window every now and then as he told us the news we had missed.

"Mr. Malik? He's dead."

MORLS had made another call to the newspapers, this time to make a curt announcement. Malik had drowned while trying to escape his guards in what was described as a needless state of panic; it had not been possible to recover the body. The government agencies had since confirmed the death, Sanat said, though he had no idea how they knew unless there was someone in the group keeping them informed. "There," Sanat called out to us from the window. "They're taking her to the government guesthouse. With VIP-level security. Come and see." There were jeeps with armed policemen and an Ambassador with a flashing red light toward which Malik's wife haltingly made her way, her slight figure even more diminished by the policemen swarming around her and fussing with their walkie-talkies. As two of the officers helped her into the car, she looked like a traditional bride about to make her way to her husband's house for the first time, and I almost expected to see a band party somewhere ahead, ready to strike up a tune as the convoy began moving. It was a cruel thought, and I stepped back from the window. Sanat too turned away with a shake of his head, but Meghen stayed on, watching the exit of the public figure who fascinated him so much — as close an introduction as he was ever likely to get.

I could hear the rumbling of army and paramilitary convoys late into the night, the sound of the trucks like some deep underground tremor that cut into the clicking of my typewriter. The sense of closure provided by finding out the details of Leela's life had only been accentuated by the news about Malik, and my mind inevitably turned to what was waiting for me in Calcutta, to the life there that I'd left so abruptly it felt as if I too had disappeared. The man whose face stared at me from the identity card issued by Sema at the *Nagaland Post* agreed; he had nothing in common with the journalist suspended by the *Sentinel* for breaking off contact in the middle of a routine assignment.

There is a school of Indian philosophy that says the condition of our existence verges on nonexistence, that we are more absent than present, creating a fragile material trace at one point in space that does nothing to alleviate our utter absence from all other spaces. Imphal with its ruins, crumbling currency, masked rickshaw drivers, and disappearing individuals attested only too well to the tenuous nature of material existence. It was a town dissolving bit by bit into a state of nothingness, crumbling into an ocean of absence, with each one of us in the town seceding in his or her own way from the blinding presence of the republic.

A march was organized to protest against Malik's killing the next day, a slow, mournful procession carried out at night with lanterns and torches. It was led by the women of the cooperative market, and Malik's wife walked in front with the matriarchs like some feminine deity come to life in a time of great evil. She looked up as she went by the hotel, but it was hard to tell whether she was waving at us or at someone else, and soon she disappeared from sight, trailed by the ubiquitous armed escort and the television crew that had flown in from Delhi for the day.

It seemed as if a large section of the town had turned up for the march, and I couldn't help thinking that Leela would have been right at the front of the procession if she'd been around. There was something touching about the show of humanity in the march, its condemnation of the death of a man who had really been a stranger, its mourning for a project that most of the people marching had never seen and whose lives it had never affected — but it was a temporary, limited gesture for all that, and it couldn't have been otherwise. The marchers halted some distance from the hotel, at the point where the edge of the town began giving way to rice fields, from which bodies of the disappeared were occasionally recovered. Those shouting slogans for peace faltered, their voices dying abruptly, and it was not until they turned and passed the hotel again that some of their earlier confidence reappeared. The march headed back toward the center, leaving the dark night to flow over the town as swiftly as Malik's watery grave had closed around him.

Of course, no one would ever be certain that Malik had drowned—either while trying to escape or after being shot and pushed into the lake—but the exact manner of his death was no longer significant. MORLS retracted its statement the day after the march, even as the government continued to insist that Malik was dead, killed in a state of panic by the unit guarding him. Dead, not dead—it didn't matter. The pendulum swing of MORLS's statements was no longer in control of the mechanism that had been set in motion around Imphal, and the course of events had run far ahead of the question of Malik's presence or absence.

NONE OF THIS made any difference to me. What I had to say about Leela to a distant foreign audience had been entered into my machine and processed as neat rows of typed words, whited out in places where I thought they verged too close to what I really felt about her. The story was finished, if not complete, and the rumblings of troop convoys or the uneasy rumors in the valley about a deal between Naga insurgents and the Indian government would not influence me or what I had written. My bags were packed, and the finished article had been xeroxed by Sanat to provide a couple of extra sets. He had also bought me a ticket on a bus going to Silchar the next day, and from there I would catch a flight to Calcutta, where I could either resume my old life or begin a new, uncertain state of freedom.

I spent some time with Meghen on my last day in Imphal, walking around the town with him, letting him show me what he regarded as its important features. These included friends of his gathered around their two-wheelers, an old temple devoted to Krishna, and a man standing on one leg at a little public square near a cinema hall. His other leg, bent at the knee, was resting on the shin of the first leg. "They make the shape of the number four," Meghen informed me with a professorial air. This was clearly the sight he had been saving for me till the very end. "He is a drug dealer selling heroin, which goes by the name Number Four in the region." The drug dealer, an unshaven man of indeterminate ethnicity, looked at us without blinking or changing his posture, his attitude that of an ascetic who was suffering serious penance and couldn't be bothered by the trivial concerns of more worldly creatures. Meghen was unable to tell me how the terminology had come into being and if *1, 2,* and *3* stood for even more potent drugs. We left when the dealer began scowling at us and started hopping around, his initial patience quite exhausted by our prolonged scrutiny.

I RETURNED TO the hotel to find a message waiting for me. Robiul had called and said he would try again. I waited for his call, aware of the news being broadcast on the television downstairs, the hotel quite empty apart from Sanat and me. When I heard Robiul's familiar falsetto once more, I felt as if I had indeed come full circle.

"You are finished, Amrit? Of course, I had heard reports of your excellent progress."

"From whom, Robiul?"

He avoided the question.

"In and out quickly. Without complications. That was my earlier recommendation to you. Now I am suggesting you make a small detour, one further trip, up to the border."

"Too far, Robiul."

I knew he was surprised by my terse response. He began stuttering, apologizing for not being in touch for so long, speaking of difficulties with his position working for the Marwari trading agency. I didn't want him to think that I was ungrateful for his help, but I couldn't tell him why I was reluctant to make that one extra trip. I was afraid—afraid of new complications, afraid of losing what I'd gained, the knowledge of Leela that let me hold on to some semblance of achievement and success. Lying in the hotel room, with the typewriter packed away and the article finished, I possessed a sense of equilibrium for the first time since setting out on this journey, and I did not want to ruin it with further thought or action.

This state of calm was precarious, I knew that: when I cashed the last of my traveler's checks earlier in the day, I realized I had barely enough money left for the hotel bills and transportation back to Calcutta. The advance fee from the German magazine had run out in Kohima, and I didn't know if there would be anything for me at the *Sentinel*. All I had to show for this attempt was a suspension order, an article that perhaps wouldn't make it into the magazine—and what Herman the German would have called a life-affirming experience.

"Yes, you have gone further than most, Amrit. Very far. Still, I had thought—given your obstinacy and your refusal to turn back—that you would want to meet Leela."

I looked out at the highway, at the dark outline of the mountains wedged against the sky. What could I possibly say to Leela if I met her?

"There is a man waiting for you in Moreh. If you can show up within the next few days, he will get in touch with certain people. He will then take you to see Leela, and she will be able to answer your questions for about an hour. The man's name is Yaima, and he will be at the Sunrising Club, quite easy to find, right next to the Bank Republic. You follow me? She is now living with Burma dissidents who operate from the Indian side of the border. Pro-democracy activists of Aung San Suu Kyi. Many are doctors, you see, so they provided medical care for Leela. They have agreed to let you visit for an hour. No longer than that."

"How did you do all this while sitting so far away?"

"Ah, I had said I would help. But the matter was made more urgent by your suspension from *Sentinel*. Sarkar even called me to find out if I had seen you around. You have burned your bridges, it seems, Amrit."

"These bridges have a way of burning themselves."

"That is what I thought when I broke my long-standing ties to the paper. Better this way, I said to myself, better a break with the past, but then I realized the new bridge that I had planned to take toward the future didn't exist, and so I was marooned on an island, unable to proceed in any direction. That is why I would have been happier if you had turned back to Calcutta when you met me, and I tried hard to convince you not to proceed further when I found the flights had been canceled. It seemed like a sign to me, but you insisted and pushed on, and before you knew it, your life had changed. So then I thought, since you have no choice, why should you not finish the story? Hear what she has to say, tell the people what she looks like, how she is coping with the tumultuous events in her life. You are destined to meet, I think."

I didn't know what to do after talking to Robiul. Do we always want to finish a story, or do we prefer to stop at a point where the story still makes sense to us? In every way, Imphal had seemed to be the end of the line, and here was Robiul nudging me further, pushing me off the map. In Moreh, among the Burmese activists, Leela would be a stranger to me, as remote as when she first appeared in the office morgue, and to find her in person would be to lose her all over again. These were my thoughts, and yet I found myself picking up the article, wondering how I would change the story when I met her, and before I knew it, I was taking the stairs to tell Sanat to cancel the ticket to Silchar.

"I'm going to Moreh for a day," I said in response to his incredulous look.

"Don't want to leave Manipur, hah?" he said sardonically. "It happens to everyone. Look at me. Holed up in a hotel with my one guest. Don't worry about the bill. I'll hold a ticket for you on the bus to Silchar a couple of days from now. You might need to stay one night in Moreh if they close the highway off early. So, Moreh? Have fun. Good luck, good shopping, but be careful out there in Burma."

• 3 •

The rickshaw driver taking me to the makeshift taxi stand was muffled up against the early morning cold, but he kept turning around to look at me. "Taxis for Moreh. Taxi stand, Moreh," I repeated, thinking that he was unsure of my destination but didn't want to take his scarf off in order to ask me questions. He nodded, but when we reached a slight downhill stretch, he stopped pedaling and straightened up on his seat, letting the rickshaw glide along on the wide road approaching the fort. He moved the scarf aside and turned around, so that I had a clear view of his face, heavily pockmarked and tapering off in a wispy beard that trembled in the wind.

"From Delhi?" he asked, and I nodded in affirmation. It was as good an answer as any. His eyes surveyed me sadly and then he pointed hesitantly at my beard; he wanted to know if I was a Muslim. I shook my head, but he didn't seem to be disappointed. With the mask off and the first words already spoken, he was determined to continue the conversation. From his halting statements, made between quick glances to the front to see that the rickshaw was proceeding in a straight line, it was possible to gather that he was a Manipuri Muslim, one of a very small number in the state. He wanted to know if I had seen the Jama Masjid in Delhi, and when I told him I had, he asked me to describe it to him. His face became furrowed in concentration as I told him about the mosque, his rickshaw quite forgotten even as the road began sloping upward. He listened like a man entranced as I, nominally a Sikh and by belief an atheist, described to him the glory of the Jama Masjid and the bazaar surrounding it, with kites fluttering above the minarets, riding on wafts of wind that bore the smell of Karim's kebabs from the alleyway in which his restaurant was located. When I'd finished, the rickshaw had long since come to a halt by the side of the road, its momentum exhausted by the indifference of the driver.

He didn't want any money when we reached the taxi stand, but he did adjust the scarf around his face, becoming a masked rider once more.

The drivers of the taxis were in no hurry. There weren't enough passengers to fill up a van, and I couldn't afford to hire one on my own, so I could either stay till more people showed up, or catch the local bus—heading for Moreh in a few minutes. The rickshaw driver, who had waited, took me to the spot where the bus would halt to pick up more passengers.

Unlike the vans, the bus was packed, and I had to make my way through the empty suitcases, bags, and baskets piled along the aisle. They would be full on the way back, after people had finished buying Chinese battery inverters, foreign brand-name clothes, and foreign sneakers at the markets along the border: many of the mostly female passengers appeared to be employees of small businesses, given the errand of picking up supplies. A young man who moved up to let me sit next to him was the one exception, dressed like a fashionable college student in new jeans and shiny leather jacket, and he looked at me with frank curiosity.

The sun was rising over the rice fields, but it was still chilly and the windows were shut; most of the passengers dozed in their shawls. The initial flat stretch of road bisecting the farm plots had given way to a mountain track curling around slopes that were thick with shrubs and trees, the plants exploding in a profusion of yellows and reds. It wasn't that far from Imphal to

Moreh, the border point where the highway starting from the refinery town finally petered out, but there was no telling when we would get there, and there were convoys of large trucks, roving foot patrols, and a series of checkpoints to be negotiated en route.

I still had Robiul's note, his list of government forces operating along the final stretch from Palel to Moreh — 1 Army, Assam Rifles, BSF, Customs, Manipur Rifles, Manipur Police, and Manipur Excise — and each unit had its little hut and signboard and barrier and uniformed personnel. Just before Palel, the bus came to a halt next to an open wooden shelter. The passengers, more awake now, took the opportunity to sit by the road, catching the morning sun, while my youthful fellow passenger gestured at me to join him. He was throwing stones, tossing them into a ridge of trees wedged between two slopes. The highway was visible on the slope opposite, quite empty of any traffic. There was a checkpoint somewhere in between, the young man said during a brief pause in his stone-throwing. We were waiting for other traffic from Imphal to catch up with us because the army liked to check vehicles in groups rather than individually; they claimed that it was safer for everyone to travel in a convoy, but it was really to make their work easier, he said.

The sun had flooded the area ahead of us with an even blue light, and I could see flat rice fields beyond the hills and forests, an open stretch of land fading into a pale horizon. "Golden Valley, Burma," the young man said, throwing stones with greater vigor as a couple of older men joined him in his pursuit. "Burma now, but not always. It was all ours when we were a kingdom. But Nehru gave it away to the Burmese. Now we have nothing." He stopped his stone-throwing abruptly, as if he had realized the futility of his efforts. Slightly before we reached Palel, he got off the bus, turning once to wave at me before he disappeared into the forest.

GOLDEN VALLEY, a fairy-tale name, an enigma like Leela, was occasionally visible in the distance before it slipped away and left me with the squalid wounds of my immediate surroundings. In Palel, where passengers separated carefully into hotels advertising themselves as Hindu, Muslim, and Christian, the owner of the nondescript tea stall I stepped into talked of hearing gunfire in the hills the night before. He thought it had something to do with the man who had been kidnapped and killed; he had often seen the Director driving by in his project jeep, looking—in his words—like a king. The traffic had grown heavier with daylight, and there were many trucks heading the other way, toward Imphal, logs protruding from tarpaulin sheets tightly lashed at the back. The wood was Burma teak, the tea stall owner explained, and each mile away from the forests added more value to the timber that was logged. Of course, it was illegal, he said, but the Burmese military and government agencies on this side made good money from it.

There were police and customs officials strolling through the maze of parked trucks, and some rushed toward a bus that had arrived from Moreh, crammed with people bound for Imphal. Many passengers had television sets or music systems balanced on their knees; sacks of rice had been stuffed under the seats and along the aisle, and colorful umbrellas were suspended from the ceiling, due to lack of space elsewhere. A fat woman in the uniform of the customs department, her feet encased in rubber slippers, boarded the bus with difficulty. She helped herself to one of the umbrellas, while a knot of policemen waited near the driver for their fee to let the bus pass.

The passengers sat calmly while the harassed-looking driver bargained with them to produce the cash. "Fifteen rupees each," he said to his audience. No one moved, except for a woman who grabbed a case of beer cans back from the fat customs woman. "Ten each?" the driver asked hopefully, addressing a man in dark glasses and long sideburns sitting near the door, who did not deign to reply. Eventually, some of the passengers began taking out money from their purses and pockets, a collection of small notes and loose change that made its way toward the driver. The policemen shook their heads and laughed, slapping the bus a couple of times to indicate that it could move on.

It was hard not to wonder how Leela would have reacted to these sights as she made her way toward the Prosperity Project in Malik's jeep, and I attributed to her a sense of liberation at being out on the road at last, a response quite different from my own. But it was precisely these thoughts that made what lay ahead in Moreh so difficult for me. Since Kohima, I had felt as if Leela were someone I knew well, as if she were a part of my past in some inexplicable way. That we should have been in Delhi at the same time, searching in our own different ways for a foothold in the world, brought her close to me. Too old for fantasy, I still found it impossible not to wonder if our lives would have been different if we had met, but all of this was now threatened by the encounter arranged for me by Robiul.

The bus bumped on toward Moreh, circling the slopes cautiously. I had a glimpse of armed men in camouflage at a clearing in the forest, but it was impossible to tell if they were a government unit or an insurgent outfit. My sense of unease deepened as I considered the woman I would be talking to in Moreh, someone who had Leela's name and personal history but was, for all practical purposes, far removed from the character I had built up over the past month.

I had nothing to say to her, I realized. The journalist's questions I would pose to her could convey little of how her story had become so central to my life and the extent to which I had come to believe I knew her, and I felt a brief flaring of anger at Robiul for having talked me into this. He was right; I had changed since setting out from his city, and so had my goals. I did not want to find, on meeting this woman, that she was not after all the person I had created in my mind, that she was frivolous or stupid or shallow or simply inept.

There was an insistent tapping at my window, and I looked out to see that the bus had stopped again. It wasn't a checkpoint—merely a spot with a few shacks visible ahead where a track branched off the highway and crossed a stretch of fallow land before disappearing into a line of trees—and the tapping at my window came from a knot of young men with open cans. There were others dispersed along the side of the bus, and a particularly large group gathered near the driver's window. The men gesticulating at me had a blankness in their eyes, a way of not really seeing even when they were seemingly looking directly at me. Some were no more than teenagers, dressed in patchwork clothes much too big for them, restless figures pressing leaflets against the window and rattling the coins in their cans.

They moved around too quickly for me to read the leaflets clearly, but all were requests for money, appeals made in the name of unheard of organizations: churches, social groups, political parties, and sporting clubs. I took some coins out of my wallet and began to slide the window up. The youth outside grew excited and held his tin higher, but the man sitting next to me reached out swiftly and slammed the glass down, nearly catching the boy's fingers. The figures on the road became frenzied, hammering on the bus and pressing their faces against the glass. I looked back at the man beside me, and he gestured at the other passengers, all of whom had their windows shut, and were avoiding making eye contact with the men outside, even as the tapping became an insistent banging and pounding of fists, and the bus jerked ahead with a blare of its horn. There were a couple of cars behind us, and the crowd raced toward these, blocking their progress with flailing arms and sticks. The bus picked up speed, and I saw more young men coming out of the shacks, gazing at the highway with that blank look in their eyes.

As we passed the road branching off from the highway, I saw the sign, faded but distinct: "Welcome to the Prosperity Project. That brings hope where none was to be found." As the bus picked up speed, the sign blurred, but there were other such signs ahead, some looking relatively new. There were more shacks, an occasional fire in the open land just beyond the highway, and many ragged figures charging toward the bus and jumping away at the very last minute when it became clear to them that the driver wouldn't take his foot off the accelerator. For nearly ten minutes I watched this play between prosperity and its opposite, between the promise of it and the reality, and when the road began climbing and the open land gave way to the hard walls of the mountain, I heaved a sigh of relief and began to think of Leela once again.

CHAPTER ELEVEN

❖ 1 ❖

There were a few surprises waiting for me in Moreh when I got in around noon—the bus having taken over four hours to cover the distance between Imphal and Moreh. The Sunrising Club was closed, and a handwritten sign pasted on the door announced that Yaima, general secretary of the club, had left for Palel because of a family emergency. There was nothing about me, although the note did state that the carrom competition scheduled for that weekend had been postponed indefinitely. I also discovered, almost immediately, that there were no buses or vans going back to Imphal that day.

The guard outside the Bank Republic, an old Nepali sitting with a Lee-Enfield across his knees, had been watching me with interest as I read the sign; when I turned away, he told me there was a curfew in Imphal because of some disturbances there. He couldn't give me the details, but there had been a demonstration and perhaps some firing from the police, and bank staff had just been told about it by their head office in Imphal.

The news of the violence didn't affect me at all. My mind was elsewhere, caught up in a nagging sense of frustration that I had come all this way for nothing. If I had been on the bus to Silchar, it would have been easy enough to let my mind play with the images it had of Leela, each mile away from the region fixing her more firmly for me. But she remained in flux as long as I had to be in Moreh; it was too difficult to be content with what I knew of her — or what I thought I knew of her — when she could be here, perhaps no more than a few feet away from me.

I looked around, hoping to see her. There were trucks everywhere, parked deep in the slush of the town, blocking the entrances to shacks and buildings crowded along the alley-ways. I felt utterly abandoned as I watched the truckers trudging through the mud, the buyers and sellers going about their business without faltering. I should make a phone call, I thought when I saw an STD booth tucked away between a couple of restaurants, but I didn't know who I wanted to call. Instead I made my way to the bus service counter, and when they confirmed the Nepali guard's news, I began walking without a clear sense of where to go.

The town was busy, seemingly unaffected by the disruption of traffic or the trouble in Imphal. I hadn't grasped the layout of the town, but knew I was close to the border gates leading to Tamu. The alleys were narrow, their width further reduced by the trucks parked on both sides, and I bumped into people as I walked, evoking protests and complaints. I didn't care, and when I roughly shouldered past a man who had stood his ground, people began to give way in front of me. The street became narrower still. I saw a stream of faces passing by as in a dream, and almost expected to recognize Leela at any moment as she stepped out of a doorway, except that the

pedestrians were mostly men, a mix of Kukis, Burmese, Meiteis, and Tamilians intent on their errands. A man standing
against a wall put out a hand toward me as I passed, and when
I turned to look at him, I saw a northern build and face much
like mine, except there was a gaping hole above his mouth: his
entire nose was missing, probably eaten away by syphilis. I
slapped his hand away and kept going.

The lane led into a marketplace that resembled a Calcutta
fish market, with raised concrete platforms for the vendors.
But instead of the fish and the large open blades I would have
found in Calcutta, there were consumer goods displayed, an
array of electronic items, sneakers, and cigarette cartons that
seemed markedly incongruous in that old-fashioned setting,
with bare lightbulbs strung from overhead wooden beams and
shallow gutters running along the passageway. There was the
steady hum of bargaining voices, with sharp cries of competing prices rising above the monotone as I walked past the stalls
and sellers tried to catch my attention.

Before I knew it, I was out of the market area, standing on
an unbuilt stretch of land next to a metaled road, blinking as I
tried to adjust to the sunlight. Ahead of me was a border gate,
security booths on either side, and a metal barrier lowered
over the road. I kept going, trying to make out what lay beyond the gate, expecting a mirror image to be reflected back at
me, showing me the outlines of a Burmese town virtually indistinguishable from Moreh.

It wasn't like that, though. The area beyond the gate consisted of an open network of fields and irrigation canals, the
road becoming wider and heading for a row of trees on the
horizon. There were some vans parked just beyond the Burmese guard post, but few other signs of activity. As I drew

closer, I could see horse carriages next to the Toyota vans; the reins of a horse jingled softly as it shook its head, and smoke from a cigarette drifted up from the outstretched hand of a coachman lying on his back.

I stepped up to the booth of the Indian border guard, who handed me a form to fill out and a receipt for the five-rupee fee required to cross into Burma, hurrying me through the process because other people were waiting behind me. "Don't buy anything in Burma," he said as he waved me on.

"Why?" a man behind me asked in a querulous voice.

"They won't let you bring anything back," the guard said, pointing over his shoulder. A burly Tamilian in a purple shirt and blue jeans had been lying on a bench behind the guard.

He sat up, yawned, and began picking his teeth. "It's bad for business on this side," he said, still picking his teeth. "Buy from our market. If you bring anything across, we'll throw it into the river."

"But you charge higher prices," the man behind me complained.

"Only a few rupees extra. And you just pay it if you want to go home with your nice things."

I didn't hear any more because I had reached the Burmese guard, a man in reflector sunglasses and bush hat who wanted to know if I had a camera with me. He looked at the slip his Indian counterpart had handed me and gave a slight nod of his head to indicate that I could continue. The men behind had caught up, and the one with the querulous voice approached the Burmese guard. I recognized him and his two companions now. It was Glaxo, Pfizer, and Hoechst, all of them carrying large duffel bags. "Sir? They will not let us buy goods from your country," Glaxo said to the guard. "This is disgraceful. You must do something."

The man looked at Glaxo without saying a word. "No Hindi," he finally said in a tone of such contempt that Glaxo was silenced and Hoechst and Pfizer began walking away immediately.

They spotted me as we approached the vans and the horse carriages, and little shouts of jubilation broke out as if we were meeting for a picnic we had arranged way back in Joseph's hotel. "Such a long time since our last encounter," Glaxo said, smiling widely, all his difficulties with the Tamilian instantly forgotten.

"Here to sell medicines?" They looked nonplussed for a moment and then began laughing very hard, Pfizer and Hoechst slapping each other on the back.

"Not here, sir, no, not in Burma," Glaxo said. "That is unfortunately not part of our selling territory, though no doubt people need medicines here as well. No, this is a simple shopping expedition. But in Manipur we have sold more drugs for cerebral malaria than in the rest of the entire country. I am sure there is very high incidence of cerebral malaria outbreaks on this side of the border also."

Pfizer and Hoechst nodded in the background, looking sober for a fleeting moment. It was not a time for serious matters, however; all three were wearing T-shirts and jeans instead of their usual salesmen's clothes and bright ties, exhibiting the air of men who had worked hard in a good cause and were now determined to enjoy their leisure. I let Glaxo bargain with the van driver about the ride to Tamu, and once everyone had settled on a price, I clambered into the back of the open van with them. The salesmen chattered on enthusiastically, but I didn't pay any attention as the road became busier and the huts gave way to shops and concrete buildings.

My first foreign country, I thought, as I saw the outline of a pagoda on a hilltop, visited in such a strange manner, and that too only because there were no buses running in what was supposed to be my own country. My sailor father would have been disappointed it had taken me so long, and that this was the furthest I had managed to come in all these years.

Tamu was not a mirror image of Moreh. It was a place with straight metaled streets and traffic lights, with modern-looking shops displaying their goods behind glass showcases. There were hotels, teahouses, and air-conditioned bars everywhere, their neon signs flashing out names and rates. The pharmaceutical salesmen could barely contain themselves, and began quarreling noisily about which shops to visit first.

"What about the Tamilian waiting for you at the border gate?" I asked as I got out of the van.

Glaxo gave me a canny laugh and rubbed his paunch. "We will not use that gate to return."

"There might be others elsewhere waiting to check your bags," I said, playing the spoiler.

Glaxo shook his head, and his accompanying chorus spoke out from behind. "We anticipated the problem."

Glaxo leaned toward me. "You should do the same, Mr. Singh. We will wait till it is nearly five, when the border gates close. There is so much commotion then, with so many people crossing over because they do not want to be trapped here at night without the proper papers."

"They will never have time to look at our bags," Pfizer and Hoechst said, and burst out laughing.

❖ 2 ❖

I was a stranger in Tamu, but I set off as if I knew exactly where I was going, following the highway until I had left the main street with its shops and hotels far behind. What I saw around me now was still a very modern town, but the buildings became more widely spaced out as I progressed, with gardens or open fields in between. In the distance, I could make out a low line of hills, their pale blue form speckled with yellow pagodas. The sun on my back was strong and my shirt stuck to my body as I kept walking. An occasional car or motorbike went by, but the highway was sleepy and quiet in the afternoon heat, barely touched by the faint breeze rustling through the gardens.

It was like being in a dream, with no way of measuring time and distance apart from the fact that when I looked at the hills again, they seemed to be a little closer. I could tell too that what had initially appeared to be a string of separate pagodas was actually a kind of temple complex on top of the highest hill, with buildings of different sizes, some topped with brightly painted concertina roofs that glimmered in the sun.

I kept going. When I grew tired and thirsty, I stopped at a small teahouse by the highway. The other customers were all Burmese, and after taking a quick glance at me as I entered, they ignored me, and I sat on the verandah instead of joining them. Everything was very clean, with touches that suggested a place designed with Western tourists in mind. But there were no tourists in Tamu to appreciate the James Dean poster framed on the wall, and the Burmese men inside the shop played cards or talked in low voices or dozed in their chairs. A young woman in a long yellow skirt came and placed water, tea, and a tray of savories on the table. When I had finished, she took the Indian hundred-rupee note I'd put on the table and returned with change, a collection of Burmese notes that included denominations of fifteen and ninety, with portraits of sinister-looking generals on them.

As soon as I felt refreshed, I left. Some instinct must have been guiding me, because I saw few places to get a drink after that; the land around the highway was quite bare, and dust rose off the fields in gray plumes as the wind grew stronger and a few dark clouds stained the sky. A flight of steps became visible far to the right of the hill, ascending steeply toward the pagoda complex. I left the highway, following a narrow road that seemed to skirt the base of the hill while, on the other side, the land dipped down to form a large depression, a bungalow with a garden located at its center. Apart from the wire fence ringed all around it, the bungalow looked like the teahouse I had been in a while ago, but no customers were visible.

A tall metal gate stood where the fence met the road, a sign hanging over it in the form of an arch. "Golden Valley Tea House," it said, but the paint was peeling in many places, and the padlock on the gate was rusted. I was drawn to the place in spite of its deserted air, and when I found a gap in the fence, I slipped in after a quick look around. The going was hard because of the weeds, puddles, and piles of refuse in the garden, but eventually I reached the wooden stairs leading up to the verandah of the bungalow.

They sagged heavily as I went up, and I found the verandah littered with empty Coke cans and bottles of Tiger beer. Old Burmese newspapers had been pasted over missing panes in the window, and the place smelt of rats. Back down the stairs I could see a Japanese garden on the other side of the bungalow, with bonsai plants and a little wooden bridge crossing a small stream. Whoever had arranged it had taken pains with the details. There were small pagodas, boats tied to the banks, and toy soldiers in the grass.

Water had collected in large patches on the ground, and the grass had grown tall and wild, so that the soldiers looked as if they were struggling through a tropical jungle. I don't know if it was my imagination, but it seemed as if a scene from the Second World War had been carefully arranged around the bridge, with Japanese soldiers in forage caps to one side, British Tommies and American GIs on the other. There were civilian toys too on the Japanese side, a column of refugees with carts and children and horses, and a toy mule being urged on by a family of four. I felt quite sick, overwhelmed by cramps in my stomach as if something I had eaten in the teahouse had not agreed with me, and I splashed through the small stream to rest in the shade of the bungalow until I felt better.

The last thing I saw before turning away from the war scene was the three British soldiers who looked as if they were approaching the couple with the children and the mule, wading through the tall grass as they converged on their prey.

THE SUN HAD NOT MOVED when I opened my eyes, and I knew I couldn't have passed out for very long. The man bending over me was Burmese, his eyes magnified by thick glasses. He smelt of alcohol, and he held a bottle of beer toward me, making little encouraging sounds that indicated I should drink. He sat on his haunches with a smile on his lips while I sipped the beer, but he wasn't looking at me. When I'd finished, he straightened up, a short, slightly overweight man in a white shirt and a checked blue *lungi*.

"Inj'an?"

I hesitated.

He smiled at me, pointed at himself, and said, "Writer. Nobel."

"Nobel?" What Nobel? There are no Nobel laureates around here, I thought, wondering what had brought him to this deserted spot.

"Nobels," he repeated, looking annoyed. "Forty-eight no-bels. Writer."

I understood and was duly impressed, and the Burmese writer of forty-eight novels expanded on his talents.

"Filmmaker. Documentaries. Artist. Dissident." He swept an arm around the verandah to illustrate.

It was three o'clock by my watch. "I must return to the gate before five," I said.

He nodded and pointed to the bungalow. "We will go around from the back entrance."

I decided not to extend the conversation, grateful as I was for his drink. I reached for my bag and saw that Robiul's en-velope was sticking out of the book I'd tucked it into, suggest-ing the filmmaker had rifled through my bag while I was unconscious.

"Yes. Reporter, I assume," the filmmaker said, looking at me very gravely and suddenly speaking in a crisp accent. He reached into the pocket of his shirt and took out the photo-graph of Leela surrounded by the MORLS guards. His gaze was distant and sad as he spoke to me. "Leela, and that man who told us his name was Malik. The Prosperity Project." He looked at me and said, "Come. We will sit inside. A long story, but I will make it a short version for you. Before the border gate at five."

I followed him as he climbed down the stairs and made his way toward the back of the bungalow.

• 3 •

I never quite caught the filmmaker's name in spite of the long conversation I had with him, and although it was supplied to me subsequently by others, it seemed an insignificant detail. Freed from the exigencies of the article with which I had once associated all my hopes, freed from the constraints of being a journalist, I was no longer perturbed by such trifles as name and occupation, all those basic biographical details intended to nail a source down to his or her statements. The Burmese filmmaker was not a source from which my story could originate but a whirlpool into which the images and stories and characters I had collected could be abandoned, a final destination that promised nothing more than the complete silence of an anonymous repository.

Enough was communicated, though, for me to grasp the pattern of his life, especially at the points where it overlapped with that of Leela's, and I wondered what brought me to his abandoned outpost in the town of Tamu to listen to his account.

He led me around the garden and into the bungalow through a narrow door giving access to a small passageway, bathroom, and kitchen. The teahouse had belonged to a man suspected of dissident activities, the filmmaker said; it had been shut down just a few months ago by the military government. He himself had moved in only a month or so ago, picking out a small room at the back for his den while leaving the remainder of the restaurant intact.

The place no longer had any electricity, but the kerosene lantern he lit revealed both the original character of the teahouse as well as its present state of ruin. The bamboo tables and chairs were still in place, with the tea crusted over in delicate little china cups. There were lacquered trays on some of the tables, but the food on the trays had been picked clean and rat droppings left in exchange. Cobwebs filled the corners and hung from the ceiling next to the posters and prints, while the floor was layered with dust that revealed the meandering footprints of the filmmaker and the smaller but more numerous tracks of the rats.

There was one empty table in the front, near the boarded entrance, and this appeared cleaner than the rest. It was to this that the filmmaker invited me with a certain ceremonious air, brushing crumbs from the table and opening two bottles of warm beer. Then he bowed and sat down and handed the photograph back to me. He kept the lamp turned low, but his face was quite clearly visible in its light, the flame reflected in his thick lenses as if his eyes were on fire from the intensity of his recollections.

He did not live in the abandoned teahouse, he told me, but on the outskirts of Tamu with his sister. "Over there, beyond the hill," he said. "No choice in the matter. The government wants me where it can keep me under observation, although I slip away every now and then." He was their man almost all of the time, and there was even a strong possibility that he would end up making a propaganda film for them, he said. This hideout was the only place where he could display his real self, usually with no audience other than the rats and the toys.

"Funny, do you not think, that I can have subversive thoughts — dissident thoughts — here? In this teahouse the military think is cleansed of all subversive activities?" It was the only way to live in the region, he went on rapidly. "To conceal surfaces under other surfaces is necessary," he said. That, he had come to understand, was how governments operated, and to deceive them it was necessary to have a mask of one's own. He pointed to the roof to illustrate his point, but he was referring to the pagoda complex on the hill above us. "Go to the pagoda. You will see a monastery, yes, and monks in saffron, yes, and even shrines with the Buddhas glowing in fog of incense, yes. All of it a front for the military." The complex functioned as a collection center for the government and headquarters for intelligence operatives. It had been sited carefully on the hill so as to block the view of the military airport below. I must not be fooled by appearances, he said earnestly. Even the town was quite fake.

He had memories of Tamu from an earlier time, when it had been a real place, a messy and anarchic frontier town where dissidents, insurgents, and smugglers collected to work on their discrete projects. Only the big smugglers remained now, he said, working with the patronage of the government. The dissidents and insurgents were gone, either in prisons or holed up across the border. The government had moved out the local Kuki populations, expelled most of the Tamilians and Nepalis, and brought in people who could be trusted. They had razed the old structures to the ground and put up the fake Tamu I was seeing now, a tourist town to which no tourists ever came and where every fifth person seen on the street was working for the military government.

"Filth," he said violently. "Under the cleanness, heaps of

filth. This place, Golden Valley Tea House, is more honest. What you see is what is. Not like the rest of Tamu. No more Golden Valley, only filth." This was how power was retained, he said, by creating fake towns and societies and projecting attractive images that concealed what lay beneath, and how well this worked he had come to understand by being with Malik. But he was getting ahead of himself; he had to explain to me how he had arrived in India and ended up with Malik.

HE HAD BEEN a filmmaker and writer, making a small name for himself with his novels. Not all of them were good, he confessed shyly. "Popular nobels, romance, lobe," he said dismissively. "But they attracted money that could be used to finance political art, dissident art." He often worked on these popular romances two at a time, and when he was done with them, he would turn to a documentary project or novel intended to expose the regime and uncover Burma's history. The past was clearly visible in the workings of the Burmese military state, he said, and in his serious writings he had often referred to Burma's colonial past and the subsequent Japanese invasion. In those days, when he walked around Tamu, the old war was still present in the pockmarked buildings of the town and the graves of Japanese and Allied soldiers on the hillsides, and children playing in the forests sometimes came across artillery shells. He liked being able to explore the connections between the modern military state and its precursory colonial regimes, and he had hoped that when these connections became evident to all, the people would rise against their masters.

The expected rising did not happen. Instead, a massive crackdown took place, catching him and the other dissidents by surprise. They had thought the regime was beginning to lose its grip; it had done little to curb political activities in recent times, and there were rumors that General Ne Win, head of the State Law and Order Restoration Committee, was getting old and feeble, and that his underlings had sensed the end of his rule. When the soldiers and police arrived, many of the dissidents, taken unawares, were easily rounded up from teahouses and clubs. The military targeted the Kuki and Karen insurgent groups as well, smashing their jungle camps and executing leaders on the spot. The filmmaker made it across the border just in time, slipping into Moreh through an unmonitored passage in an old graveyard.

He sighed and took off his glasses, polishing them with a corner of his shirt. "Escaped from SLORC. Went to India. To land of democracy." He made it sound as if democracy were a topographical feature like a mountain or river. He had expected to be free, and had intended to go all the way to Delhi, where he had heard of a socialist trade union leader who let Burmese dissidents stay in his house. But when he made further inquiries, he found out that the socialist had turned right-wing, and the filmmaker became too unsure of himself to make such a long journey after that. Twice he went to the train station with a ticket the dissident network had bought for him. Both times he stood helplessly on the platform, panic-stricken at the thought of being cooped up in the train with strangers, watching the carriages inching forward with a heavy clanking of wheels as he stayed wrapped in his misery, aware of how short he had fallen of his conception of the artist as an activist. "Hollowed out," he said, rubbing his chest.

So he drifted, spending time in Moreh, in Imphal and Dimapur and Kohima and Shillong, a foreigner among foreigners, although the Indian soldiers who made him squat on the road and strip to his underwear did not distinguish between his face and that of the Indian hill tribals. It was a sign of his freedom that no one any longer understood who he was. The person he had been bore no relationship to the life he led in India, where his efforts were mostly concentrated on finding occasional odd jobs and living off the reluctant kindness of strangers. He had hoped to return to making films and writing, he said, just as he had thought he would take up the cause of Burmese democracy with the help of Indian comrades. But there was no way for him to insert himself into the complicated politics of the Indian states, and neither his novels nor his dissident politics could be translated into the lexicon of the region through which he floated like a ghost.

He walked up and down the dark tearoom smoking a Burmese cheroot, appearing very much like a ghost in his white shirt, vanishing behind the counter momentarily as if intending to take orders for tea and then changing his mind and floating back toward me through the smoke. He had felt disembodied, even though he became bloated from the cheap liquor he drank whenever he had the money. He hated the smugness of the Indians he encountered, their self-involvement and their ignorance about his abilities, and he detested the other Burmese he met on his travels. Even when they helped him out, it was always in an atmosphere of sour distrust. Now when he looked back at it, he did not blame them. His ties to the organization to restore democracy had been loose, and since the crackdown, many former dissidents had become government agents, sent out to infiltrate the network. But he was incapable of thinking with such clarity at that time; he had been in despair and yet held on to some semblance of hope, and this was a state of being in which he could not think properly. "Now I have no hope, and so I can see things clearly as they are. It is like this." He gestured at the tearoom we sat in. "All quite dark, some light here and there, a room to rest in, a few hours of free thoughts, memories."

He remembered getting off night buses in strange Indian towns often under a curfew. Even the barking of the dogs sounded foreign to him as he stumbled along in the cold, still half-asleep from the bus ride, so that the pine trees bleached white by the moonlight seemed like some blurred landscape from his disturbed dreams. He would knock on the door of an unknown house with a sinking feeling, listening to the invariable whispers and murmurs inside before he received a cautious response, knowing that even after the passwords and common names had been confirmed by the muffled figure at the door, the only welcome he could expect consisted of a cold bed and grudging acceptance.

"It was like dying," he said. "And like a dying man, one is possessed by delusions in such a state, fantastic images toward which one tries to crawl because they look like life as opposed to the darkness one is falling into." Although he hated other Burmese exiles and would avoid their company unless he needed money or shelter, he had begun to grow nostalgic about the country he had left behind, his treacherous memory softening the military regime's worst excesses. "The pull, the pull backward," he said, shaking his head in exasperation. And so he retraced his earlier route, but in reverse, returning to Imphal with the intention of then reentering Burma, thinking of giving himself up to the military, when he met a man who said he had a job for him.

The filmmaker seemed to have a vast supply of beer in his

inner room; he had been fetching bottles periodically to replenish our stock, and the table by now had become overrun by empty bottles. He pulled one of the other tables toward us to create an additional surface, adding its little china cups and plates to our vast confusion of beer bottles, so that the setup became vaguely reminiscent of the Mad Hatter's tea party, awaiting only a final charge from the toy soldiers to end our session. But we still had a while to go, because all he had said so far was only a preliminary to the subject closest to his heart.

◈ **1** ◈

He had heard the rumors even as he was making his way toward Imphal: of a new development project somewhere off Highway 39 that was remarkably well funded and had the support of army, politicians, and insurgents. When it was finished, it would be built of steel and glass, and there would be technically qualified staff in charge of the modern machines humming inside the clinics. No one knew where the machinery and staff were coming from, and how they would be transported along the problem-ridden highway to such a remote site, but the project was considered a certainty, and the drifters and losers the filmmaker naturally gravitated toward told him of the amazing jobs to be had from the man who ran the project. It was one of these disreputable characters who took him to meet Malik.

He hesitated before continuing, looking at me with a silent appeal that was surprising. He had been unreserved while denouncing himself, but now needed some kind of encouragement to keep talking.

"He impressed you," I said. "He made you feel less lonely. You thought you were useful once again."

"He blinded me," the filmmaker whispered. "With his intensity and his charisma and his energy. With all his talk of needing my artistic skills to do something new. He wanted me to shoot a three-minute film on his development project. I would have all the equipment and assistance I needed, he said, and although I was a hungry and lost man, I saw myself in my former guise, holding the camera, planning my shots, arranging the lighting. He was like an answer from deep within my dreams. I did not then fully understand the kind of dream he came out of."

He took out the photograph of Leela at the MORLS press conference and spent a long time looking at it, turning it over to study the caption and then returning to the picture again. "Even now, at this moment, knowing everything that I do, I cannot assure you that I would not succumb to his spell if you were to bring him in front of me again." He shuddered. "But he is dead?"

I nodded, and after a look at the darkness of the tearoom, the filmmaker went on. "I would have worked for free when he offered me the job because it was such a relief to meet a man who seemed above the usual things happening in the region, someone with knowledge and intelligence and authority, someone with a vision of a new world rising from the trampled wilderness everywhere. He was the first person I had met since the crackdown who seemed undefeated, almost a fellow-artist with his belief that it was possible to create something here."

Even though the room had been screened off from the world outside, it was possible to sense the sun beginning to set beyond the hills. I could hear a distant ringing of bells from the pagoda complex above, as if intended to signal to me that the border gates would close very soon and I would undergo some irreversible transformation if I were to stay any longer to listen to the filmmaker's disjointed story.

I must try to understand the attractions of boundless hope in an area of such hopelessness, he said. When he arrived at the project to find just a ramshackle office with an attached shack overlooking a weed-choked lake, he did not feel disappointed or perturbed. He was introduced to two other men and shown into the shack, where there was a new xerox machine. When he was told about the counterfeiting project he would be working on temporarily, he remained convinced it was all in a good cause. Malik said he intended to break the deadlock between the Indian government and its insurgents, and the filmmaker thought he would learn something useful as an apprentice. Painting the security threads into Indian currency notes one by one, he reasoned that he would be able to take this expertise to the other side of the border and so weaken the general whose face was portrayed on Burmese notes.

The largely empty project office and the shack where he and his colleagues turned out the fake notes appeared to be the beginning of something grand. Why else would army officers, government officials, and insurgent leaders come to visit, holding long discussions in the afternoon with Malik, shaking hands vigorously as they took leave of the Director of the Prosperity Project? He saw evidence of money, real money, in the new jeep Malik and his local assistants drove around in, in the phone line installed in the office, and in the Pentax camera Malik handed him one day. He was asked to take photographs that would accompany a report to be sent to funding agencies in Delhi and in foreign countries. They needed to be given a sense of the scale of the project, and his film expertise was required.

The project was yet but a dream, Malik said, but surely a filmmaker and a writer of forty-eight novels was capable of capturing a dream? First the dream, the idea, the vision, the desire; then, from the sheer force of the conception, a reality that would become undeniable, sending a message across the region that the previous stalemates had been dissolved and all the old models shattered. So the filmmaker took pictures of an AIDS clinic, laboratory, rehab center and classroom, even though all that really existed was a small shabby office with a bright signboard outside.

He grew agitated when I said I didn't understand. "Surfaces, I have said earlier. That was what it was about." He had worked in filmmaking in Rangoon, and knew enough to build the basic sets Malik's project required. "Plywood, tin, cardboard, paint, wires," he said scornfully. They looked real enough in the photographs he took, with MORLS insurgents playing the parts of addicts and project workers. "All a game, but a convincing one, and the reports and pictures went out to the world. Who would come here to investigate the reality behind those words and images?"

That was all there was to it: fake notes, a fake project, a false promise of prosperity. It was enough. Throughout the region the word was spreading about a man so powerful that he had befriended both army and insurgents, had built a tower of hope in the very heart of despair. People believed in the project. Junkies and AIDS patients and unemployed youth and abused women got off local buses at the fork on the highway, trudging through the wilderness along the narrow path to the

Prosperity Project where they would be admitted to its clinics and classrooms and get their share of prosperity. He saw them being turned away by the MORLS sentries, their belief in the project somehow untarnished by their rejection and the sight of the shabby building overlooking the lake. They were patient, content to believe that they were undeserving, returning with memories that convinced them they had glimpsed hope and grandeur. The more people were turned away, the more the project fed on its own myth and prospered, with rumors among the rejected about the fortunate, about those privileged enough to be admitted into the grounds and given a new life.

"It was a nightmare posing as a dream," he said. More guards were posted by MORLS as the project became well-known, and he heard that some of the hopeful strangers who had been turned away had built shacks near the highway, perhaps expecting to benefit by their very proximity to the project. A boundary constructed of false hopes and misery, while at the center of this was Malik, placing his phone calls to the project office in Imphal, planning more brochures, newsletters, announcements, and signboards, flying around state capitals collecting the applause and eager partnership of important people.

Had there been a point to the Prosperity Project beyond its success? He didn't know. He didn't understand the close cooperation of MORLS, their foot-soldiers assigned as Malik's bodyguards once he grew increasingly important. He never understood, for instance, where the money went, either the real money or the fake stuff, and why Malik was so closely involved in the cease-fire negotiations with insurgent groups in the region. He didn't know if Malik was working for the government, or MORLS, or himself, or some idea, and sometimes, sitting by himself in the abandoned teahouse, he thought Malik himself hadn't known, that he had abandoned any understanding of the plot even though he was capable of coming up with devious twists to the very end.

There was, however, one person on whom the project lost its hold as time went on, someone who grew worried at the lack of interest in accepting the medicines and materials offered by faraway organizations, someone who called from Imphal even when Malik wasn't around. Usually it was a MORLS thug who answered, speaking in monosyllables, but at least on one occasion the filmmaker spoke to Leela. She was very nice to him, but he also got the sense that she was worried. She asked questions about the project to which he could give no answers, even though he wanted to confide in her immediately and tell her: there were things bothering him too; he knew, for instance, that a reporter called Thoiba had tried to visit the project office. The MORLS guards no longer let anyone approach the project area unless they were approved by Malik, and the reporter had to be turned away at gunpoint.

The filmmaker had also heard what sounded like a quarrel between Malik and the MORLS leaders, and although this ended with laughter, he felt things were coming to a head. He had the impression that the MORLS leaders, such as they were, had become confused about the negotiations between the government and the major insurgent groups. They had at first enjoyed their liberty, free from the constraints of the cease-fire observed by other groups, and they listened to Malik willingly enough when he suggested they should play hard to get. There were great rewards waiting for them if they were the last group to join the bargaining table—but the filmmaker had no idea what these suggested rewards might have been. In fact, he was quite certain that the MORLS leaders had not known either. It could have been more guns and cash, more men, posts in the government, maybe a little country of their own, but he couldn't see them doing much more than they did for the project, lolling around and planning punitive new measures against the moral corruption of the people, carrying out occasional petty raids or forays of extortion into the countryside.

But the thought of missing out on the favors being given to other insurgent groups by the government began to make the MORLS leaders edgy. They talked about the Naga and Meitei representatives invited to Delhi as official guests, of the convoys and armed escorts and five-star-hotel accommodations given to these men, and they became discontented about their long wait. They wanted to join the negotiations, preferably after carrying out a spectacular act of violence that would demonstrate to the government and the bigger outfits that they were not a fringe group, after all. Malik held them back, and suggested a more dramatic act that would bring them attention as well as taking care of a problem with a certain worker in Imphal who had apparently become suspicious about the existence of the Prosperity Project.

The filmmaker opened a window looking out on the verandah, saying it was quite safe to do so in the dark. He leaned out over the cans and bottles and rubbish as if he were breathing in clean, refreshing sea air, and when he turned around again, he did not look at me.

"I had no courage to stop them. Neither did the men who worked on the counterfeiting operation, although they did not like what was happening. We saw them bring Leela to the project and take her into the office, and he sounded so reasonable, so avuncular and generous and concerned, as he told her that MORLS would charge her with immoral activities at a press conference. A minor punishment would be meted out to show that MORLS meant business, and no one would ever believe her after that if she said anything against the project."

They didn't worry about producing evidence. No one would challenge them or ask why a smart young woman working for a development project should be willing to work as an actress in a porn film; they would assume they hadn't known what lay beneath the surface, and that it was yet more evidence of the world they lived in—where everyone wore masks to cover the unpalatable tasks they carried out in order to carry on. Discredit the woman, and everything else falls into place, Malik explained to MORLS. It was an old, time-tested strategy, and it would work well for their plan. He took pleasure at his inventiveness, and like the director of a film giving himself a small role as an in-joke, Malik attended the press conference as a representative of civil society. He negotiated with the MORLS leaders in the presence of the local press, convincing them that they should not go ahead with their execution and instead should mete out a smaller, gentler punishment—although this had been decided by him long before the conference.

Malik's role wasn't mentioned in the local papers, but people found out anyway. The fact he had bargained with the MORLS leaders to save the life of the woman added to his aura as a man who was both kind and courageous, and his stock as a peace negotiator rose dramatically. It must have pleased him greatly to have been spoken of in this manner. What he had not anticipated—or had he?—was that the reaction to MORLS and their charge against Leela was quite different from what had been suggested. People did not appreciate a young woman being shot in the legs, nor did they care for the attitude of the group toward the negotiations. If they had no great faith left in the Indian government, they had little to spare for a group that staged such random acts of violence. The worry in the valley was that the Naga insurgents would strike a deal with the Indian government, adding Naga-inhabited parts of Manipur to an autonomous Naga state much larger than present-day Nagaland. This was not a time for a Manipuri insurgent group to stay away from the card table.

MORLS, acting under Malik's advice, said it had nothing to do with the press conference. But they began to think that Malik had been setting them up in some way, because he had come out of it very well, while they had not, and they suspected the press conference to be part of a vast conspiracy.

The filmmaker paused, looking hesitant, as if he had lost the thread of his story. "We must get going soon, so that you can get back before nightfall," he said, as if he were an old friend I had casually dropped in to see. He turned the flame higher on the kerosene lamp and asked me to follow him: he wanted to show me the room he worked in.

There was a thin mattress on the floor on one side. Bottles of beer and cheroots and packets of biscuits were piled on the floor, along with a few cheap-looking Burmese paperbacks with glossy covers. The filmmaker shook his head sadly when I asked if any of the books were by him. "I can no longer write, so I read trash." But he was working on a project of his own, and the center of the floor was occupied by paint boxes and brushes and small clay figurines like action figures.

"You put the toy soldiers in the Japanese garden?" I said.

"My last project. A history of Burma, and a story of my travels."

He hadn't got far, he said, because he worked slowly and surreptitiously. His material was simple, but buying brushes and paint too frequently could lead to questions. Besides, he had plenty of time.

"Rest of my life, unless they move me to Rangoon."

He showed me a figure that represented a younger, more hopeful version of himself, slimmer and without glasses, its left arm raised, fist clenched. He had crafted Leela too, from his brief glimpse of her when she was brought to the project and the photograph taken at the press conference. But he had given her a happy expression, not that cautious, reserved look imprinted into my memory, and there were no other figures near her, as if she deserved her own space. He was also creating a tableau around a plastic jeep, with two men in fatigues, their faces masked. "They escorted him into the jeep, hands tied behind his back, blindfolded. The other MORLS men began destroying the equipment in the office, smashing the telephone and xerox machine and firing a few rounds through the walls and the project signboard. Before the main group left on foot, they told us to get out, me and the others who had been hired by Malik, and we headed out through the forest, careful to avoid the shacks on the highway."

"Are you re-creating the Prosperity Project?"

He nodded. "Small cardboard cutout, painted to look like buildings. And the MORLS men taking him into the jeep." He pointed at the unfinished figure lying on its back.

"That's supposed to be him?"

I looked at the doll without picking it up. It was smaller than the soldiers, nondescript in its shirt and trousers, looking dead in the horizontal posture forced upon it. The filmmaker hadn't painted in Malik's face yet, only the body with very long arms, and the head was no more than a little round blob of clay, waiting for his touch to knead some life and character into it.

"I find it hard to remember his face, so I postpone," he said. "His voice I recall very well, it is always in my head, but the face eludes me constantly."

❋ 2 ❋

The street where I had been dropped off earlier by the van was quite deserted, emptied of the customers shuttled back and forth between town and border gate all day long. Some of the shops were closing, and with the shutters down and neon lights turned off, it was possible to make out the fakeness the filmmaker had talked about.

The filmmaker stayed a little ahead of me because he did not want to draw attention to us. His head was lowered and he walked steadily, moving with the slightly mincing gait of a plump man, ignoring the occasional laughter directed at him by the men drinking in front of the shops.

I felt responsible for drawing him away from Tamu, but he was adamant that his minders wouldn't miss him for a night; he had insisted on accompanying me because it was well past five and he did not want me to risk getting back on my own. It was too late for the vans to take me to the gate, he had said, and he was right. We would try a shortcut through the forests, a path used by villagers and poor people living on the outskirts of the town, and if we could avoid running into policemen or guards, it should be possible to slip across.

A motorcyclist approached from the opposite direction, on

the wrong side of the road. He was dressed in the usual Burmese outfit of shirt and *lungi,* but he was a big man riding a big motorcycle, confident of his right-of-way as he scanned the storefronts. The filmmaker stumbled as the motorcycle came closer, but the rider ignored us, and we were soon out of the fake, orderly grid of Tamu and walking along a dirt track that could not have been more real. The track weaved through an area much like the neighborhood Leela's aunt lived in, with scattered huts and shops dispersed along thick groves of trees, the traffic consisting mostly of pedestrians and bicyclists. The beer bars, neon signs, and shiny electronic goods visible in the town were quite absent here, and the shops we passed were little more than village stores, shabby and dimly lit, their everyday wares piled on narrow countertops and stacked at the back of the shop.

The filmmaker paused at one of these stores and bought two cans of beer, handing me one when we were out of the sight of the storekeeper, walking alongside of me as we drank. He thought it would take us at least another hour to reach the border. We passed a large bungalow surrounded by a concrete wall, a black Mercedes gleaming in its driveway. He grimaced and said, "Country home for lower-level army general." Here he began walking ahead of me again, asking me to follow at a distance, even though the settlements and shops had disappeared and we were climbing toward a teak forest with no one else in sight. We moved silently, each of us thinking his own thoughts, bound together by no more than the common direction of our journey and the beating of our hearts.

It was dark and muggy inside the forest, the trees leaning toward each other and blocking out any view of the sky. When we emerged again, I saw that the sun had not yet set over the hills straddling the border, so that the pale dusk seemed suspended, afraid of the emphatic certainty of the coming darkness. I felt as if we were suspended too, toy figures making our way up a tiny incline on the surface of the earth that to us was an almost insurmountable hill on the route to India. Villagers passed by, heading in the other direction, but even the children skipping ahead of their parents could not puncture that fabric of stillness, their cries and shouts swallowed up as soon as they went past a bend in the road. The valley was already shrouded in darkness, while the river before us was shallow and motionless, another surface of concealment. There were scattered huts by the track on the opposite bank, and Burmese women were setting up their cooking fires outside the huts, fanning the coals with their aprons. Tamu, stripped of its face paint and unable to extend its performance any longer, had drawn a blanket over itself and withdrawn into sleep.

My breathing grew more labored as I tramped on, following the white shirt still faintly visible in the dusk like some specter leading me through purgatory, and I felt incapable of clear thought even when the track widened and the outline of another group of shacks appeared in the distance. The filmmaker paused, mopped his brow, and smiled wanly to indicate that we were now in the realm of democracy.

IT WAS JUST ABOUT SIX as we made our way to a stall in the Morning Market. The place was getting ready to close, and people were emptying the open stalls rapidly, pushing past each other and wading through the slush to load their things onto the carts and vans waiting outside. Entreaties, insults, and orders overlapped in the hubbub of last-minute bargaining, but the squalor and chaos was a relief after Tamu's carefully arranged mask, and I let the sounds sweep over me as I sank into a chair, sitting for a while by myself at a long table in the middle of the tea shop.

The filmmaker had headed out as soon as we got there, saying he would be back in a few minutes. Half an hour passed without his reappearance, while I watched the steady dismantling of the market: bulbs taken out of their sockets, counters and tables stripped down, and table fans carried out. From the talk around me, I realized there was more to this than the usual end-of-day hurry. All businesses and offices would be shut the next day because of some kind of demonstration throughout Manipur, but I was too tired to ask for details.

The lights went off suddenly. It was like a heavy curtain dropping before my eyes, and there was a momentary hush when it seemed as if the figures gathered all around had become petrified by some unnamable calamity. A chair turned over with a crash, and voices began calling out for candles and lamps and torches. In the pinpoints of light beginning to appear in the market, I saw a group of shadows climb into the tea stall and approach my table. The filmmaker had returned.

The tea-stall boy brought over a candle as the four young men accompanying the filmmaker looked around carefully and arranged themselves in a row across from me. The filmmaker regarded me with nervous excitement, gesturing with his head at the men. Two of them wore glasses, and they were all dressed neatly in shirts and *lungis*, with a way of holding themselves up that distinguished them from the more disheveled, frantic petty traders and smugglers in the marketplace.

The oldest spoke first, addressing me in English, "You were supposed to meet us hours ago," and I realized they were the people Robiul had mentioned when he arranged the meeting with Leela.

"Where's Leela?" I asked.

The leader shook his head slightly. "She's gone back. She had work to do."

"Is she well?"

"Very well. We took care of her. We are medical students."

Nothing had quite prepared me for the tenor of my conversation with them, their calm, detached manner quite unruffled by the things happening around them. Their claim of being medical students in a place that had neither medical school nor hospital would have been preposterous coming from anyone else, but they made it seem unexceptional. They had been medical students working to restore democracy in Burma when the crackdown happened and they fled across the border—and they were still medical students, undamaged somehow by events.

The filmmaker had ceased to be a filmmaker after crossing the border. By his own admission, he had become someone other than himself in that process of crossing over, diminishing steadily with each day he spent as a refugee or hired hand working on Malik's project of illusions. But the same was not true of the medical students: they had faith still, although it was impossible to tell the exact nature of that faith. They spoke reasonably, if carefully, about their work and their objectives, unwilling to make any grand claims for themselves or their restoration. Their faith had to be deduced from their quiet manner, and perhaps it was more impressive because it had to be gleaned from tiny gestures, their understated concern for each other, their patience toward the filmmaker, and their kindness toward me. I wondered what kept them going. Their faith was certainly not based on the belief that they would return soon to Burma, or that democracy would displace the rule of the tottering old general, or that—having established itself—democracy would prove more honest and just than the forms it had taken elsewhere.

It was not even an uncomplicated, personal motivation, a belief that they would eventually be able to complete their medical training and become doctors with expensive private practices. Their belief was both simpler than that and more elusive, and it was expressed in the way they spoke of themselves as nothing more or less than medical students. Without saying a word about it directly, they helped me understand why Leela was with them and the direction in which she was headed. She too had faith, that sense of selfhood both the filmmaker and I lacked, and that Malik had never thought worth possessing.

"You understand. Good," the oldest of the four said. "She will be glad."

They finished their tea and stood up, bowing briefly to me before slipping out into the night. The filmmaker sat with me, seemingly quite calm and happy to have helped me meet the medical students—but in his heart he was with the four of them as they made their way through the alleyways, accompanying them to their huts and still continuing the long, unforgiving struggle that he had in reality abandoned the very first time he crossed over into Moreh.

* 3 *

There wasn't much else after that in Moreh; just the film-maker's tearful departure, an overnight stay in a hotel on the roof of a warehouse where I was let in by a ten-year-old

boy with the wizened face of a day laborer, and a brief encounter early in the morning with the pharmaceutical salesmen. Still triumphant from their successful shopping trip and
unfazed by the prospect of violence, they wanted to know if I
had heard anything about a development project nearby, a
place they thought might prove to be a good customer for some
of their new drugs. They had bought fake Ray-Bans in Tamu,
and the sunglasses gave them a vaguely sinister air as they
crowded around me with their questions. I told them I found it
unlikely there was any such project, but they chose not to believe me, moving away with dissatisfied expressions as though
I were trying to cut them out of a lucrative deal.

I left them to it. Rumors take a long time to die, and it was
quite possible that the project would never be forgotten in the
region, quickening the pulse of some traveler or newcomer
long after the signs had faded and the surrounding shacks had
crumbled to the ground. Appearances and illusions are important everywhere, but perhaps nowhere more so than in a place
where illusions mask an unbearable reality. Even with my recent knowledge, it was possible to fall under the spell of those
illusions on my return journey to Imphal: the distant glimmer
of the Golden Valley rice fields and the bright signs of the
Prosperity Project along the highway made what I had learned
feel completely unreal, while the clear sunlight and the empty
highway seemed to augur the beginning of a journey rather
than its end.

Yet the end was shaping itself carefully as the bus rolled
along a highway increasingly deserted except for army patrols.
The settlements along the road were boarded up, with paramilitary units waiting among the posters announcing a demonstration in Imphal that afternoon. The demonstration was

intended to preserve a necessary illusion, that of the territorial integrity of the state of Manipur. The Naga insurgents and the Indian government had at last agreed to a cease-fire, but the boundaries of the cease-fire included those areas of Manipur where the Nagas were in a majority.

To the outsider it seemed like an innocuous detail; what did it matter where the peace extended to as long as the guns fell silent? But people stripped of all power hold on to their few illusions all the more desperately. Frustrated with the continuing violence in their own state, the apathy of the Indian government, and the inability of the Manipuri rebels to present a united front that would give them as much weight as the Nagas at the negotiating table, the people of the valley feared a conspiracy in the making. They remembered the talk of the Naga insurgents about a "Greater Nagaland" that would include all those areas of Manipur where Naga tribes were dominant; now they were heading for Imphal to show the government that Manipuris could not be left out of the peace process.

I realized even before I entered Imphal that the demonstration was going to be a serious affair. There were young men looking for rides near the bus stops, and a stream of cars, jeeps, buses, and trucks passed us, becoming a massive and chaotic column of traffic on the outskirts of the town. There had been an attempt at a protest near the fort the day before, but the group had been small and easily driven away by the police; the people gathering now were determined that this time the numbers would be too large to be dismissed without thought.

Most of those going to Imphal were young men, perched on the roofs of buses and vans and waving banners. They possessed something of the manner of a Calcutta football crowd, with the same combustible violence bubbling under the air of easy camaraderie. They leaned down from the roof and slapped other vehicles on the side, urging their drivers on as separate lines of traffic from different districts converged on the main axis of the town and came to a complete halt near the Hotel Excellency. Some of the young men dismounted and joined the throng of people forming a loose procession of sorts that was heading for the state legislature building.

I got off the bus and made my way along the edge of the crowd, trying to catch up with the advance guard of the procession. The people around me moved slowly, but Imphal was a town under siege, its houses and trees and canals obscured by the exhaust of vehicles and the dust thrown up by thousands of feet, the ramparts of the fort barely visible over the massed heads. I remembered the last march I had seen here, when people had come out to protest Malik's abduction and death. My new knowledge of Malik did not diminish that march and its spirit of solidarity and reconciliation. In retrospect it seemed a brave act, that slow wave of flickering candles and lanterns moving through the night, faltering at the edge of the town and yet remaining there for some time to show both abducted and abductors that their darkness had not taken complete hold yet.

It was a strange recognition for me, and it made it easy to believe that a touch of grace, of wisdom, had been conferred upon me by Leela and the medical students and the filmmaker, because Imphal and the region never looked as beautiful to me as it did then, in those fragile moments before the madness took over. After weeks spent struggling through the bewildering profusion of images and voices in the region, I saw things with as much clarity as if I had freed myself from my body and was suspended high above, the clamor of contending voices fading away to the rush of the wind and the gentle, barely perceptible movement of rivers and trees and villages and towns and the people. I slowed down, and in what I had so far thought of as a homogeneous crowd, I began to see distinct, individual faces, some calm and resigned, others wracked by doubt, faces that were here not just to defend some boundary or the other but to show the uncaring, unheeding world that they existed and could not be forgotten.

THE PRESS OF BODIES became thicker, and I found it increasingly hard to push my way through. There was a confusion in the crowd, people turning this way and that, some craning their necks to see ahead. Beyond, the state legislature building was just visible. The local Manipuri politicians were meeting there to discuss the situation, and it was at them that this demonstration was directed. The Indian government and the Naga rebels were distant, powerful entities, but local politicians were accountable. The protesters wanted them to come out and answer questions, but there was a barrier between crowd and building, a line of armed policemen defending that generic institution with the melancholy Indian flag fluttering on top.

It was a symbol of the realm of democracy, I thought, recalling the filmmaker, and I tried to find a way out of the crowd. I made my way toward the barriers and, holding the press card issued by the *Nagaland Post* in front of me, ran toward the policemen. They didn't object when I climbed over their barriers, and let me through with a quick glance at my card. Over to the side, where another road approached the legislature building, there was a smaller, younger crowd pressed right up against the barrier. Scuffles had broken out, and the policemen behind the barricade were using their sticks to hold the crowd back. A reserve company of paramilitary arrived in trucks and began heading for one spot in particular. I followed and, from the corner of my eye, saw a group of masked men who had broken through and were gathered around some PVC pipes left near the building. The reserve policemen began running toward them, but the young men set the pipes on fire, producing a chemical smoke that rapidly fogged the surrounding air and the skies. Tear-gas canisters arced toward the crowd, and then the policemen charged with their sticks and shields.

I had my handkerchief out, because even though I was behind the line of policemen, I was afraid of a tear-gas canister or two being tossed back. In front of me, the crowd was fleeing before the charge of the policemen, running from the sticks and the smoke and the tear gas, some of them being trampled in the course of the mad rush away from the area. I smelt more smoke, and I turned to look at the legislature, quiet and inviolate amid all the chaos, a few curious politicians peering out from the windows on the top floor. I think I was the first person to notice the flames on the ground floor.

❖ 4 ❖

In time, the curfew lifted over Imphal, revealing the smoldering ruins of the state legislature building, more soldiers on the streets, and people rushing to form lines in front of grocery shops and the trucks that had finally come into the town with basic supplies. "It will get back to normal in a few weeks," Sanat said. "Why worry? Things always get back to normal."

I was no longer a guest of Sanat's. My money had more or less run out, with just enough left for a bus ticket to Silchar and for the plane to Calcutta. When I mentioned this to Sanat, he shrugged. "You were the best guest I had. I made a lot of money from you. What's a few extra days?" We had been the only two people staying in the hotel during the curfew. The telephone had stopped working, so our news of what was happening came mostly through the television. We took turns at cooking and watched television and played cards. There were even some books to read. Sanat had a collection of Victorian novels, fat books into which one could retreat to follow the slow progression of time, the deeds of the characters taking years to come to a resolution. It had been an expansive world for those authors, I realized. Even when the immediate surroundings of the novels were provincial, every small town and city depicted in those books was the center of an empire, quite unlike this spot on the periphery where I found myself without knowing how I had got here, as if I had sleepwalked my way to the edge of the republic.

I slowed down as I read those novels and chatted with Sanat, and the interlude in the hotel was a pleasant, domestic phase after all the violence and the rioting, the calm inside the hotel untouched by the convoys that passed by or the loudspeakers on government jeeps that made noisy but indecipherable announcements.

"You like it here," Sanat said. "You don't want to go. Or you want to come back. It's the charm of the place." We were standing in a long line of people when he said this, empty jerricans in our hands, hoping to get some kerosene for the oil lamps and

the stove on which we made our meals of rice and boiled pota-
toes. The supply of cooking gas had run out a while ago, and we
didn't think it worth trying to queue for gas cylinders.

Gradually, as a week passed after the curfew had been
lifted, the lines in front of the shops became shorter. The telephone connection was restored, and Sema called one evening
to tell me that Minister Vimedo had died of a heart attack.
Maria's husband was back, he said, trying to talk to the Naga
rebels about continuing with the peace process without pressing their demands for the cease-fire to be extended to Naga-
dominated areas of Manipur.

I prepared for my homeward journey. Sanat had advised
me to head out before a sixty-day strike was called in Manipur,
and I made my way to the bus station one morning. "You'll
come back, I know," he said to me before I left. "It grows on
you, the excitement of living here. You can't wait to be back
before the next spell of riots or abductions."

The first signs of autumn were in the air, the sky appearing
freshly washed and the road littered with dead flowers and
leaves. There was a man bargaining with the taxi drivers about
the fare to Moreh, accompanied by a small woman with a ten-
sion about her shoulders that I recognized instantaneously. It
was Malik's wife, and the man with her was Meghen.

"I am going to Moreh," she said with a smile. "Meghen is
coming with me. He insists on helping me." Meghen looked
embarrassed.

"But the reports . . ." I said.

"The reports don't matter," she said earnestly. "You must
believe. You must believe in him, just as I do. Of course he is
alive. So much confusion about the way he is supposed to have
died, and they took it all back, didn't they?"

"You're going to look for him in Moreh?" I asked.

"We've heard that someone there may know where he is. People say they have seen him, and me, I believe fully that this is my mission, this search for my husband."

"The driver is ready," Meghen said hastily, trying to avoid my gaze.

I waved at them as they walked toward the van. Malik's wife turned around once to look at me, disregarding the traffic around her. Two rickshaw drivers swerved to pass her, and I knew I would always remember her like that, seeing her as if she were in a photograph, standing in the middle of the road with that serious, abstracted look on her face, framed by the two masked rickshaw drivers bent over their pedals.

The return journey was inconsequential, although it seemed to take a long time. More soldiers, watchtowers, and rickety bridges, with one bridge that had collapsed, so that all of us had to scramble across the gorge to the other side where enterprising young Mizo men were waiting with vans to give people rides to Silchar. A night at the hotel there, and then a morning flight on a small Boeing to Calcutta airport, where I was struck by a sense of dissonance at the sight of the crowds outside. People going about their frantic business in the harsh sunlight, gathering on the pavements and roads, running to board crowded buses, emerging from their offices at lunch hour, they seemed unreal, like shadows created by the smoke and fire of a giant conflagration.

My body knew the city instinctively, my feet leading me with practiced ease to the *Sentinel* building hidden behind a mass of bamboo scaffolding, to the local market and the STD phone booth to call Herman, but my mind was somewhere else, unsurprised when Herman didn't answer the phone or when Sarkar refused to see me.

I ran into Sarkar one afternoon near the Grand Hotel, and he smirked as he said that he couldn't discuss my suspension until a labor committee had been convened. "What's your problem, anyway, Singh? You are getting the checks, aren't you? Half pay for no work sounds pretty good, if you ask me." He lowered his voice, as if the crowds on the pavement were listening eagerly to every word of his. "If you really want my opinion, Singh, perhaps it's time for you to move on. There's been a lot of change since you've been gone—have you noticed we're painting the front? No?—and it takes a certain mind-set to be able to adjust to change. We're leasing out the ground floor to a foreign bank. And we're fully computerized these days, Singh. No more noisy, dirty typewriters in the reporting room, but clean and modern computers. The stories come directly into my computer, and they get sent to the editors in the newsroom only after I've checked each one personally. It's all very exciting, Singh, and I wish you could sense the potential, the possibilities. Somehow, though, I feel you're not the type. Can you use a computer?"

"It's just a glorified typewriter, Sarkar," I said. "And it's still not going to be able to write an editorial for you, is it? What you really need is a machine with brains, with intelligence, with perception, but the computer can't quite do that for you yet."

His face darkened and he clicked his fingers at his driver to bring the car forward. I walked on past the pavement vendors, ignoring the thin men with their weighing machines and their paper rats darting between the feet of slow-moving tourists. I walked home, pausing at the stairway to check my letter box for some sign that the magazine in Tubingen had accepted my exemplary story on the woman who embodied the mystery and sorrow of India.

One day, giving way to a sudden impulse, I took myself to the Max Muller Bhavan. I asked to meet the director and persisted long enough to be led into the office of a large, bearded man with an absentminded air about him. I told him a little about the magazine in Tubingen and the story they had asked me to do, explaining that I was curious about the magazine more than anything. He had never heard of the publication, he said, nor of a man who had written on the sewers of Calcutta for the *Wochenpost*. He offered me beer and thought aloud about what I had asked him as if he were contemplating a difficult but abstract philosophical question. Then he asked me more questions about what had happened in the region, and I told him some of the story, including my suspension from the *Sentinel*.

He perked up when he heard this. "You have some German? No? But you could learn, I am very certain, and then you know Calcutta, the city, the culture." He was looking for a press officer, he confessed. He invited me to a dinner he was hosting the next evening for a visiting German theater artiste and some Indians who had taken part in her theater workshop. If I came by for drinks and dinner, he would see what he could discover about the magazine in Tubingen.

I showed up late for the dinner at his Alipore residence, making my way hesitantly toward the giant colonial bungalow concealed from the empty roads by thick lines of shrubbery.

The theater people inside were having a good time, arguing loudly while waiters in white uniforms circulated with drinks. The director of the cultural center was the perfect host, with words for everybody, even for the raggedy-looking young man who was both entranced and ill at ease amid the cultural opulence of Europe.

The director pulled me aside when I arrived and took me to his study. He had looked into the magazine in Tubingen, and his advice to me was to forget about the assignment or the money they had given me. "You spent it in good faith, in order to do the story they wanted. Who knows what they really wanted? If they get in touch with you someday, I would avoid a conversation. We cannot be absolutely certain that this is the same publication we are talking about, but I do wonder how many magazines with such a name exist in Tubingen? The one I know of is not a magazine, not really, more of a newsletter for a somewhat evangelical church, and your friend Herman too was almost certainly of that persuasion."

He looked embarrassed on behalf of his evangelical countrymen, and began playing around with the papers in his study. Had I ever heard anything about a developmental project in Manipur during my travels? He seemed to remember a letter from the man in charge, a most impressive letter describing what sounded like a very worthwhile project. "They put up AIDS clinics and drug rehabilitation centers there," he said. "Must have taken quite some doing, don't you think?" I agreed with him. "I cannot remember the name of the man who wrote me the letter," the director said, frowning. "I don't usually forget names, but his eludes me. Seems an amazing man, though."

He must be to have achieved so much, I replied.

The director asked me to think again of the press officer

position before we parted, and I said I would drop in on him the next week.

The roads navigating their way through Alipore were quite deserted as I walked homeward, my path taking me past the white lions of the long-dead empire standing guard outside the National Library. There were sounds of laughter from the other side, where cars were pulling up under the blaze of lights coming from the lobby of the Taj Bengal hotel. It became quiet again as soon as I had passed the hotel, and I stood for a while when I came to the fork where I had to turn right to go home. Ahead, to my left, I could see the new bridge the Japanese had built over the Hooghly. I turned left, knowing that if I kept going I would come to the river.

a c k n o w l e d g m e n t s

One of the pleasures of writing a novel is that it requires nothing in the way of footnotes or bibliography. It stands or falls on the merits of its fictional world, and this is particularly true of *An Outline of the Republic*. Although the region where the novel is set takes much from India's northeast, including names of real towns and states, it is so much a product of my mind that anyone wishing to replicate Amrit's journey would be hopelessly lost. A trip to the northeast had always been part of my plans for the novel, but the usual obstacles—not enough money, not enough time—forced me to depend entirely on the characters who showed up in the narrative. They are responsible for all inaccuracies, of which there are no doubt many.

The novel takes equal liberties with chronology when actual events are referred to. The story is generally set in the early nineties, as should be clear from the portable typewriter Amrit takes along. I therefore refer to Indian cities by the older names of Bombay and Calcutta rather than by their newer variants.

I assume less explanation is required for the historical element in the novel. Sutherland's narrative is entirely fictional, and the *Imperial* or the *Sentinel* do not correspond to any actual newspapers in Calcutta. Nevertheless, Ian Stephens's *Monsoon Mornings*, a memoir of his years as the editor of the *Statesman*, provided important background information on a Calcutta newspaper during the war. The seeds of Jim's story can be found in his memoir. David Rooney's *Burma Victory* and Gerald Hanley's *Monsoon Victory* furnished useful details of the World War Two campaign on India's northeastern front, but I doubt either of the authors would be pleased with my cavalier treatment of their military histories. Michio Takeyama's novel *The Harp of Burma* gave me a different perspective, that of the Japanese experience of the Burma campaign, and I found its melancholia and wisdom refreshing in thinking of the war.

A number of people helped me in different ways during the course of this novel. My wife, Amy Rosenberg, was always on hand with advice and ideas; I am grateful to her for that and for everything else. I would like to thank Hartosh Singh Bal, Shruti Debi, Pankaj Mishra, and Mary Mount for reading the manuscript and offering useful suggestions, and Kishalaya Bhattacharya for patiently answering my questions about names. David Miller was an ideal literary agent, and I am grateful to him for his friendship and exquisite literary taste. Finally, I would like to thank editors in England and the United States who provided me with book review and feature article commissions over the past couple of years. I cannot name them for obvious reasons, but their assignments and checks showed faith in my writing and bought me time to work on this novel.